CANKERED ROOTS

NEW EDITION

OTHER BOOKS BY G.G. VANDAGRIFF

Regency Romance

Rescuing Rosalind
Miss Braithwaite's Secret
The Taming of Lady Kate
The Duke's Undoing

Women's Fiction

The Only Way to Paradise

Pieces of Paris

Historical

The Last Waltz

Alex and Briggie Mysteries

Hidden Branch

Poisoned Pedigree

Tangled Roots

Of Deadly Descent

Non-Fiction

Deliverance from Depression

Voices In Your Blood: Discovering Identity Through Family History

CANKERED ROOTS

NEW EDITION

A Mystery

G.G. Vandagriff

The Orson Whitney Press
ISBN: 0-9839536-0-0
ISBN-13: 978-0-9839536-0-9

PRAISE FOR G.G. VANDAGRIFF'S WORK

The Last Waltz

G.G. Vandagriff completes her story using vivid word pictures. Ms. Vandagriff's latest offering is very appropriately titled. Like the waltz, the storyline picks the readers up and twirls them from plot twist to plot twist in what is, at times, almost a dizzying rate of speed.

Although the tenor of The Last Waltz is somewhat different than this author's previous books, it does have one trait similar to the author's previous writings. For those readers who like to "cheat" by peeking at the end of the book, it is almost a guarantee that they will put two and two together and come up with nine. With many authors, one can skim through the final pages of a book and sum up a story. One thing that seems to be common throughout Ms. Vandagriff's books is her ability to weave so many elements so tightly that one cannot arrive at the proper conclusions without actually reading her books from cover to cover.

The Last Waltz illustrates the value of so many different kinds of love . . . companionship, empathetic love, protective and secure love, and of course, that vibrant first love. This book is not necessarily the happily ever after type of love story that causes teen hearts to flutter. Although the sheer determination of the heroine makes one feel that the endings scattered throughout this book are not necessarily tragic, this is truly a romance of more than the star struck lover variety.

—AML Review

What is by far the strength of Ms. Vandagriff's writing is her ability to create characters that pull you into the story, until you become a part of that story yourself. I read somewhere that if a reader wants to see two characters fall in love, then they have to fall in love with both of those characters. And I find that this is a truism for all of fiction—and doesn't just relate to the event of falling in love. The more enmeshed the reader becomes with the characters—the more wrapped up they will be with the story itself. And in this book there is little doubt that this was the case. There were times I wanted to throw the book against the wall, times I was deliberately ignoring people because they were interrupting the "best part," (which, by the way was nearly the whole book—and there were certainly more than one.) and at times I would laugh, cry, mourn, and rejoice with the characters. But what is amazing is how well the characters worked into the historical setting itself.

—The Bookworm's Library

I was immediately drawn into a chaotic world of love and war—an interesting juxtaposition. I kept reading if only to discovered how the story would end. But along the way I encountered several themes which ran throughout the novel. What does it mean to be in love? Is it true that you can give yourself completely to another person only once, as Amalia's uncle states? What does it mean to be part of a family—especially when family members keep secrets? How can one find strength to make good choices and persevere in the face of adversity? How can we avoid the tragedy of becoming, as one character says, "less than we were born to be"? Norman Mailer wrote the following: "I feel that the final purpose of art is to intensify—even, if necessary, to exacerbate—the moral consciousness of people. In particular, I think the novel at its best is the most moral of the art forms." I think "The Last Waltz" confirms Mailer's statement: It asks us to look inside ourselves and to examine the state of our own moral consciousness.

—Joan Petty (Five Stars)

Pieces of Paris

"It was the simple things that undid her, Annalisse had discovered. Something as ordinary as the scent of lilacs when the air was heavy, a brief measure of Tchaikovsky, or a dream. A dream like the one she'd awakened from last night— so real she could smell the Paris Metro in it. Any of these things could revive in a moment the memories she'd spent the last six years burying. They crept under the leaden shield around her heart and found the small, secret place where she still had feeling."

From the first paragraph Pieces of Paris gripped me. The story, by G.G. Vandagriff, didn't matter then, the writing had enchanted. And then, I realized, the story did matter. Very much. I was carrying this book around with me everywhere I went.

Pieces of Paris is about environmental abuses, narrow-mindedness, narcissism, bigotry, tragic memories, loyalty, vindication, rediscovered faith, love, resolution, and peace. It's about a husband and wife, who learn that the best way to resolve the challenges of life is with each other. And with God.

—Susan Dayley, Looking Out My Backdoor (Five Stars)

GG Vandagriff once again explores the intensity of human emotion, delivering a powerful story of second chances, the gift of forgiveness, and the depth of true love. This well-crafted story is absorbing from page one and the characters powerful and relatable.

Pieces of Paris is a literary symphony, a cacophony of words that delves into the hearts of all of us, as Annalisse and Dennis fight to reestablish the rhythm of their marriage. An emotionally engaging and unforgettable journey.

—H.B. Moore, Multi-Award Winning Novelist (Five Stars)

Weaving together powerful truths and psychologically driven fiction, GG Vandagriff's Pieces of Paris takes readers on an emotional ride that winds through the darkest recesses of painful memories, plunges into unexpected realities, then climbs to breathtaking vistas of understanding, forgiveness and love.

Vandagriff has a true gift of words and paints glorious scenes and intense emotion in this well-paced, gripping drama. This powerful story of second chances, the gift of forgiveness, and the depth of truth will resonate with readers of all ages and stations in life.

—Michele Ashman Bell, Best-selling Romance Novelist, author of the Butterfly Box Series (Five Stars)

If it sounds like there's two stories going on here, you'd be correct. But Vandagriff is an accomplished and skilled writer, and she manages to weave the two threads together to form a compelling and utterly wonderful story of hope and redemption.

There are so many interesting aspects to this story. It is, in a sense, a love story. But in the broader view, it's a tale of pain, memory and loss, but it is also a story of redemption and hope.

"Pieces of Paris" is a lovely work. Vandagriff just gets better and better with each book. Give it a look.

—AML Review

For my accomplice,
David.

A LETTER TO READERS

This book was the first fiction I published. This is a new edition of the original 1993 publication, but the content of the book remains the same.

I wrote this novel as light relief, never knowing that it would spawn a series of at least five books. (I have one up my sleeve that makes a ten year leap into the future.)

Cankered Roots takes place in 1994. To you, it may seem like a historical relic, for it was written before genealogists used the kind of internet technology we take for granted today for their research. My heroines, Alex and Briggie are definitely "old school," but that really makes it much more fun.

These characters have become much beloved by many readers over the years. I sincerely hope you will enjoy them as much as I do, and make them part of your family of favorite fictional characters.

Happy reading!

G.G. Vandagriff
August, 2011

Hate is fear and fear is rot
That cankers root and fruit alike.
— Robert Graves

PROLOGUE

Crouching in the overgrown shrubs, the stocky, ginger-haired man consulted his watch for the fifth time in the past half hour. Where was she? Waves of shimmering humidity rose like steam from the dense yews surrounding the old brick apartment building that radiated heat like an oven. No place on earth could be hotter than Kansas City in August.

Then he heard it—the slap of sandals against the old brick sidewalk. Forgetting his discomfort, he gripped the butt of the gun in his pocket with something close to glee. It was his quarry, all right. One, two, three, darting out into the open, he fired.

His victim whirled, eyes round with shock. Looking down, she saw the spreading stain darkening the red of her shirt.

"Daniel! This is silk!" she shrilled, bunching the fabric in her hand.

Dropping her groceries, she leaped off the steps, kicked off her sandals, and struck the squirt gun from his hand with a roundhouse kick. The toy skittered onto the steps. Before he could react, she executed a karate chop to the collar bone, felling him to the ground.

Sprawled on the grass, he watched ruefully as she ran back to the steps, retrieved the gun, and commenced firing without mercy. Daniel grinned as water mingled with the sweat on his face. "Your reaction time's improved, Mrs. Campbell."

The woman aimed the spray at her own face. "This was a truly inspired idea, Daniel."

"Actually, I was angling for an invitation to dinner."

She turned the gun on him again. "Do you realize this blouse cost forty dollars?"

"Well then, how about dinner at the Bristol?"

"That's a much better idea. You can buy me a new blouse afterwards."

Hoisting her groceries, he asked, "Did they fix your sink yet?"

Alex squirted his ear, her lapis eyes alight with mischief. "Who knows? There's nothing quite like the suspense of coming home to The Baltimore."

Daniel surveyed the old apartment building that an enterprising young developer had modernized by adding the square sunrooms that jutted out from an old brick exterior. Straddling the borderline between fashionable, gentrified Westport and the slummy mass of decaying brick housing reaching north, The Baltimore was the most desirable residence on the block. That wasn't saying much.

"For the same rent you pay here, you could have a nice, clean apartment in Overland Park," he told her.

Passing through a white-tiled lobby reminiscent of men's lavatories, Alex led the way out the back door to the fire escape. The elevator was permanently out of order.

"Overland Park hasn't got a soul," she said with a grimace. "Where else could I live next door to a Hispanic cellist, a Japanese karate master, and a West Indian silversmith?"

Later, as they were finishing raspberries topped with almond cream, Alex tossed a document across the table. "There," she said. "I've been dying to show you this all evening. It finally came today."

Daniel sighed and picked up what appeared to be a death certificate. "Dead people sort of ruin the ambience, Alex. Can't I finish my dessert first?"

"It's not as though you knew him."

He studied the document reluctantly. "There doesn't seem to be anything fishy about this. Your grandfather died of pneumonia twenty years ago. I'd say that was a relatively peaceful death."

Alex nodded. "The death does seem fairly straightforward. That's not what's fishy. It's his birth."

"How can someone's birth be fishy?" Daniel smothered the last of his berries in cream and finished them with regret.

"Notice the parents' names?" she persisted.

"There aren't any."

"So. Fishy Thing Number One: My father gave that information. Why didn't he know his grandparents? Now. Look at the place of birth."

"La Salle County, Illinois. What's wrong with that?"

"They started keeping birth records in La Salle County in 1877. According to that certificate you're holding, Grandfather was born in 1895. I called the La Salle County clerk today. No birth record."

"Maybe your father was wrong about the year."

"I had them check the years 1890 to 1905. That makes Fishy Thing Number Two." Alex polished off the last of her berries without appearing to taste them. "Besides that, there's the census. He would have been five in 1900."

"Let me guess. No grandfather in La Salle County."

"According to the 1900 Soundex there was no Joseph Borden, age five, in all of Illinois!"

Settling back in the comfortable booth, Daniel extended his arms along its back and studied his dinner companion. When Alex got full of her subject, no one else was more passionate. Her eyes sparkled, her cheeks flushed carnation pink, and she talked volubly with her hands, running them through the curly black mass of hair that fell to her shoulders.

"I don't know how I ever could have conceived of genealogy as dull," he remarked.

"I'm boring you," she said without contrition.

"Not at all." He grinned. "You forget I've known the risks of this relationship from the beginning. No one can say you're not up-front about your profession."

"Unlike some people I could mention."

He laughed. "Come on! Should I wear a warning sign or something?"

"You intentionally misled me! For weeks I thought you were a lawyer."

"How was I to know you would leap to such an unwarranted conclusion?"

"I did meet you in your father's law office," she reminded him. "You were wearing a white shirt and tie."

Pushing the raspberry dish aside, he positioned his coffee cup in front of him. "Back to the non-birth of your grandfather. I don't think your fish make much of a stink, Alex. Your father probably just made those things up on the death certificate. I'll bet lots of people do that. They're embarrassed. They ought to know and they don't. There doesn't have to be a deep, sinister reason."

Alex looked away and began pleating her napkin between her fingers. "Anyway, I'm going to Winnetka tomorrow."

The atmosphere suffered a palpable change, as though the temperature had suddenly dropped forty degrees. "Why?" he demanded before he could stop himself. "What possible good do you think it's going to do to talk to your parents?"

"Calm down, Dr. Grinnell," she said quietly. Her body had gone rigid. "You may be a shrink, but you're not my shrink. It's time I faced up to things and saw my parents. Dr. Brace agrees."

Daniel drank the dregs of his coffee, forgoing comment. The silence between them was strained.

"I might find something in the house. Some kind of clue," she said finally.

"Nancy Drew has a lot to answer for," he remarked darkly.

She grinned slightly. "There *is* a mystery, Daniel. Grandfather lived with us all my life. Why won't my parents talk about him? I was fifteen when he died—old enough to have the impression that we were a fairly ordinary family. I mean no Mafia connections or anything like that. Once they got him buried—presto! He's a non-person. They got rid of everything that belonged to him. They even took up the rug in his bedroom, for heaven's sake."

"Then what makes you think there are any clues to find?"

"Genealogists learn to find clues in ordinary things other people might overlook."

Daniel ran a hand over the hair on the back of his neck. Thinking of Alex going to Winnetka was to picture her making a polar expedition in street clothes. "Why are you so hung up on this Mormon stuff, Alex? Why can't you just get on with life as it is?"

"Don't drag my religion into this," she warned, her eyes flashing. "Apart from what I happen to believe, there is every reason for me to try to connect somewhere. My husband is dead. I have a mother and a father who have virtually denied my existence for the past fifteen years. I want some family, Daniel. Is that too hard for a psychologist to understand?"

"I'm sorry, Alex."

For a few moments there was silence, and he wondered whether his apology had been sufficient. Why *had* he made that crack about her religion? Because the idea of her going home had enraged him. Maybe she was right. Maybe he couldn't keep his profession out of their relationship.

"And then there's the genetic side of things," she continued, throwing up her hands. "I mean, what if it turns out I'm descended from the same genetic pool as Lizzy Borden, for heaven's sake? I could turn into a homicidal maniac at any time, hacking up all of Westport, maybe even Overland Park."

"Cheer up," he said bracingly. "There are other Bordens. Astrid, the senator, and the canned milk people, for instance. Cows are so wholesome. Why focus on Lizzy?"

"An obsession, probably. Who's Astrid Borden?"

"The rock star with the bald head and the breastplate."

Alex blinked. "She's a Borden?"

He nodded, and she grinned, sinking back into the upholstery of the booth and folding her arms across her chest. "No genetic similarity whatsoever. Nor do I have the slightest reason to believe I'm related to the senator or the milk people. My parents would certainly have claimed the relationship, had there been one."

Shrugging, he decided to make one last attempt. "If you haven't got the rent paid this month, you might be interested in the fact that Dad's got another missing-heir case for you. Dog food fortune. Legitimate business. Twenty-five dollars an hour."

She folded her hands primly on the table in front of her. "I've already paid the rent, thanks."

ONE

The Chicago Skyway had to be the weirdest place on earth. Breathing as little of the yellowish air as possible, Alex gripped the steering wheel and glanced through her car window at the factory-scarred landscape below. A sudden nostalgia for Scotland pierced her, as it did all too often.

High summer in Inveraray was the very best time. Against the sapphire waters of Loch Fyne, the little white-walled town sparkled on the occasional sunny day. Sweet peas, snapdragons, and pansies danced indiscriminately through the tiny flower garden on each side of the solid black door. Fresh from its daily shower, the earth smelled sharply of peat as Alex weeded the lettuces and collected the writhing brown worms for night fishing. In the long summer twilight, she and Stewart donned mackintoshes, stashed a thermos of hot chocolate with their fishing poles, and ventured out in their tiny boat. The stillness, the whispering, ghostly magic of the loch at midnight . . .

. . . was a million miles away. Reality: She was stranded in time between Stewart's death and her own, suspended at this moment above a brutalized landscape, on her way to the last place on earth she wanted to go.

Squaring her shoulders, she told herself, "I'm going home." But in spite of her resolutions, her heart bounded in panic. Winnetka wasn't home! Home should mean Stewart with his snapping black eyes, curly black beard, and sexy, one-sided grin. It should be a peat fire glowing on the hearth, fish frying in the pan, and the cold wind whistling outside the door—not a hollow, neo-Georgian house; not a place where no one knew or cared who you were. The panic clamped tightly around her chest.

In the apartment in Kansas City, Stewart was always there, waiting to be summoned in the middle of the night while she was potting plants or hanging the museum posters he had photographed. His blithe spirit still spurred her on to the outrageous activities that kept her sane—starting her improbable business, taking karate lessons, renting her crazy, run-down apartment in the once-grand Baltimore. And now this. Going to Winnetka. Taking the bull by the horns.

Unfortunately, Stewart's influence had been on the wane for the last hour, at least. Her happy memories were thinning, her bravado vanishing, her persona of the past fifteen years falling away like armor, suddenly too large. In Chicago, she wasn't Stewart's Alex. She was someone else—a scared little girl he had never known.

Could she do this after all? Maybe Daniel had been right. The thought roused her, and she felt a spark of anger. Daniel was always right. He saw straight through to the heart of her.

But she *wasn't* going to harbor this scared child forever. It was time for the little girl to grow up. She would walk into that house. It was going to hurt, but she would live through it. What could her parents do to her, after all?

With these thoughts, her panic began to subside. She tried to prepare herself for the meeting ahead in Winnetka. She had reached the Edens Expressway, so it wouldn't be long now.

Taking a deep, steadying breath, she remembered how years before, in the safety of their little white cottage, she and Stewart had hashed everything over and decided that it was useless to try to make sense of her parents' behavior. For whatever reason, they didn't want her, and she needed to accept that. But they couldn't deny her a heritage.

Grandfather was the only other family she had known, the only person she could visualize being with in eternity. Genealogically, she must start with him and go back, linking the generations, discovering the voices in her blood. Perhaps some healing would be possible. Maybe at last she would feel connected with the universe instead of hanging out in space all alone.

In dealing with her parents she must simply be all business. After all, genealogy was her business. A crazy business maybe, but RootSearch, Inc. paid a few of the bills, helping to stretch the small income from Stewart's life insurance.

"Your mission," she told herself firmly, "should you choose to accept it, is to uncover, by fair means or foul, your Grandfather's ancestry."

If she had to probe the family secret, she wouldn't shrink from it.

* * *

No one was home. The black-shuttered, brick Georgian mansion was deserted, its ornamental evergreens clipped to perfection and lawn uniformly green and closely mown. Relieved at the impersonality of it all, Alex fished her old key out of her purse. How long had it been since she'd used it? She'd been twenty when they'd sent her off to Paris. Now she was thirty-five. Had they changed the locks during those fifteen years?

Apparently not, because the door opened easily. Everything looked exactly the same—the black-and-white tiled entry, the vase of pampas grass in the corner next to the Picasso.

Picking up her overnight bag, Alex went upstairs to her old room. Here she paused. It wasn't the same at all. A bare clothes form confronted her like a truncated human. Needlepoint, embroidery, and inexpert oil paintings covered the beige-painted walls that had once displayed flowered paper. The bed was covered with a different spread, fitted corduroy, and was stacked with winter clothing, patterns, and skeins of yarn. It was a catchall—an overflow room for her mother's fill-time projects. Nothing of hers was left.

Acid tears stung her eyes. She'd been gone for fifteen years. What did she expect? Some sort of shrine complete with her candy-striped bedspread and all her stuffed animals?

Proceeding down the hall, she looked into the other rooms. The guest room would have to do, though she had always hated it. Windows were shrouded by an enormous evergreen, and the room was dark and depressing with an olive green bedspread and wallpaper. In her imagination, she had always associated it with the Brontë sisters.

Admonishing herself to hold tightly to her sense of humor, she went downstairs. The kitchen, which had been remodeled in dazzling white, offered little in the way of food. Soup was it. Heating it up on the Corning surface of the stove, Alex felt suffocated by the deadly quiet of the house. She had not quite forgotten that terrible quiet.

Switching on the little black-and-white TV on the counter, she filled the room with the voice of the news commentator.

"Hearings are set for mid-October to investigate allegations that Senators Bacon, Carpenter, Borden, and Teasdale received illegal campaign contributions from savings and loan magnate Cornelius Presley.

"Authorities remain puzzled by the Tranquilor cyanide killings that are terrorizing Chicagoland. Another strong warning was issued today by Cook County sheriff, Otis Brown. If you have the drug Tranquilor in your possession, you are advised to discard it immediately. The latest victim in the seemingly random killings, twenty-nine-year-old Gwenda March, was found dead today in her Mt. Prospect home by her eight-year-old son returning from school. Police discovered a bottle of the over-the-counter pain killer Tranquilor by her body. Three of the remaining capsules were found to contain potassium cyanide. According to neighbors, Gwenda March was a widow, raising her son Bobby and struggling to put herself through college while working a graveyard shift at the local cheese plant. They know of no one with a motive for killing her . . ."

Enraged, Alex snapped off the television. The words of the newscaster echoed in the room, hammering in her brain, but the picture in her head wasn't of a poisoned young widow being discovered by her son. Instead, she saw an enormous jet diving toward the earth. Shutting her eyes, she still saw it and then heard the deafening crash followed by a roaring explosion, hell-fire, and searing heat. The burnt-out plane.

Stewart!

She gripped the edge of the counter to steady herself and opened her eyes. Only a person as neurotic as she was would ever make the connection between a random cyanide poisoning in Chicago and a plane crash in Scotland!

But there was a connection. The same type of hideously warped mind had conceived both disasters—a depraved, psychotic terrorist.

Would she ever get away from it? Would the vision ever stop haunting her? Dr. Brace promised it would fade in time, but it had been two and a half years.

With tremendous effort, Alex dragged herself back to the present. She was heating soup in her mother's kitchen. Soon her mother would be home, assuming they had gotten the letter, of course.

Had they gotten it? If not, it was going to be even more awkward than she had imagined.

Leaving the soup, she went into her mother's little study at the back of the house. Yes, there it was, sitting on top of the desk. She reread it: "Dear Mother and Father, I will be coming to Winnetka on Wednesday to see you. I hope it will be convenient. There are some things I would like to discuss with you. Alexandra."

Bald. To the point. But what else could they expect?

Glancing around the room, her eyes rested on the bookcase. Drawing closer, she saw with some surprise that Stewart's book was there. She pulled it out and was immediately comforted by the photograph of Holyrood Castle that looked out from the glossy cover. Stewart had taken that picture on a sparkling day when Edinburgh had been full of marvels. To start with, the sun had shone, and that was rare enough. She remembered that the light falling on the old city was different from any light she had ever seen. Opening the book, Alex paged through the photographs, mentally recreating the occasion when each one was taken. Stewart had captured the light beautifully.

A welcome warmth spread through her chest, easing the panic that had threatened to tighten its grip. So, Stewart's book was here in Winnetka. Why? Her parents had declined every opportunity of meeting him. They hadn't even come to the funeral. But they'd bought his book.

"Hello, Alexandra." Her mother's voice made Alex jump. Turning around she saw that her parent was standing in the doorway, holding herself carefully erect in the way she did when she had had too much to drink. Her hair was strawberry blond now, still perfectly coiffed, blending nicely with her coral suit.

"Hello, Mother. I was just looking at Stewart's book." Summoning a smile, she put the volume down and went to kiss her mother's cheek. It was the automatic act of a younger Alex, but she felt nothing.

"You look well," her mother said, studying her daughter at arm's length.

The look in her eyes puzzled Alex. If she hadn't known better, she would have thought it was pride. "So do you. Would you like some soup? I've got some on in the kitchen."

"Heavens, no! It was my bridge day today, and Caroline served lobster salad. I couldn't eat another bite." She started back toward the front of the house. "In fact, you'll have to excuse me. I've got to get out of my girdle *this minute.*"

And have another little nip, thought Alex grimly as she watched her go. Perhaps this wasn't going to be so bad. Amelia Borden didn't feel like her mother anymore. She was only a middle-aged, North Shore alcoholic. One of hundreds.

Alex went back to the kitchen to eat, but the soup wasn't very satisfying. Foraging in the pantry, she found some stale Rye Crisp. *Don't they eat?* she wondered. *Even Briggie, who hates to cook, keeps frozen burritos or something on hand.*

The thought of Briggie was surprisingly comforting. Alex could see the stout, motherly figure of her friend, sporting her Royals T-shirt, surveying the kitchen in awe.

Her mother reappeared in a bright cotton Mexican shift. "Don't ruin your appetite, dear. Your father will want to take us out."

"What time does he get home?"

"Oh, you know your father." She sank into a chair. "It'll be close to eight, I expect."

Even today, Alex thought. Even the day his daughter comes home after fifteen years.

"Did Grandfather work as hard?" she asked.

Her mother looked startled at the question. Then, glancing away, she said, "Why do you ask about your grandfather?"

"That's why I'm here. I wrote years ago, telling you I was a genealogist," she said lightly. "Don't you think it's time I did my own genealogy?"

Her mother sighed and then sagged a little. Alex saw suddenly how she had aged, shrunken. "It's that Mormon church, isn't it? What more can you want to know about your grandfather? You knew him when he was alive, didn't you?"

Alex was momentarily stunned. How on earth had her mother known of her conversion? After an awkward interval, she managed to go on. "He died when I was fifteen. All I have is his death certificate, and I think it's wrong."

Amelia got up, and Alex, depositing her empty bowl and spoon in the sink, followed her mother back to her sitting room. They sat on the red flowered couch. "Did you have a nice trip?" her mother asked.

"It was fine. I'd forgotten how terrible the traffic was."

"Yes. It's gotten worse. I don't go downtown much anymore."

There was a little silence. Her mother had picked a rose out of the vase on the coffee table and was pulling the petals off. Alex might not have been there. Now was the time to ask her mother questions—while she was drunk, but before she passed out.

"Please, Mother, tell me about Grandfather. I didn't get to ask him anything."

"Like what?" Amelia demanded, her voice suddenly sharp.

Too sharp, Alex thought. At this stage, she should be enjoying a nice, comfortable blurring of reality.

"Well, to start with, I've sent for his military papers," said Alex. "I remembered he was in World War I. That's how he got that scar on his temple. I'd like to know how it happened. Did he ever tell you?"

Her mother's hands were unsteady as they picked at what remained of the rose. "You'll have to ask your father about that. But I doubt if he knows. It wasn't discussed."

"Do you still have anything of his? Personal, I mean. Letters, pictures?"

Her mother shook her head. "Nothing."

"Why? What did you do with everything when he died?"

Amelia looked nonplussed. "Do with everything? What do you mean?"

Suddenly irritated with her mother's stonewalling, Alex demanded, "I mean, did you burn his things, store them, throw them away, put them down the disposal? What did you do with them?"

"Alexandra, this is an absurd conversation. After all, we haven't seen each other in a long time. Aren't there other things to discuss?"

Gritting her teeth, Alex persisted, "I want to know where I came from, who I am. Why does it have to be a mystery? Why won't you ever talk about it?"

Amelia shredded the stem in her hand, thorns and all.

Alex persisted, "May I look in the attic?"

"By all means!" Her mother tossed the mangled flower on the coffee table. For just a moment, the veneer slipped and she looked very drunk. "Try the cellars, and the dungeon, too. Perhaps you think we murdered him and put him under the floor?"

Alex got up and left the room. It was ridiculous to feel like an intruder in her childhood home. She knew suddenly that she must do this before her father came home. He might not allow it, and she didn't want to be forced into a midnight foray. That would be too much like the Brontë sisters for comfort.

August is not the time to search attics, she decided. *It must be over a hundred degrees up here.* Her memories had told her not to expect much, but she was surprised to find the attic so empty. Light from the 60-watt bulb revealed only a few items—the old chest of drawers she associated with her grandfather, some long boxes that probably contained formals, a stack of cardboard file boxes, and her mother's old Singer sewing machine.

The file boxes seemed the most promising. Lifting the top one down, she opened it expectantly and saw that it was neatly packed with files, labeled in her father's precise block capitals. Canceled checks, 1989. Canceled checks, 1988. Canceled checks, 1987, and back through the decade to 1980.

Sighing, she pulled down the next box. This, she was surprised to see, contained her school papers. Alexandra's senior essay. Alexandra's history project. Alexandra's term papers. These were also neatly labeled in her father's hand. She felt an unexpected emotion beneath her numbness. Why had he done this? Why had he cared about her papers? Had he read them? If he cared enough about her to salvage even these dry memories, why had he sent her away?

Scrapbooks, photograph albums, and baby books filled the next box. She had forgotten all about them. Carefully turning the pages of the photo album, she couldn't connect the pictures with herself. Here was a distant childhood recorded in photographs—the Halloween costumes her mother had sewn, ski trips to Colorado at Christmas, a summer in Minnesota.

At first, her recollection was dim, as colorless as the black and white snapshots. Then, somewhere in the middle of the summer in Minnesota, she began to feel, and memory returned. She was on Daddy's shoulders in the middle of the pond they called a lake, chicken fighting with her cousin Bob. Her feet dangled in the warm, murky water while the wind blew her bathing suit, gritty with pond mud, cold against her skin. She was winning! Uncle Richard wasn't nearly as good at this as her father. He didn't really like it. Bob was yelling, "Dad!"

Attack, attack!" while she and her father pursued them across the pond.

She leaned far out to seize Bob's hair, her father's hands strong on her legs. With a great jerk she pulled her cousin toward her. "Yow!" Falling headfirst, Bob made a huge splash as his fat, white body smacked against the water.

"Hooray!" her father cheered, parading her triumphantly onto the shore. "Hooray for Alexandra, Queen Chicken of Loon Lake!"

Alex bit her lip. She didn't want to feel *this*.

Tears prickled behind her lids as she opened her baby book. There was a lock of her hair, her first lost tooth, pictures of her in her crib—odiously chubby, but cheerful.

She had told Dr. Brace that her parents had always been remote. But here was evidence that it wasn't true.

When had everything changed? When had her parents' adoration cooled? What had she done to cut them off from her? It had happened long before Paris. Presumably, it was another of the things she had blocked out. Hadn't she, until this moment, forgotten that there *had* been a time when she was a happy little girl?

Now that was strange. Someone had removed a picture. Peering closer, Alex had difficulty reading the fading ink of the caption. She carried the fragile book over to the 60-watt bulb. "Grandfather Borden and Alexandra, age 6 mos."

Puzzled, she went back to the box, taking out the books one by one, paging through them rapidly. *All the pictures of Grandfather have been removed.* Why? Gooseflesh prickled her arms and legs, even in the oppressive heat.

The final box contained her letters. This surprised her most of all. Except for an annual Christmas card, she and her parents had ceased correspondence altogether after she and Stewart were married, making her monthly allowance obsolete. These were all her Paris letters.

Opening one, she was swept out of the attic, over the sea, into her funny little pie-shaped room on the Left Bank. The reek of garlic drifted up from the kitchen below, and her friend Mika was giggling as she made herself up to resemble a Modigliani painting. There was a hoot from a barge on the Seine and the soft sound of rain on the flagstones below her tiny window.

20 April 1974

Dear Mom and Daddy,

Spring in Paris is as wonderful as everyone claims. Why don't you come for a visit? Mika and I have met lots of French students and even some other Americans who hang out on the Left Bank. The Americans aren't at the Sorbonne. Most of them have lived here several years. It's rather sad, really. Some of them would like to go back to the States, but they can't because they're draft dodgers.

Some of them write novels. One of them is a photographer . . .

This was irrelevant. Hastily cramming the letter back into its envelope, she threw it into the box and shoved the whole mess away from her.

Why had her parents kept her things but rejected her? It just didn't make sense. And she didn't like the way it made her feel.

But she was a professional doing a professional's job. Standing up, she dusted her hands and moved over to the long boxes. They did contain formals. Her formals. She went quickly on to her grandfather's dresser.

The first three drawers contained paint, stain, wood putty, brushes—all apparently used in remodeling the kitchen and her room. The last drawer contained more mementos of hers: childhood books, dolls, and the trophy she had won at the modern dance contest in Chicago her senior year. Of her grandfather, there wasn't a trace.

Her stomach was twisting with the familiar anxiety, and the hot attic suddenly became unbearable. She was perspiring all over. Nothing was making any kind of sense. Her chest was growing tight. *It's time to leave this place. Now!*

Slamming the bottom drawer shut with unnecessary violence, she heard something drop and scrape the floor underneath the dresser. Alex retrieved a small, yellowing studio photograph of a woman she had never seen in her life. This was more like it. Forgetting the knot in her stomach, she carried it over to the light and read, "To Harold. Forever, Sarah."

Who was Harold? Who was Sarah, and what was she doing in Grandfather's chest? She must have been there for years, crammed against the back of the dresser. It was like something out of a gothic novel.

Looking closer at the portrait, Alex made out the tiny gold imprint of a photographer in Des Moines. The woman was pretty but not beautiful. She had a round face, wide-spaced eyes, a short nose, and a tiny mouth. Her hair was worn in a chignon at the nape of her neck.

Hearing a heavy tread on the stairs, Alex hastily stuck the picture in her skirt pocket.

Her father appeared in the doorway. "Xandra?"

"Hello, Father."

The man who approached her was so different from her memory of him that Alex was shocked. He was stooped, gray-haired, old. As he walked over to her, she saw tears standing in his eyes. Trembling, he kissed her on the cheek and then stood looking at her.

"You look wonderful," he said.

Alex cleared her throat and spoke with difficulty. "It's good to see you, Father. Has Mother told you why I'm here?"

At this, her father's face transformed, settling into the starker lines of her memory. "Yes. You'll find nothing up here."

"So I've discovered. What did you do with his things? I mean, this was his home. There must have been tons of stuff."

"You must be thirsty," he said firmly. "We'll discuss it downstairs."

Following him, Alex fingered the photo. "Grandfather's name was Joseph, wasn't it? I mean he wasn't Harold Joseph or anything like that?"

Her father paused on the staircase, then took another heavy step down. "Harold Joseph? Whatever gave you that idea?" he asked.

"I don't know. I just want to make sure I have it right."

Suddenly, she was fed up with being made to feel like a snooper "You've always been so closemouthed about him; he could have a dozen names for all I know."

"Just the one. Joseph Borden," her father replied with irritating calm.

In the living room, Joseph Borden, Jr., went to the bar.

"What would you like?" he inquired, his voice remote.

"Nothing alcoholic, thanks."

He raised an eyebrow. "Oh, yes. I'd forgotten. You've become a tee-totaler, haven't you?"

She had to fight this. He had turned as cold as ice, treating her like a child again. "One alcoholic in the family is enough, don't you think?"

"Alexandra." Her father faced her, his voice frigid. "You are not to make judgments about your mother."

Hot blood scalded her cheeks as she accepted the tonic water he held out to her. "Where is Mother?"

"Gone to lie down. Your hostility was a little hard for her to take." He seated himself calmly on the couch.

"Hostility?" Anger overwhelmed the child in her who still wanted so badly, so futilely, to please. What had happened to that happy little girl in the attic? Why had they taken everything away—the security, the happiness, even the memories?

"What did I ever do to you?" she cried, hurling the words like stones. "What did I ever do to make you reject me? Why did you stop loving me?"

Her father was staring as though she had struck him.

"And what did you do to Grandfather? Wipe him off the face of the earth? Make a bonfire in the backyard and burn up every trace of him?"

He sagged heavily into the couch and looked past her into the hall. "Alexandra," he said tightly. "Sit down and stop this."

"No! I won't stop. You've taken everything away. I won't let you take Grandfather away too."

He deflated suddenly, dropping his head into his hands. "Xandra, believe me, you don't want to know about your grandfather."

Sitting down across from him, she demanded, "He wasn't a crook, was he? Or a murderer? What could be so bad that I shouldn't know about it?"

"It has nothing to do with you. We've always wanted you kept innocent."

"I'm too old to be innocent!" she protested, balling her fists. "Don't you understand? *I'm thirty-five years old!* I've been married and widowed. I earn my own money, pay taxes . . ."

"You will remarry some day," he said heavily, "and hopefully have children. We would prefer if the truth died with your mother and me."

Alex jumped up. "*What truth?* Whatever it is, however horrible, I have a right to know. It's part of me. Part of who I am. Don't you understand? *I want to have some family.*"

Planting herself in front of her father, she fought to keep her hysteria down. "I can't believe that any knowledge could hurt me worse than what you've already done."

At this, he looked up at her, opening his mouth to reply, but she overrode him. "Have you any idea, any idea at all, what it's like to feel completely alone? To feel that no one, not even God, cares about you? Two years ago I was that alone."

Horrified, her father was shrinking away from her.

"Fortunately a wonderful woman found me in time and saved me from doing something stupid. She taught me about God and love and the way families are supposed to be."

Her father's eyes were swimming. He dropped his head. "I'm sorry, Xandra. I didn't know."

Alex gripped his shoulder, forcing him to look at her. "You couldn't, by some wild stretch of the imagination, guess what Stewart's death would do to me? Couldn't you have given me even one word of comfort? No. You sent a wreath and a check, and that was it. Period." He flinched. She couldn't stop. She knew she was hurting him, but her anger had a momentum of its own. "But then, what did you do the last time I was depressed? You sent me away, didn't you? Clear across the world to Paris! What kind of a parent are you?"

He was rigid under her hands, looking at her as though she were a stranger.

Amelia Borden appeared in the doorway, eyes bleary and confused.

"What've you done, Alexandra? What've you done to your father?"

Pushing past her, Alex bounded up the stairs to the guest room. She grabbed her bag, ran down the back staircase, and rushed blindly through the kitchen door to get to her car.

For the first hour, she didn't even know where she was driving. Turning corners automatically, she tried to block out the vision of her father's stricken face by thinking of all the other things she could have said—all the hurts, all the anger, all the emotions that had accumulated in her like dynamite over the past fifteen years.

"I didn't know." Why did her father's pitiful denial echo so tragically in her head? Why wasn't anger enough to blot out the memory of all those relics of childhood, so carefully preserved in an otherwise ruthlessly sterile house?

She eased to the curb, clutching the steering wheel like a life preserver. Her heart felt as though it were under some tremendous pressure, as though at any moment it would explode, blowing her apart into a million pieces.

TWO

That night, in her strange hotel room, Alex dreamed of Stewart. She was standing on the dock of the marina near the Winnetka house. A powerful wind was blowing off Lake Michigan, whipping the water into white-capped waves, and she could see Grandfather's big mahogany boat coming in to dock. Dressed in a navy pea jacket, Stewart was at the helm, looking in her direction but not seeing her. His curly black hair was blowing back from a frowning brow, and his eyes were as stormy as the lake. His lips didn't move, but she heard his thoughts quite plainly. "Alex? What are you doing?"

Then she was running up and down the pier, waving, flapping her arms, struggling to call out, but the words wouldn't come out of her throat.

The boat turned sharply away from her, into the approaching storm.

"Stewart!" The scream finally came, and Alex jerked awake.

It was dark. Her empty arms reached across the bed, but there was only a pillow there. She was alone.

But Stewart had been *here!* Just a moment ago, he had been here—so tangible she could have touched him.

"Stewart!" she moaned, anguish sweeping over her in its familiar black tide. He was gone. Again and forever. She gathered the empty pillow into her arms and cried.

Finally exhausted, Alex lay still, looking up at the unfamiliar acoustical ceiling, remembering where she was and why. Now an image of her father's face came as she had seen it the night before. Was that why she had dreamed of Stewart? To fill the emptiness?

She willed herself to block out the memory of her father's stricken face, but it stayed there, imprinted unforgivingly on her mind. It would probably be there until she died.

No. She wouldn't let that happen. She would find out what she needed to know about Grandfather, and then she would take that knowledge back to her father. Once the truth was out in the open, maybe they could be honest with one another. Maybe they could be a family again. Anything would be better than this. However bad the truth was, reality had to be faced and dealt with. If she had learned nothing else over the past two and a half years, she had learned that.

A thin paring of dawn glimmered through the blackout curtains. Her watch told her it was almost five o'clock—too early to call Briggie, but not too early to be on her way. The first thing to do was to find the woman in the photograph. Sarah.

At seven o'clock, she stopped at Princeton, Illinois, to eat breakfast and make a phone call to Brighamina Poulson, the other half of RootSearch, Inc.

"Briggie?"

"Hello!"

"Is there any reason why you can't meet me in Des Moines?"

The older woman laughed. "No good ones. The Royals aren't even in town. Why? What've you found out?"

"I've got a picture." Alex explained about Sarah.

"And your folks? How did things go with your folks?"

"Not well. Are you sure you can come?"

"It'll be a lot more fun than putting up blackberry jam and mowing the lawn. Where should we meet? The main library?"

"Yes. I've got at least four hours ahead of me, so by the time you get ready and drive there, we ought to arrive close to the same time."

"I'll just take Maxie over to Marigny." Marigny was Daniel's daughter. "That child loves the darned cat, and it makes me feel not quite so guilty about leaving him."

Alex laughed. Maxie was a tiger-striped terror who made his feelings known. It wasn't the cat Briggie worried about so much as the damage he would do if left to himself.

As she restarted her car, Alex thought of Briggie, the woman who had taught her about the gospel of Jesus Christ. A distant relative of Stewart's, Briggie was on a genealogy foray into Scotland when Alex met her. Briggie was the only person in Stewart's family who seemed to understand what his death had taken from her. In her brisk and sensible way, Briggie had scooped Alex up and taken her back home with her to the big house in Independence, Missouri, that had once housed her husband and nine children.

It was only intended to be a visit, but as the light grew in Alex's desolate life and she accepted the hope of the gospel, the visit had grown into a two-year stay. Alex had insisted on paying Briggie room and board after the first month, and she had gradually decided not to return to Scotland. While the memories of that place were bright and painful as knives, life with Briggie was comfortable and the new surroundings reassuring. The panic attacks still came, but they were fewer and farther between. Her psychiatrist thought that her present surroundings were much more conducive to full recovery than Scotland would be without Stewart.

Then there had been her new hobby that had turned into a profession—genealogy. Though Briggie and the gospel had heightened her passion for the subject, it was actually Stewart who had originally kindled it years before with his sudden whim to see his ancestral home.

Alex grinned as she recalled that trip. They hadn't been married then. Hitchhiking from Paris to Calais, shelling out a few precious francs for the Channel crossing, and then changing most of their remaining money into pounds for the train journey north, they had arrived in Inveraray on a rainy summer's day. Stewart had never doubted that they would be taken in by overjoyed relations, and he had been right. Before a year had gone by, they were absorbed into the family, "sorted out," and married properly in the village *kirk*.

There were Campbells everywhere. To Alex, with her sparse experience of family, Campbells seemed to occupy most of Scotland. For something to do and as a way of further defining and understanding her new relations, she had begun to group the progeny on paper, sorting out who descended from which great uncle—Jock, Iain, or Duncan. This had led to an interest in the next generation back and so on, until she had become hopelessly hooked on family history. Those first years of research had been quite a struggle, for the never-ending religious conflicts had destroyed a heartbreaking number of ecclesiastical and civil records. Scottish genealogy depended mostly on land records because there had been a tax on entries recorded in the parish register during various periods. Many thrifty Scots trusted the Lord would recognize the baptism of their infants without the costly benefit of an entry in the official register.

Then Briggie had come to Inveraray on her visit from the States, bringing all the expertise Alex lacked, and between them they had traced Stewart's and Briggie's common ancestors back to 1686. From there it had been easy to go back and discover that they were descended from King Malcolm, better known as the father-in-law of Macbeth.

Smiling in anticipation of the hunt that lay ahead of them today, Alex turned up the radio and pressed the gas pedal closer to the floor. Her red CRX leaped ahead. Those happy, halcyon days were gone, but when she and Briggie were together, building another pedigree out of scraps and bits, something of that old joy revived. Today they would have fun.

* * *

Halfway through Daniel's eleven o'clock session, which was already running fifteen minutes behind schedule, the intercom buzzed. Frowning, he apologized briefly to his client and went into the next office to take the call. Only emergencies impelled Debbie to interrupt sessions.

"Dr. Grinnell?"

"Speaking."

"This is Lieutenant O'Neill of the Winnetka Police Department. We have information that you are taking care of a cat for a Mrs. Brighamina Poulson?"

Winnetka? Police? Briggie? "I am?" With Briggie, of course, anything was possible.

"You *are* Dr. Daniel Grinnell?"

"Of course I am." Of that, at least, he was certain.

"We have information from a neighbor that Mrs. Poulson left to deliver her cat to your house around eight o'clock this morning."

"That's possible. My daughter usually tends him when Brig . . . er, uh, Mrs. Poulson goes out of town. You're calling about a cat?"

"Not exactly. We need your help, Dr. Grinnell. We're trying to locate a Mrs. Alexandra Campbell, whose last known address was with Mrs. Poulson. The neighbor also told us that you are friendly with both women. Can you give us any idea where Mrs. Campbell might be right now?"

"I am a friend of Mrs. Campbell's," he admitted, shaken. Why were they trying to find Alex? "I may be able to locate her. Could you tell me what this is all about?"

"I'm afraid not, Dr. Grinnell. Police business."

"What kind of police business?"

"Now then, Doctor, are you going to help us or not?"

Daniel took a deep breath. "Look, Lieutenant. I'm a therapist. Mrs. Campbell has been very ill. I need to know what this is about before I turn you loose on her."

"Been ill, has she? Mentally ill?"

Why had he given that away? His professionalism was clearly shot where Alex was concerned. "I'm afraid I can't help you, Lieutenant."

"Even a doctor can't obstruct justice." The policeman's voice had turned grim.

"I'm out of your jurisdiction, Officer. Not even the same state, in case you hadn't noticed."

"In cases of suspicious death, we have ways of getting around things like that."

"Suspicious death? You mean murder?" His stomach did a somersault. "Who's been murdered?"

"Heard of the Tranquilor killings?"

Dumbfounded, he could only reply, "On TV?"

"Yeah. Could be we've got another one. Or could be something else."

"Who's dead, for crying out loud?"

"Just tell me where to find her, Doc."

In a split second, Daniel saw what he needed to do. "Look, Lieutenant. How about this? You tell me what's going on, and I'll find Mrs. Campbell and bring her to your doorstep."

There was a heartbeat of silence, then, "You don't have her here by tonight, and you're in trouble, Doc. Her father's dead. Mother says it's suicide. We're not satisfied. Could be one of the Tranquilor murders or something more specific."

Closing his eyes, Daniel felt the room go upside down.

"I'll have Mrs. Campbell there as soon as possible."

"Tonight."

After the connection was cut, Daniel sat for a long time, phone buzzing in his ear. What in the world was going on?

* * *

When she pulled into the library parking lot, Alex's watch told her it was nearly noon. She had made excellent time. Recognizing Briggie's Bronco by the gun rack and license plate—ROOTS 2—she headed for the genealogy and local history room, anticipating what she would find. She wasn't disappointed. In her Nike track shoes, Royals T-shirt, and white polyester slacks, her friend and partner was easily distinguishable as she talked animatedly with a librarian in steel-rimmed glasses. Grinning, Alex eased up stealthily behind Briggie and tweaked her ear.

"Hello, Briggs. Have you got the layout?"

Turning around, Briggie looked at her over the tops of her half-glasses. "Hello, honey. Have you eaten?"

"A shake at McDonald's."

Before Briggie could remonstrate over her diet, Alex produced Sarah's picture and introduced herself to the librarian.

"Can you tell me anything about this photographer?" she asked, handing Sarah over.

"Hmm. Simms. I don't know the name. Let's have a look in an old directory. From the hairstyle, I'd say it was made somewhere after 1914. This kind of style with the chignon low on the back of the head was popular then. It went with their hats. Before that time it would have been more elaborate."

"You're probably right, then." Alex was impressed.

The directories showed a Simms Portrait Studio near the old Fort Madison Hotel. Further checking revealed that it had apparently gone out of business sometime during 1919, as it was not in the 1920 directory.

"Good. That gives us the limits then," Briggie declared. "It was made between 1914 and 1919."

"Do you have an index of marriage announcements in the *Des Moines Register?*" Alex asked hopefully. "Harold was probably her husband. This may even have been an engagement photo."

"Seems reasonable," Briggie agreed thoughtfully.

"Well, we have an index," the librarian said doubtfully. "But I'm afraid it's going to be a long job without a surname. Harolds and Sarahs were pretty common back then."

Pulling out the little loose-leaf notebook she carried in her purse, Alex followed the librarian back to the microfilm area.

"All the indexes are in this drawer." She indicated a tall gray metal cabinet. "Put used films on top of the cabinet, and if I can be of any more help, let me know."

So they began the tedious job of extracting Harold and Sarah marriages from the index. To begin with, Briggie looked through the 1914 index, Alex through the 1915. By three o'clock, they had the wedding dates of ten possible couples.

"I'm going to start looking these up in the newspaper," Briggie said. "If we get lucky early and find her picture, we won't have to go through all those indexes."

"It would be nice, wouldn't it?" Alex yawned as she inserted the 1916 microfilm in the machine. The tormented night was taking its toll with a throbbing headache and gritty eyes.

Only five of the ten wedding announcements had photographs; none was Sarah. Briggie printed the announcements for the five others on the reader-printer and stuck them in her blue canvas carry-all.

Alex handed over the 1916 index entries and began on the next year. She was tired, there was no doubt about it, but she was also at peace. They were going to get to the bottom of this mystery. They always did.

At six o'clock, Briggie called a halt. Alex had just completed the 1917 index. Altogether, she had accumulated twenty-five possible couples, and Briggie had eliminated fifteen on the basis of photographs through the year 1916. It was time to eat.

Over waffles and bacon at the Village Inn, they reviewed the photocopies Briggie had made of the remaining ten possibilities.

"I think we can eliminate this one," Alex said, crumpling it with pleasure. "Second marriage. The bride was a grandmother."

"Okay," Briggie said, peering through her half-glasses. "This is doubtful, too. The bride was from Chicago. Probably would have had her portrait made there." She set it aside temporarily. "That leaves us with eight." She took a bite of waffle and whipped cream. "It would be nice if we could find her, picture and all, but I'm beginning to think it won't be that easy. The ones who had pictures seemed to be pretty prominent in society. For some reason, Sarah strikes me as being fairly humble."

"Me, too. And it's odd, isn't it? Because Grandfather was very wealthy. How would he have met little Sarah from Des Moines?"

Briggie swallowed the last sip of her orange juice. "We'll find out. Nobody's defeated us for long." Taking Sarah's picture from the table where Alex had placed it, she continued, "You know, even if that studio hadn't closed, I'd have said 1919 was the upper limit. Women started bobbing their hair after the war."

"That's right. Suffragettes and all that." Alex was thoughtful. "You know, my grandfather was in the war. Do you think that could be it?" Pushing her half-eaten waffle away, she said, "Grandfather may have known this Harold in France. Perhaps he died or something, and Grandfather got the picture."

"Why?"

"I don't know. Maybe he wanted to return it to her in person, recount Harold's last brave moments."

"That is an idea. Let's see. The Americans got into the war in 1917. You've done that year, haven't you? How about if we cross-check the Harolds in your marriage index with the obituaries for 1917 to 1918? If Harold did die in the war, we could find him that way."

"It's just a crazy idea, Briggie."

"But worth checking out," her friend assured her. "It could save us a lot of work. Besides, it makes a lot of sense, don't you think?"

Once back at the library, they planned their method of attack. "We've got eight possibles, right?" Briggie asked, counting the photocopies.

"Right." Alex agreed.

"If you're right about Harold, there's a way we can pare this list down even further," Briggie said, heading for the librarian with the steel rims. Alex followed.

"Do you have any lists of Polk County men who served in the First World War?" her friend inquired.

Leading them back through the stacks, the librarian handed them a heavy Polk County history. Alex checked the index, her hands not quite steady. Suddenly, she had that feeling—that wonderful, glorious feeling that meant they were getting close.

"Read the eight Harolds' surnames, Briggie."

"Brown. North. Oakley . . ."

"Yes!"

"Okay, that's one. O'Hara. Rogers . . ."

"Another one!"

"Simpson . . ."

"All right!"

"Summers. Temple."

"Okay." Jamming the history back onto the shelf, Alex checked her watch. It was seven-thirty. Just thirty minutes until the library closed. "Oakley, Rogers, Simpson. Obituaries."

They nearly ran back to the newspaper index cabinet. Starting with 1917, they checked the obituary index for the three Harolds.

At five minutes to eight, they found it. With trembling hands, Alex removed the film carefully from the reader and took it to the reader-printer. Harold Simpson had been killed in early November 1918, a week before Armistice.

Had they really found Grandfather's Sarah's Harold? He had left two children, Harold, Jr., and Mary. While she copied the obituary, Briggie was already looking up Harold, Jr., in the telephone book.

THREE

Where was Alex? It was almost nine hours since Daniel had talked to O'Neill, and he still had no idea. The most obvious genealogical haunts—the Chicago Public Library, the Winnetka Public Library, the Family History Center in Wilmette—had yielded nothing. Did she know her father was dead? Was she in a blind panic, heading for Canada or something?

Briggie had probably gone to meet her somewhere, but the neighbor who had been so helpful to the police had no information to add when he talked to her. Wherever they were, maybe they would head home tonight. He would put O'Neill off until the morning, anyway. Popping an antacid tablet into his mouth, he went to the basement for his workout. Weight lifting had kept him sane when his wife had run off with her golf pro, but murder was another matter. He doubted whether anything could dispel his anxiety tonight.

After Daniel left the study, Maxie stalked into the room and settled himself beneath the edge of the desk. Rolling onto his back, he batted the telephone cord with his paws. The receiver skittered off onto the hardwood floor. Jumping up, Maxie nosed it disdainfully and prowled away.

* * *

Harold, Jr., if still alive, did not live in Des Moines. "That would have been too easy," Briggie said bracingly. "Which route do you want to take to find Mary?"

"We can't do anything without her married name. I don't remember if Iowa has a statewide index of marriages, do you?"

"Let's ask Ms. Steel Rims."

Iowa did indeed have a statewide index. It was in the Lucas State Office Building, which would open at 9:00 a.m. Ms. Steel Rims drew a map.

"Let's find a hotel and then have a little snack," Briggie suggested.

After checking in at the Super Eight, they located a Perkins Coffee Shop around the corner and ordered hot-fudge sundaes. Traveling with Briggie was always a highly caloric proposition.

"Okay. Simpson's obit says he went to France in August 1917," Alex began. The index says they were married in July 1914. You have the copy of that announcement, don't you?"

"Yes. Nothing there except the names of the parents and attendants, if we need them later." Briggie was doing sums on the napkin. "Here's the general picture. According to the obit, they had only the two children. Probably one in 1915 and one in 1917. If Mary is still alive she could be anywhere from . . . seventy-three to seventy-five."

"She would probably have married around 1935," Alex added. "So if she has children, they would be in their mid-to-late fifties."

"Right." Briggie's face lit up at the arrival of her sundae.

* * *

Back at the hotel, Alex took a much-needed shower. When she emerged, Briggie was immersed in a Royals game. "They've got no business being in the basement!" she said, punching the imaginary glove on her right hand. "Don't they know they've got the highest paid pitchers in the majors?"

"Where are they playing?" Alex asked.

"Toronto. Blue Jays are in first place, if you can believe that."

"How's George doing?"

"Don't ask," her friend grumbled. "He's injured again. It's enough to make me take up sports medicine. The score's six-zip, in case you're interested."

The Royals' pitcher proceeded to walk the bases full. Disgusted, Briggie aimed the remote and zapped the whole game into hyperspace. "I've been trying to reach Marigny," she said. "Just to make sure Maxie isn't climbing the living room curtains or something. But the line keeps being busy. Either she's got a boyfriend, or it's off the hook."

"It's probably Daniel. Someone's in crisis. His patients call him day or night."

* * *

The next morning, they were delayed by forms and friendly Iowa bureaucrats. Finally, having paid $10.00, they got the marriage certificate of Mary Simpson, born 1915, Des Moines, daughter of Harold and Sarah Simpson. On 20 July 1934, she had married Timothy Montgomery, auto mechanic, son of Michael and Esther Montgomery, also of Des Moines.

Racing to the public telephone in the downstairs lobby, they checked the directory. Timothy Montgomery was not listed. There was no Mary, nor even an M. Montgomery. Alex could have wept with frustration. They had come too far to end with disappointment.

"Perhaps we need to spring for a death certificate. Another ten dollars," she groaned. "Then back to the obits."

Briggie was thinking. "I've got an idea. Does that book have yellow pages?"

"No. But there's a separate book here. All yellow pages."

"Look up nursing homes, retirement homes, or whatever they're called."

"Briggie, you're brilliant!" Alex revived.

There were thirty such homes in the metropolitan area. Getting change from the nearby pop machine, they divided the list between them and began calling.

With her fifth call, Alex struck pay dirt at the Lilac Haven Nursing Home.

"Yes, we have a Mary Montgomery here. Who's enquiring, please?"

"I'm a genealogist, Alexandra Campbell. Is Mrs. Montgomery allowed to have visitors?"

"Oh yes. She's very lonely. She enjoys visitors."

"Wonderful! Perhaps you could have someone prepare her for our coming. My friend and I have some questions to ask her. Is her health good?"

"She has good days and bad days. Congestive heart problems. But a visitor will be good for her. I'm afraid her children aren't too attentive."

Excitement trembled through Alex's fingers, making it difficult to jot down the directions. At last, she hung up and threw her arms around Briggie. "We did it!"

But on their way to the home, Alex's elation deflated somewhat. "We've assumed an awful lot, Briggie."

"It's the only way to work," her friend reminded her. "We're not accountants. We've got to go on our hunches, or we'd never get anywhere."

"I suppose the old soul won't be the worse for a visit, anyway, even if we are wrong. The Lilac Haven lady said her children don't pay her much attention."

"Thank the Lord I'm not seventy-five and in a rest home!"

"You'll never go to a rest home, Briggie. Your kids and I will be fighting over who gets you. I'll win though. I'm the only one who lives anywhere near the Royals' stadium."

Lilac Haven proved to be a run-down establishment not far from the stockyards. It had obviously been built as cheaply as possible. The vinyl siding was buckled, and the asphalt roof lacked more than a few shingles. Inside the door, the nasty smell of disinfectant and dirty linen hit them in the face. Alex's stomach tightened. What a horrible place it was! The linoleum was scuffed and dirty; the acoustical ceiling tiles stained by water leaks.

The receptionist, a brassy blond wearing a coral polyester uniform, greeted them cheerfully. "You must be Mary's visitors."

Alex pulled out one of her business cards, handed it to the woman, and introduced her partner.

"Is she expecting us?"

"Yes. She's quite excited. It's one of her better days, but I had to explain to her what a genealogist was."

Leading them down the dim hallway, she stopped before room 10 and gave a little knock. "Your visitors, Mrs. Montgomery!"

Alex held her breath, fingering Sarah's picture in her pocket. When the door opened, she saw a tiny, white-haired woman sitting in a wheelchair and reading a luridly jacketed romance.

Flashing an amused glance at Briggie, Alex felt all the tension in her drain away. Hadn't she unconsciously expected the woman to be crocheting a doily?

"Mrs. Montgomery?" she inquired. "I'm Alex Campbell, and this is my friend Brighamina Poulson. May we talk to you for a few minutes?"

Carefully marking her place with a Precious Moments bookmark, the woman peered up at them. "I don't know much about genie . . . whatever you call it, but Janice here says it just means your family tree." The woman's speech was accompanied by heavy wheezing, as though she had to make an effort to grab the air necessary for each word.

Alex suddenly realized she had no idea what to say. How on earth was she supposed to account for her interest? She decided to stick as close to the truth as possible.

Pulling the picture out of her pocket, she said, "A member of my family found this picture in a drawer and asked me if I could find out anything about it. You see, my job is tracing people's families. I wondered," Alex passed the old woman the picture, "could this be your mother?"

Doubtfully, the woman shifted her bewildered gaze from Alex's face to the picture she was holding. Her initial glance was blank, but slowly a look of recognition and pure joy lit her features. "This is Ma! This is my ma! Well, how do you like that?" she wheezed excitedly.

Elation surged through Alex. She felt as though she'd just won the sweepstakes. Briggie winked at her. They'd done it! They'd found Sarah! It was only with great difficulty that she was able to preserve a professional facade.

"To Harold. Forever, Sarah. Well, now. I never saw anything like it," Mary Montgomery was saying.

"Could you tell us something about your mother?" Alex asked hopefully.

Mary's eyes had clouded over with emotion. Alex fished in her bag for a tissue, but Briggie was quicker. Sitting on the bed next to the old woman, she handed her a clean handkerchief and admired the picture. "She was pretty, wasn't she?" Briggie murmured sympathetically. "And you have her eyes, haven't you?"

"That's what she always said," Mary sniffed. "Poor Ma."

"She had a hard life?"

"Yes, looking back. Not that I ever thought much about it then. Kids don't, you know."

Alex detected a grievance here and hoped Briggie could avoid the trap. Looking around the room for the first time, she noticed a complete absence of photographs. It was a grim little room, in fact—one bed, one chair, one chest of drawers, and only a small window with a depressing view of an empty parking lot, except for her own little red CRX. It was enough to drive anyone to romance novels.

"This must have been taken before her marriage, don't you think?" Briggie inquired gently.

The other woman harrumphed. "Probably."

Sensing a change in the old lady's mood, Alex raised her brows at Briggie.

"You never knew your father, did you?" Briggie's voice was sympathetic now. Alex knew the emotion wasn't feigned. "Didn't he go to France right after you were born?"

The woman's lips set in a hard line. "You know an awful lot. What's this all about anyway? My ma's been dead over sixty-two years."

Alex took over. "Why don't you tell us about your children?" She opened her notebook. "We have to put them on the family tree, too." It was a purely diversionary tactic, of course, though one never knew what might come in handy.

"Well, now." Mary Montgomery settled herself back in her chair. "My youngest is the clever one. Named him Robert, after the actor, you know. Calls himself an ontri-penure. Works in Vegas. Just as well, 'cause he has his Dad's temper." She looked around the room smugly and indicated the color TV. "He pays for this place. Bought me that TV last Christmas."

Guilt offering, Alex decided. "When was he born?"

"Forty-one. Pearl Harbor day. His Daddy enlisted the day after, and we never saw him again."

"So, history repeats itself," Alex murmured.

"What?"

"Nothing, just talking to myself. Your daughter's name?"

"Patsy. Was married, but she kicked her husband out. She's a cashier out to the truck stop on the highway. Could've married again lots of times, but she's down on men. Can't say I blame her."

"And she was born in . . . ?"

" Thirty-five. Right smack dab in the middle of the Depression. Her daddy was out of work. We were livin' with his folks."

Alex decided she'd laid her groundwork well enough. "Let me ask you a few questions about your mother. One thing is really puzzling me. Did she ever mention the name Joseph Borden to you?"

"What do you want to know for?"

"He was my grandfather."

The old woman looked Alex over as though seeing her for the first time. "So, you're a Borden. Thought you said your name was something else."

"Borden is my maiden name. You have heard the name, then?" Alex's heart was thudding in her throat, but she tried to keep her voice casual, patient.

"Man named Borden was in the war with my dad. He wrote mother. Used to send us money." Mary gave the information grudgingly.

Taking a deep breath, Alex darted a glance at Briggie. "Did anyone save his letters?"

"Well, we found them in mother's things when she died. I remember bein' surprised. First I'd heard of him. I don't know where they are now. Always thought there was something fishy about the whole thing."

"Why?"

"Rich people don't get that way by giving away money to people they hardly know, now do they?" There was acid in her voice, detectable even through the wheezing.

Alex wished she'd known her grandfather better. Wasn't it possible that he would have done something like that out of

Christian charity? "My grandfather always kept this picture, Mary. Perhaps he promised your father he would take care of your mother."

"Don't seem likely to me."

"What do you think the reason was?"

"Not charity, anyway," the woman said, her look caustic. "The letters . . ."

Before Alex could even react, the woman's expression froze and her eyes bulged in panic as she began gasping for air like a landed fish. In an instant, Briggie had grabbed the oxygen cylinder in the corner and was pressing the mask over Mary's contorted face. "Get that woman," she commanded tersely, indicating the hallway with a jerk of her head.

Badly frightened, Alex flung open the door and ran down the hall towards the front desk. Janice looked up at the sound and made her way toward her. "Is something wrong?"

"Yes. I'm afraid . . . I'm afraid Mrs. Montgomery got a little excited. My friend is giving her oxygen . . ."

With a look of weary resignation, Janice made her way unhurriedly down the corridor toward Room 10.

"Isn't there a doctor, someone we should call?"

"We only call Doctor in emergencies." Janice said firmly. "I think you and your friend had better go."

Surely this was an emergency? But Alex did not reenter the room. The sight of her might only make the woman worse. What had she been going to say that excited her so much?

In a moment, Briggie came out, Sarah's picture in her hand.

"Thank heavens. I was afraid she wouldn't give it up." Alex took the photo and stuck it in her bag. Somewhat guiltily, they made their way out of Lilac Haven.

"Well, what do you make of it?" Alex asked as soon as they were under way.

"I'm afraid we're not any forwarder," Briggie sighed. "It's pretty much as we thought. They met in the war. He wanted to do the widow a good turn."

"Mary certainly didn't seem to think so. Why do you suppose she had that attack?"

"Spite. Once she heard who you were, her whole attitude seemed to change."

"Really, Briggie. This isn't Shakespeare. People don't choke on spite."

Her friend shrugged. "Nasty feelings raise your blood pressure. That increases your heartbeat. Hyperventilation . . . and there you are. In her condition she has to fight for every breath."

"But why should she have nasty feelings toward me?"

"Daniel could probably tell us."

Alex sighed, exhaustion descending on her like a heavy blanket. "It's been fun, but I'm afraid we've wasted a lot of time."

"We don't know that. Maybe the letters would tell us something. Then there's Sarah herself. Should we look up her obit? Mary said sixty years ago. Around 1930."

Alex looked at her watch. "Do you realize it's lunchtime?"

"Now that you mention it, I'm starved. Let's find that Perkins again. I want to try their Philly Cheese Steak Sandwich."

Twenty minutes later, they pulled into the restaurant parking lot.

"I think I'll just try calling Marigny again," Briggie said, sighting a pay phone inside the entrance. "You go ahead and get us a table."

Briggie was gone a long time. By the time she returned, the waitress had brought their water and was hovering, anxious to take their order.

Alex thought she looked worried.

"I'll just have a bowl of soup," her friend told the waitress.

"The fruit salad, please."

Sticking her pencil behind her ear, their waitress departed, and Alex inquired, "What's wrong? I thought you were going to have the steak sandwich?"

Briggie unrolled her silverware from the napkin. "I don't know. Daniel wouldn't say. He's on his way up here. We're to meet him at the airport. He'll be on the first plane from Kansas City."

"What? But what did he say, Briggie? What reason did he give?"

Her friend's eyes were serious. "He said he wasn't going to tell us over the phone. He's been trying to get us since noon yesterday. That darned cat of mine knocked the phone off the hook last night." Briggie fidgeted with the corners of her napkin. "Do you suppose it's one of the kids?"

Alarm shot through Alex like an electric shock. Briggie had nine children and thirty grandchildren scattered between Boston and San Francisco.

"But how would anyone know to call Daniel?"

"The cat. I told Frances next door that I was taking the cat to Marigny so she wouldn't worry. She hates it when I go away. Maxie whines at her door until she lets him in."

When the food arrived they ate only half-heartedly. "It's an hour to the airport from Daniel's office, Briggie. Don't you want a sundae? He won't be arriving for a while yet."

"I just want to get to the airport," her friend said.

They paid their check and left.

Driving south to the Des Moines airport, Alex racked her brain for comforting phrases. She owed her life to Briggie, and her sanity. When Stewart had died, she had felt bereft in Scotland. She hadn't known where on earth she belonged. Stewart's relatives had been more than kind, but they had their own way of dealing with grief. They shut it away, never speaking of it, never speaking of Stewart. She had thought she'd go crazy if she couldn't talk about it. Briggie, recently widowed herself, had understood. In addition to taking her home with her and introducing Alex to the gospel, Briggie had found Dr. Brace and had driven Alex to the appointments that she would have skipped. When money was low, Briggie had somehow miraculously worked the details out with Dr. Brace so Alex could continue treatment. For two years, she had lived with Briggie, only recently venturing out into a life of her own.

"I love you," was all she could think of to say. Reaching across, she squeezed her friend's hand. A wave of helplessness choked her.

Arriving at the airport, they ascertained that the next flight from Kansas City was on U.S. Air arriving at three-thirty. Would he make it? Probably. They had called him shortly after noon. It was now one-thirty.

The time dragged. Through the glass of the vending machine, Alex scanned the headlines of the *Des Moines Register.* There had been another Tranquilor murder. The S & L campaign funding scandal was still front-page news, along with continuing upheaval in the Russian Parliament. Depressing, boring, scary. She decided to pass up the paper and browsed through the magazines instead. Astrid Borden winked at her from the cover of *Penthouse*. Grabbing the offending magazine, Alex turned it backward in the rack. Finally settling on *American Photographer*, she joined Briggie, who was pretending to concentrate on Tom Clancy's latest thriller.

Finally, Daniel's flight was being announced. Alex didn't know whether to be relieved or not. Her stomach was turning flips, and Briggie's hand was clammy as she held it tightly in hers.

There he was at last, running a hand through his ginger hair, his stocky, wrestler's body taut with some new tension. His worried eyes scanned the little crowd of those greeting the plane and homed in on her face. He pushed his way through. Ignoring Briggie, he looked at Alex with obvious concern.

"Daniel? What is it? What's wrong?"

"Alex, I'm afraid I have some bad news."

Bad news? She heard Briggie make a little sound next to her.

"For me? It's not one of Briggie's children then?"

"Briggie's children?" He looked at Briggie in confusion and then dawning realization. "Is that what you thought? Oh, Briggie, forgive me. It never occurred to me . . . I just didn't want to tell you over the phone. No. It's Alex's father."

"My father?"

Daniel put both hands on her shoulders. "Yes. Alex. I'm afraid your father is dead."

"Dead?" she echoed blankly. "No, he isn't. I just saw him day before yesterday. He wasn't dead."

"He's dead. He died the same night."

Looking frantically from Briggie to Daniel, she felt her throat closing and clutched at her windpipe. "No. You're making this up! It isn't true! Why are you saying this?" She jerked away from them, walking blindly down the hall, her hands still fumbling at her throat.

Daniel came after her, "Alex, I'm sorry, but you've got to listen. There's more."

His voice was coming from far away. "No!" she insisted. "He isn't dead. He can't be dead. Somebody's made a mistake!"

People were beginning to stare. She had to get out. Briggie was running after them.

"Go away," she told Daniel. "Get away from me."

Breaking into a run, she sprinted wildly through the terminal doors. Air! She had to have air! She was suffocating.

Darting between the cars lining the curb, she didn't even feel their bumpers snagging at her skirt. She dashed across the street, heedless of the oncoming traffic, looking frantically for the entrance to the parking lot.

Suddenly she felt sick. Grabbing desperately at a signpost, she tried to hold herself up, but everything was spinning, and the sun was going out. Something was wrong with the sun.

FOUR

Opening her eyes, Alex found that Daniel was carrying her.

She was going to be sick. Don't, she told herself, closing her eyes again. Don't get sick all over Daniel. She felt people staring, crowding around her.

At last. A place with a bed. It smelled vaguely medicinal, and, opening her eyes, Alex saw a tiny white room with a large metal first-aid chest. She was lying on a cot.

"I'm going to be sick," she told Daniel. Promptly hauling her off the bed, he held her over a stainless steel sink while she heaved. She couldn't stop. The retching went on and on until it was nothing but dry spasms.

Then Briggie was there, holding her, rinsing her cold, sweaty face, laying her back on the cot. Where had Daniel gone?

"Daniel?" The room seemed dark, though it was flooded with fluorescent light. "Where's Daniel?"

A shape resolved itself at the foot of her cot, broad shoulders and square chest. "I'm here, Alex." His voice was heavy and sad, and she remembered then about Daddy.

Squeezing her eyes shut, she moaned. Daddy was dead. She would never be able to make things okay between them. Aching with remorse and grief, she curled herself into a ball and prayed that it would be all over right now, that she would die this minute and stop hurting.

"Alex." Daniel was kneeling beside her.

"*Go away, Daniel.*" I want to die. Please let me. die. Don't make me feel this.

She heard him get up, felt him go from her. "No!" she cried, sitting up in alarm, holding out her empty arms.

Kneeling again, he gathered her to him and held her tightly. Alex began to sob.

After a long interval, she whispered hoarsely, "How did he die?"

Daniel held her away from him a little so he could see her face. Looking away, she gripped his hands.

"They're not sure, Alex. I'm supposed to take you back to Winnetka. They want to ask you some questions. It looks like it was another one of those Tranquilor killings."

She stared at him blankly. Not the headline! Not Daddy! This couldn't be real! "No!" she cried again, snatching her hands away.

"I'm sorry, Alex," he said softly. "I can only guess how it must hurt."

"There's got to be a mistake," she whispered hoarsely. "It couldn't be Daddy."

Daniel stayed where he was, making no further attempt to hold her. When he spoke, his voice was firm. "I know this is difficult, Alex. It would be difficult for anyone. But we have to be on the five o'clock plane for Chicago."

Numbly, she stared at his shirt buttons. Briggie appeared from somewhere with Alex's luggage, which had been stashed in the Bronco.

"I'll follow you up tonight," her friend told them. "I phoned the Super Eight. They'll keep the CRX."

"You're coming with me?" Alex asked Daniel.

"Of course."

* * *

The brief plane ride was a blur of impressions—holding Daniel's hand, sipping Sprite from a plastic cup, vomiting again in the airsick bag. Worst of all, the horrible idea kept drumming in her head.

"Maybe he did it himself," she said finally. "He could have rigged it up to look like one of those Tranquilor poisonings so Mother would get the insurance."

"I don't know about Illinois," Daniel spoke in his reasonable, therapist voice, "but in Missouri, if the policy's more than two years old, the company has to pay, regardless of whether it was suicide or not."

"Well, if it was, it was my fault. I was horrible to him, Daniel. I knew I was hurting him, but I just kept on doing it. It was like stabbing him over and over again with a knife."

"Get hold of yourself, Alex. You certainly can't take that line with the police," he said firmly. "If he committed suicide, it was his own choice, just as everything else he did in his life was his choice. You're not responsible for his emotions."

"Don't give me that! I *am* responsible. I hurt him. There were tears in his eyes when I left him!"

"Don't you think he was crying because of what *he* had done—what he had chosen to do to you?"

Her chest tightened in pain. "How can I possibly know? How will I ever know?"

"You'll ferret it out," he smiled faintly, his voice gentler, less professional. "Maybe your mother can tell us something."

Mother. She hadn't even thought about Mother.

But now Amelia was suddenly present, towering over her, eyes troubled and accusing: "Alexandra, what have you done to your father?"

The words taunted her the rest of the way to Chicago.

* * *

Lieutenant O'Neill was a short, muscle-bound man with thick, curly black hair and a heavy five-o'clock shadow. He stood at the end of the jet walk, watching her come toward him, beating a tattoo against his leg with a rolled newspaper.

When she got close enough to see his eyes, Alex felt uneasy. Whatever the expression was in those eyes, it wasn't sympathy.

She forced herself to greet him, "I guess you're waiting for me. I'm Alexandra Campbell."

Daniel was stiffly cordial. He extended a hand. "Daniel Grinnell."

"Lieutenant O'Neill." The policeman shook hands perfunctorily. "Afraid Mrs. Campbell needs to come with us to the police station. You got transportation?"

"I can rent a car, if necessary, but I'd rather go with Mrs. Campbell."

"You her lawyer?"

"You know I'm not."

"'Fraid you'll have to rent a car then."

Alex felt some of the stiffening go out of her, then immediately held herself straighter. She could get through this without Daniel. She'd gone through lots of things without Daniel. "Fine. Let's go and get it over with. I need to see my mother."

"Your mother's under heavy sedation. Doubt if she'd know you. They'll take care of her just fine in the hospital. That all your luggage?"

Alex nodded.

"Let's go then."

"I'll wait for you outside the station," Daniel told her as they parted by the Avis desk.

The drive to Winnetka in the back of the police car was like riding in the limousine to Stewart's funeral. Once again she was outside herself, viewing a strange, numbed woman with black hair, disheveled and pale, holding her hands tightly in her lap.

* * *

The Winnetka Police Station was housed inside a modern building with a scalloped roof. It looked oddly out of place, planted amid the town's traditional facade. Led to a small office with a gray metal desk, Alex sat down and squared her shoulders. She must keep focused on the present if she was to get through this.

The lieutenant introduced her to Sergeant Lindsey, a tall blond who would be helping with the investigation. Lindsey leaned against the door frame while O'Neill perched on the edge of his desk, ready to begin his interrogation.

"Now, Mrs. Campbell," he began, his bloodshot blue eyes probing hers keenly. "Tell us about the last time you saw your father."

She took a deep breath and began, her voice firm. "I'm a professional genealogist. I hadn't seen my parents for quite some time. I decided to make a trip up here, which I did three days ago, in order to find out more about my grandfather."

"Did you?"

"No. They wouldn't tell me anything."

"Were you estranged from your parents, Mrs. Campbell?"

It sounded exactly like an old Dragnet. "I guess so. They haven't had much contact with me since I went to Paris fifteen years ago. I lived in Scotland for ten years after I was married. When I came back to the States two and a half years ago, I lived with Mrs. Poulson, a relative of my husband's."

"What was the reason for the estrangement?"

"I have no idea," she told him coldly. "Nor do I have any idea why they refused to discuss my grandfather with me. I'm sure you've heard I quarreled with my father. That was why."

O'Neill looked down at his blotter, where he was doodling a small, neat spiral.

"You're going to have to level with me, Mrs. Campbell. Money and influence don't mean squat in a murder investigation. We're not having any Claus von Bulows on the North Shore, believe me."

"I am leveling with you," she insisted, suddenly angry. "And I haven't got money *or* influence."

"The Borden name and six million dollars don't count?"

This offensive confused her. "The Borden name? Daddy was the owner of Borden Meats, but that doesn't have anything to do with me. And I certainly don't have six million dollars."

"That's an approximate amount of the estate."

Alex was stunned. She had no idea her parents were that wealthy. Then she shrugged. "It will go to my mother, not to me."

"What's the difference? Six million buys a lot of defense."

"I don't need any defense," she told him sharply. "I didn't murder my father. Some nut put cyanide in a bottle of

Tranquilor. Or do you seriously think I'm the Tranquilor murderer?"

"There are reasons we think this was a copycat killing. Someone wanted it to look like the Tranquilor murders. We're not exactly blind to the fact that people can take advantage of these things to do their own dirty work."

She tried to take in what he was saying. "And suicide? You're sure it wasn't suicide?"

"Someone wanted us to think it was. Either that or one of the random killings, but they fouled it up."

"How?" she asked numbly.

"I don't suppose it'll hurt if I tell you. Autopsy revealed coffee in the stomach along with the cyanide. No coffee cup by the body. Cyanide kills instantly. Therefore, no suicide and no accident."

"It would have to be a pretty dumb murderer to set the whole thing up with the Tranquilor and then take the cup away," she said drily.

"Oh, we found the cup." O'Neill indicated the mute Lindsey. "The sergeant here supervised a search of the room, and they moved the couch. The coffee cup was under it. Traces of cyanide."

Alex sighed deeply and frowned. There was something wrong with this picture. "How did it get under the couch?"

"Maybe the murderer got careless when your father was choking, and kicked it under himself without realizing it."

"Or maybe it *was* suicide, and my father kicked it under."

"Pretty improbable. He died just where he sat."

Alex closed her eyes, shuddering at a vision of her father's congested face, his bulging eyes, convulsions . . . "How can you be sure?" she managed finally.

"Mrs. Campbell." O'Neill's voice told her he was through sparring. "Where were you during the period after you left your father and when you checked into your motel?"

Drawing a deep breath, Alex tried to refocus. "I was having a panic attack. I don't know where I was most of the time."

"These . . . panic attacks. What happens when you have one?"

"I don't get homicidal, if that's what you mean."

"Just tell me. I'm interested." Standing, the lieutenant went around to his chair behind the desk, sat down, and leaned back, elbows on the armrests, his fingertips bridged over his middle. He drummed the two middle fingers together.

Alex swallowed and began for the first time to be frightened. "My neurotransmitters get overloaded. I . . . it's like I lose awareness of everything. My body shuts down—it just stops working. I don't go unconscious—I can still think. But sometimes I can't move or speak or hold myself up."

"And what causes that to happen?"

"Lots of things . . . mostly fear, anger." Fighting this present fear, Alex raised her chin and looked him in the eye.

"And what were you feeling Wednesday night? Fear or anger?"

"Anger," she said briefly. He reminded her of a vulture circling his prey. Closer and closer.

"Just because your parents wouldn't tell you about your grandfather? That was sufficient to cause one of these . . . panic attacks?"

Alex shifted in her chair. Her head was beginning to feel fizzy. Her tongue was thick in her mouth as she said, "It wasn't just that. It was a whole lot of things." *Lord, please! Don't let it happen now*, she pleaded silently.

"Such as?"

The voice was caustic. Looking up, she saw the smugness on his face. The man was almost smiling. He was enjoying this! Suddenly, anger burst clean through the panic, loosening her tongue. "*I didn't murder my father.* I loved him. I was angry because I had just found out that he loved me, and I couldn't understand why he had abandoned me for fifteen years! If that doesn't fit neatly into your theory, then I'm sorry." Her voice rose hotly. "You can't just categorize me as mentally ill and then try to hang a murder on me. I'm not a homicidal maniac. My husband was killed by terrorists in a plane crash. Have you any idea how that feels? It would drive the sanest person to a psychiatrist. And there are records—two years of records. They've done every psychological test on me known to man. You have my permission to read them to your heart's content."

"You have been under psychiatric care for two years?"

"Yes." Her voice was defiant. "My doctor is Winfield Brace, Willow Creek Hospital, Overland Park, Kansas."

"I was under the impression Dr. Grinnell was your doctor."

"No. He's just . . . a friend."

"But he is a psychiatrist?"

"A psychotherapist. There's a difference. He has his Ph.D., not an M.D."

O'Neill nodded.

"Are you finished? Or were you planning to arrest me?"

"No. I have one more question. Why are you and your mother both so determined this was suicide?"

"Mother thinks it was suicide, too?"

"Yes."

"And she blames me for it, I suppose."

The lieutenant tried to look enigmatic and failed.

"She does. I knew she would."

"Why?"

"It's got something to do with my grandfather. I pressed Daddy pretty hard, but he wouldn't tell me the secret. I guess . . ." her bravado faltered as she remembered the look on her father's face." I guess I pushed him too hard, told him what he'd done to me by cutting me off." She put her head in her hands. "I blamed him for everything that's ever gone wrong in my life. No one deserves that."

O'Neill's flat voice cut through her grief. "Would that be enough to make him kill himself?"

"Maybe not. Unless he felt trapped. Maybe Grandfather . . ." she stopped. "Oh, I don't know. I just don't know."

The lieutenant looked skeptical. "Where are you going to go after you leave here?"

Alex took a deep breath, trying to pull herself together. "I'd like to go to my parents' house, if it's all right."

"Why? There's no one there."

"Maybe I can find something that will shed some light on this thing with my grandfather."

"Really hung up on that, aren't you?"

She looked him full in the face. "I'm neurotic, remember? You have to make allowances."

He actually chuckled. "We'll have to send someone with you. Are you and your boyfriend planning to spend the night?"

Her face flamed. "He's not . . . No."

"Let Officer Gentry know where you'll be. He'll meet you at the house in a few minutes. Don't try to go in until he gets there."

Alex stood up, feeling the weakness in her knees. "Is that all?"

"For now. But don't go and leave town."

* * *

By the time she found Daniel, her teeth were chattering so hard, she couldn't speak.

"Are you okay?"

She nodded, settling herself next to him in the car. Pressing her fingers to her temples, she tried to order her thoughts. "They think I murdered my father. I need to go back to the house," she said.

"Tonight?"

"Yes. I want to see if I can find anything."

"Like what?"

"Something about Grandfather."

"Alex, you're obsessing about this. What you need is sleep, food, and a lawyer."

"I want to go to my parents' house."

Shrugging, Daniel started the car. "Tell me which way to turn."

Officer Gentry was there before them, standing beside the open front door, and Alex felt more dispossessed than ever.

Without saying anything, she led Daniel to the newly remodeled kitchen. It was the only room without associations.

"I don't think this is such a good idea, Alex." Daniel was studying her, openly worried. "You're suffering from shock. It's foolhardy to heap on all the emotional baggage of this place."

"I've got to do something," she said shortly.

"You're not Nancy Drew! What good do you think you can do here tonight? Why don't we come back in the morning?"

"I just want to see his room."

"Okay, but just a quick look around," Daniel said grudgingly. "Then we'll get you to bed. You're so tired that you're ready to fold up. I've arranged for rooms with friends in Evanston, if that's okay."

She nodded and led the way to her father's bedroom. Officer Gentry, who had listened to this exchange without any expression on his face, followed them upstairs.

Opening the door, she flicked on the light and steeled herself. It was the beige and white room she remembered. The police search had been relatively neat but thorough. Her father was a fastidious man, but now the room looked like it belonged to someone more careless—drawers were half open, the closet door stood wide, and books and magazines lay scattered over the desktop.

Going through the desk, she found nothing but personal bills and correspondence, check stubs, and a file containing miscellaneous papers related to the Shriners, to which he belonged. Aside from that, there were paper clips and labels, pencils and Scotch tape. The desk might have belonged to anyone. There were no memories here, except in the third drawer down, where she found her high school picture. The girl in the portrait had long, curly black hair and looked out at Alex with solemn eyes and a tentative smile. She didn't even remember having it taken.

Wordlessly she handed it to Daniel, who had seated himself on the edge of the bed.

"This isn't where he died, is it?" Alex asked the policeman suddenly.

"No, ma'am. That was the living room. We can't let you go in there."

Alex shivered. *Why the living room?* she wondered, amazed at her own detachment. He wouldn't have committed suicide in the living room. And Daddy normally entertained friends in his study. But then, a friend wouldn't have murdered him.

The closets yielded nothing but rows of shoes, shirts, and suits. Ties were arranged neatly by color on a rack on the back of the door. Everything still smelled like Daddy. Pipe tobacco and English Leather cologne. She used to give those things to him for Christmas.

Alex shut the closet doors, blocking out the scent. This was a lot harder than she could have imagined. She moved over to the bedside table.

"Daddy used to write his letters in bed," she remarked, her voice high as she strove to override the lump in her throat. "He'd sit up late with a little desk thing across his lap like some lady in a Regency romance."

The rosewood travel desk was still under the bed. She hadn't realized it before, but it was actually a valuable bit of Chinoiserie. However if there had been anything interesting in it, the police had already taken it. The drawers contained only his gold Cross pen set, blank sheets of buff-colored paper with her father's monogram, and a book.

"That's weird." She swallowed hard.

Daniel looked over her shoulder, "The Bedside Book of Poetry for Children?"

"He used to read to me out of it a long time ago—when I was little."

"Odd to find it *there.*"

"Maybe he was remembering . . ." Tears choked her.

Daniel took her by the shoulders and steered her toward the door. "Come on, Alex. Enough is enough. Let's go. Bring the book if you want to, but let's get out of here."

* * *

The night was unusually bright as they wound down Sheridan Road toward Evanston. Full moon. Alex remembered this road well from the last year of that old life. She had driven it every day on her way to Northwestern. Now it was as though the fifteen years between had never happened. She was caught in a nightmare, enmeshed in a scenario worse than her worst fears. She looked steadily at the road, mesmerized by the beam of the headlights.

Daniel's friends had left the back porch light burning. There was a note on the table in the comfortable blue and cream-colored Victorian kitchen:

Welcome, Daniel and Alex: Help yourself to bread, cheese, juice, etc. Your bedrooms are upstairs to the right of the landing. Bathroom in between. Breakfast whenever you wake up.

Susan and Lee.

At Daniel's insistence, she choked down a piece of cheese and a glass of juice. Then, dragging herself up the stairs, Alex said a weary good-night to Daniel and retired to the four-poster bed with lavender-scented sheets. As she lay there exhausted, staring into the blackness, she remembered the book. Sliding out of bed, she took it off the dresser and opened the cover. By moonlight, she read the bold, black inscription on the flyleaf:

"To Joey, with love, Dad."

So Grandfather had given it to him! Here, at last, was something tangible, something of love. Something of Grandfather.

Her tiredness vanishing, Alex switched on the light and began paging through the book. There was a piece of notepaper—buff notepaper with her father's monogram. Hands shaking, she unfolded it, scarcely breathing.

FIVE

Wednesday, Aug 14

Dearest Alex:

I wish with all my heart we could replay the scene downstairs tonight again. I wish we could replay your adolescence again. I wish I could replay much of my life again. I had thought I was doing the best thing to let you go, let you make your own world, entirely independent of us, free of those limitations that hedged us in. But now you have shown me how wrong I was and how cowardly. As you so rightly demanded, what kind of a parent am I?

A father who loved you so much that he didn't want to expose you to painful scandal and very real danger. I didn't want you to lose the memory of the man you loved so very much as your grandfather. But now I see that, in my desire to protect you, I took away everything you had.

I will tell you about your grandfather, but you must be a little patient. It is not my secret alone, and there are legal and other messy ramifications that will be unpleasant. There are arrangements to be made. However, I hope this action on my part will begin to bridge that long rift between us, and that we will be a family again.

Love, Dad

Tears streamed down her face. She hugged the paper to her breast. In spite of everything else, here was sweet knowledge. She hadn't driven him to suicide—he had planned to make everything all right! They were going to be a family again! How many years had she longed for those words?

Switching off the lights, she curled up under the sheets, holding the letter to her. It still smelled faintly of pipe tobacco.

In spite of all the horror of that day, in spite of what she knew intellectually to be true, the little girl inside her was strangely soothed, drifting away, separate from all the adult emotions occupying the space around her. For the moment she was that little girl, denying everything but this reality.

Alex wasn't lying in a strange bed but curled up on Daddy's lap on Sunday afternoon. He was stroking her hair, and she could feel the satin lapels of his smoking jacket, smooth and cool against her cheek. The slow, steady rhythm of the heart beneath the satin quieted her own reckless pulse. She had been jumping rope. The sky had been brilliant early-spring blue, and there were poppies. Now the poppies stood on Daddy's desk, drooping in a jam jar as she heard his deep voice rumble in his chest:

Five and twenty ponies, Trotting through the dark—Brandy for the Parson, 'Baccy for the Clerk.

Them that asks no questions isn't told a lie—Watch the wall, my darling, while the Gentlemen go by!

Alex slept.

* * *

When she came down to breakfast the next morning, Daniel detected a change. Alex looked surprisingly rested and serene.

Susan Cooper stopped halfway to the table and stared at her guest, as well she might. A perfectly formed blond with a golden tan, Susan had been homecoming queen at the University of Missouri. She had also been divorced recently. All morning, she had been casting unmistakable lures in Daniel's direction.

By contrast, Alex was striking, even in her pallor. Dressed in navy-and-white polka-dot leggings, a long white T-shirt, and a scarlet head-wrap, she didn't exactly give the impression of one of life's victims. And Susan had been overflowing with such sympathy for her.

Thanking her hostess warmly for the plate of eggs and bacon, Alex handed Daniel a sheet of stationery.

"Daniel," she said, "Look."

He read it and felt a weight slide off his shoulders. "It wasn't suicide, then."

"No, it couldn't have been. He was going to make everything all right. Do you think we should show it to O'Neill?"

"Sure. I'd say it goes a long way toward letting you off the hook, too."

She raised an eyebrow and attacked her breakfast.

"Use your brains, woman. It says here that the secret wasn't only his and that it involved some legal hocus pocus. Maybe he'd already set the wheels in motion. Depending on what the secret was, it might give someone else a good motive for murder."

Alex stared at him. "I was right then. It all has something to do with Grandfather."

"I hate to admit it, of course, but your obsession seems to be justified."

Her face clouded, and she dropped her eyes. "My obsession killed him, you mean. If I hadn't . . ."

"Alex! Quit that, for crying out loud!"

Standing at the sink, Susan Cooper looked at him over her shoulder. "You quit bullying that poor girl, Daniel," she drawled, her voice warmly familiar.

Alex pushed her plate away and stood up. "He can darn well bully me if he pleases," she informed her hostess.

Daniel laughed and felt boyishly smug. "Sit down and finish your breakfast," he demanded.

"No," she replied and disappeared up the back stairs.

If Daniel was right and her father was murdered because of the grandfather issue, then there were things to do, and she was the person to do them. Pushing down a new upsurge of grief, Alex packed her few possessions and quickly made her bed. Then, hesitating, she knelt down and composed herself to pray.

It was difficult. She felt guilty for her actions, her anger. They were like a great lead wall separating her from the Lord. Despite what Daniel had said, she knew her meddling must have caused her father's death.

However, after she had been on her knees for several minutes, the feelings of the night before returned, and she felt comforted again, as though her father were kneeling beside her. Then, inexplicably, she was filled with a surge of love, warming her through, stretching her heart to the bursting point. She could not contain it, and it spilled over into tears. It was as though someone had placed a warm cloak over her shoulders. She was enveloped by peace and a sweet nurturing she had never experienced.

She knew that this must be a gift—a gift of the Spirit. Daddy was here. She was being allowed to feel his presence— to know that whatever she had done, it was forgiven. She was loved. She was on the right track.

"Alex? Oh! I'm sorry."

It was Daniel. "It's all right," she told him, getting to her feet. Wiping the tears with her hands, she reassured him, "I'm all right. I was just having a good prayer."

Looking as though he had just committed a flagrant faux pas, he turned to leave, but she was so full of love at that moment, she threw her arms around him and buried her face in his chest.

"It's going to be okay," she said. "Everything's going to be okay."

Tenderly returning the embrace, Daniel didn't speak.

"I suppose we had better call Lieutenant O'Neill," she said, meeting his eyes. "I have to go back over to the house."

He looked pointedly at her bag, packed and ready.

"Briggie is coming, remember?" she asked. "We'll stay at the house tonight. What about you? Don't you need to get home to Marigny?"

"It's Saturday. Dad's there. I already called. Everything's okay. They send their sympathy, by the way. Dad says to hurry and get this settled so you can get back to work. That dog food fortune, you know. He knows a good lawyer up here, if you need one."

"Hopefully I won't before the day's out," she said, leading him downstairs.

"What do you have in mind?"

"I'm going to take that house apart, looking for clues about Grandfather. If it weren't Saturday, I'd go downtown and have a look at his will."

Spying the telephone, she called Lieutenant O'Neill to inform him of her intentions.

* * *

When they arrived at the house, Briggie was already waiting, munching on a Danish and talking to the tall, thin policeman Alex recognized from the police station. Sergeant Lindsey.

Alex's heart lifted at the sight of her friend. "Briggie! When did you get here?"

Wiping her hands on a paper napkin, Briggie allowed herself to be embraced. "I drove up last night. Slept in some place called Glenview."

"You must be exhausted."

"Nope. Rarin' to go. What're we looking for?"

"Anything to do with Grandfather. I'm convinced he's the key to everything."

The policeman, taking his cue, walked in front of them to unlock the door.

"You know Sergeant Lindsey, I take it," Briggie remarked. "Other than being a White Sox fan, he seems okay."

The sergeant grinned, as self-effacing as he'd been at the station on the night before. Alex realized she had never heard him speak.

"Where shall we start?" her friend asked, eyeing the baroque plaster molding that crowned the entry hall.

"None of the obvious places. It's got to be something my parents have forgotten. I only hope the police won't have taken it."

"Is there a safe?"

"Yes. My father kept the key on his chain. The police will have it. But isn't that the most obvious place of all?"

"Obvious, but probable. You never would have had access to it, would you? Maybe the police got careless and left it open." Briggie seemed oblivious to Lindsey's presence. Or maybe she simply preferred to forget he belonged to the police.

Leading all three of them back to her father's study, Alex realized that because of her prayer and the letter in her bag, she felt far less oppressed by the house this morning. She was no longer the scared little girl of fifteen years ago. She was Alex Campbell, genealogist.

Somewhere Grandfather had to have left a trace of himself. He had built this house and lived in it most of his life. He had to be here somewhere.

The study had been gone through thoroughly. The safe was standing open and empty. Presumably whatever had been in there was gone. Looking at the shelves of books, the gray filing cabinet, and the large rosewood desk, Alex didn't know where to start. Idly, she began flipping through the Rolodex file that contained his addresses. "I have no idea what to look for."

Daniel had gone to the file cabinet. "Neat fellow, your father. Everything's clearly labeled. Insurance. Mortgage . . ."

"Mortgage?" Alex roused herself. "There isn't a mortgage on this house. Grandfather was always very proud of the fact that he'd paid the builders in cash. It was a thing with him. He paid me an allowance and taught me to manage my money from the time I was eight. I know there was no mortgage on this house!"

Extracting the file, Daniel brought it over to her to read.

"Taken out in September 1970. $200,000. Isn't that about the time your grandfather died?"

"Yes! But what would they want with $200,000? Surely Daddy was the principal heir. He had the business. It's worth millions." Alex's depression vanished. "Could this be a clue?" she wondered, looking at the closely printed document.

"Your grandfather would have had a pretty large personal estate?" Daniel seated himself next to her.

"Of course. He lived here with us. Never spent a dime as far as I remember, except on his boat. He never went anywhere. Mother took him to Fields twice a year to buy clothes; otherwise he would have worn everything through at the elbows. Thrift was practically his religion." Pausing, she studied the document. "Purpose of loan: home improvement."

She appealed to the mute Sergeant Lindsey, who was hovering close by. "This is odd. Weird in fact. They never did anything that major! The kitchen was done after my time. Everything else, except my room, is practically the same as it's always been."

Folding the mortgage, Alex was about to place it in her bag when Sergeant Lindsey walked over, holding out his hand. "I'm sorry, ma'am. If that document's important, I can't let you take it. Gotta give it to the lieutenant."

Alex handed it over reluctantly and thought again of the letter. She was loathe to give that up just yet. It was the only communication she had received from her father in years, and now he would never give her anything else.

Briggie, standing at the window, was looking out over the yard. "You know, that $200,000 could mean blackmail."

The word was a shock. Alex thought it over. Blackmail. It was a dirty, sordid word. But so was murder. She sighed. "I suppose you could be right. My father said he didn't want me involved in a scandal and that it had legal ramifications. Blackmail fits."

"When did he say that?"

Alex remembered Briggie didn't know about the letter, but she didn't want to give it away just yet. "The other night."

"Would your father have let himself be blackmailed?" Daniel asked. "Was he the type?"

The question brought her back down to earth. For just a moment the whole situation had been a puzzle, abstract and remote as a crossword. Now she put her head in her hands. "I have no idea."

"This isn't a game, Alex," he told her solemnly. "If we're dealing with a murdering blackmailer, playing detective might be dangerous."

The whole scenario seemed suddenly absurd. "The only danger I feel right now is from Lieutenant O'Neill. He's convinced I murdered my father in a fit of homicidal mania."

Briggie's eyes glinted fiercely. "He must be a nut."

"Certified," Daniel assured her. "By me, at least."

"Thanks," Alex said, eyeing their pet policeman. What did he think of them all? He was trying unsuccessfully to efface himself and his notebook in the corner by the potted palm.

There was a Dictaphone in the top drawer. Pressing the play switch, she listened, but the tape was blank. Dropping it on the desk top, she resumed her search but found nothing that didn't pertain to Borden Meats. "If it's a business problem, I don't know what to look for," she said.

"Dad would. We can corral him if we get desperate. Maybe we should go on to the rest of the house," Daniel suggested.

Briggie left to prowl the other rooms. Alex and the others went on to her mother's sitting room.

While she sorted through her mother's desk, Sergeant Lindsey seated himself in a wicker chair and appeared to be engrossed in his notebook.

Daniel examined the bookcases. Looking up after a few minutes, she caught him paging through Stewart's book. He had never knowingly seen any of Stewart's work before.

"So, Dr. Grinnell, was he good or what?" The defiant words were out before she thought.

Daniel refused the bait, as he always did. It was one of his most maddening characteristics. Closing the book, he laid it on the coffee table and faced her, his gaze bland. "Yes. He was good."

He didn't take his eyes away, and she began to feel uncomfortably transparent. She knew he saw the anger and the stubborn loyalty beneath it, but his green eyes challenged hers with unremitting gentleness. Alex spoke firmly, "Quit looking at me like a therapist."

"I wasn't," he said quietly. "And you know it."

Briggie entered.

"What's that building out back? Not the garage. The one next to it with the padlock."

Alex switched gears with difficulty. "Out back? A building?"

"You must know. It looks like it's been there since the flood."

How could she have forgotten? "It's Grandfather's dry dock! The boat's still there, if they haven't sold it."

Opening the French door, she ran out onto the patio, through the gate in the hedge, and across the driveway to the gray, peeling shed. Locked with a rusty old padlock, it had obviously not been opened in years.

"A screwdriver," Briggie demanded. "We can take the hinges off."

Half an hour later, they had managed to open the left hand door. Stepping down from the ladder, Daniel dragged the loosened door aside and leaned it against the adjoining wall. They peered into the gloomy interior.

"Well, I'll be!" Briggie breathed. "It's still there!"

"Why didn't they sell it, I wonder?" Alex brushed her way through the spider webs until she could put her hand on the mahogany bow. "It would have been worth a lot of money twenty years ago. Why just leave it here?"

The light inside the shed was gloomy, and the boat fit tightly, making it impossible to maneuver. "We need that stepladder and a flashlight," she pronounced.

"And bug repellent. That thing is bound to be full of spiders," Briggie prophesied.

Daniel was feeling the grain of the wood with obvious respect. "This is the real thing. They don't do wood anymore. It's all fiberglass now. What did he call her?"

Alex had forgotten Daniel's passion for antique vehicles. His collection of old cars was his way of being fiscally outrageous.

"Cecilia. Perhaps my mother will sell her to you; she certainly isn't using her!"

When he looked up, it was through a dreamer's haze.

For the first time that day, she laughed. "Earth to Daniel: Ladder. Flashlight. Bug spray."

"Lunch," Briggie countermanded. She was firm.

After a hasty meal composed of canned crab and shrimp in a base of Campbell's Tomato, Mushroom, and Split Pea soups accompanied by Rye Crisp and a somewhat hard Swiss cheese, they tackled the boat again. Their sergeant, having shared the limited repast, resumed his seat on the patio.

Using the ladder, Alex climbed up on the bow, turned on the flashlight, and explored the cabin. "Perfect set for a horror movie," she relayed as her flashlight glinted off the myriad, dusty spider webs. "It's a good thing I haven't got arachnophobia on top of everything else."

Daniel came up behind her, a second flashlight in hand. "Is there a place where he might have kept things?" he asked, his voice curiously tentative.

"Have you got it?" she demanded, turning her flashlight on his face.

"What?"

"Arachnophobia."

"Of course not." He was pulling webs off his hair and ears. "I have no human weaknesses. Get on with it, for crying out loud."

Laughing, Alex felt her spirits rise unaccountably. They climbed down into the hull where the galley and sleeping quarters were. "There's Grandfather's chest," she said after they had oriented themselves. "He used to keep the dominoes and checkers in it."

The circle of her flashlight picked out the ivory inlaid chest sitting on the floor between the two bunks. Opening it carefully, Alex was disappointed to discover it still contained only dominoes and checkers. "Well," she sighed. "At least it's something of Grandfather's."

"What about the cupboard?"

Alex squirmed. "I'm afraid of what might be living there."

"Perhaps we need to bring Briggie on board," he suggested. "She's not afraid of anything."

"Except snakes."

"Seriously?"

"Seriously."

"Well, shall we flip for it?"

"How about if we just say one, two, three and then open it together?"

Daniel was irresolute. "Did you know you can die of a brown recluse spider bite?"

"Don't worry. I'll nurse you through your final moments. But if there are mice in there, it's another story. I'll scream," Alex warned.

Together they chanted, "One, two, three," flinging open the cupboard. Except for a quantity of mice droppings, it was empty.

Gingerly, they pulled open the drawers under the bunks to find that they were also empty. Their only strange find was an old automatic pistol under a pillow.

"Probably brought it back from France. Colt 1911. Government issue," Daniel mused, inspecting the clip. "Loaded, too."

"Put it back before you shoot something!" Alex shuddered with distaste. Why on earth had Grandfather slept with a gun under his pillow?

Finally, they made their way back toward the galley. There, in what should have been the coffee tin, they finally found something of significance. It had the appearance of a closely folded document.

"It's awfully old," Alex breathed, afraid to unfold the brown, crumbling paper. "We'll have to take it down to Briggie. She knows how to handle old documents."

"Let's finish up here first," Daniel suggested. "I'm never coming back, if I can help it."

Further searching, however, revealed nothing except more evidence of spiders and mice. Gratefully, they climbed back over Cecilia's bow and down the ladder.

Alex handed their prize to Briggie. "Here's the goods. I didn't trust myself to undo it."

"Good heavens. This has been around a lot longer than twenty years!" She took it out into the sunlight. "It's the kind of parchment paper they used to make wills on."

SIX

A thrill shivered through Alex. "A will! Whose will?"

"We have to do this properly, honey, or it'll fall apart. We need two sheets of glass," Briggie told them.

"I can't imagine where in the world we could find anything like that in this house," Alex protested. "Can't we just take a peek?"

"Could the bottom one be a mirror?" Daniel asked. "There's that old beveled one in the entry."

"That'll be fine."

Then Alex remembered the glass-topped table used to hold plants in the solarium. Briggie helped her fetch the heavy, round top and maneuver it into the laundry tub, while Daniel went after the mirror. Sergeant Lindsey, who seemed to have gotten into the spirit of the thing, held the table top in place while Alex and Briggie scrubbed away years of moss and hard-water deposits with steel wool and cleanser. The whole procedure took fifteen precious minutes.

Why would Grandfather keep a will in the coffee tin on the boat, of all places? Privacy? She hadn't been allowed on the boat without him, and her mother and father weren't sailors. Perhaps it was his one sanctuary. She remembered the automatic and shuddered again.

When the mirror and table top were finally prepared, Daniel placed them side by side on the butcher-block island in the kitchen and repositioned the track lights to focus on the desired area. Sergeant Lindsey joined them to witness the procedure.

Briggie gave Alex instructions to hold down the outside edge of the parchment against the mirror while she carefully unfolded the document. It crackled a bit but remained whole. Alex saw only that it was handwritten in purplish ink.

"Now!" Briggie commanded, and Daniel and the sergeant slid the glass table top carefully over the parchment.

Four heads nearly collided as they gathered to read it. Searching first for the signature, Alex was astonished to read her grandfather's name. "Joseph Borden? But this is so old! It can't be his will. When is it dated?"

"June 1917," Briggie told her, pointing to a scrawl beneath the signature. "See?"

"It's a holograph," Daniel pronounced.

"Handwritten wills are quite legal." Briggie was tracing the lines with her fingers. "It looks like the witnesses are French, Jean-Louis Courbet and Pierre DeLavalière. He must have made it in France."

After a moment, she began to read,

"Whereas I am unmarried and whereas my parents are both dead, I, Joseph Borden, therefore will and bequeath my entire estate to my cousin, Edward Borden of St. Louis, Missouri. Said Edward Borden shall also be my executor."

"Edward Borden?" Alex repeated. "I never heard of Edward Borden! But that's Grandfather's handwriting. He used to make his B's with swirls, just like that." For a few moments, they were silent, rereading the will. "But why would he keep it? He must have had a new will, and even if he didn't, this one wouldn't hold water, would it?"

"No," Daniel mused. "I don't imagine so. He clearly states that he is making his bequest in this manner because of being unmarried, etc. Your father could have contested it quite easily."

"And that didn't happen, because there it was in that crazy coffee can instead of the probate file. Besides, if my parents had found it, they would have destroyed it, like they destroyed everything else. Why did Grandfather hide it on the boat? Why did he even bother bringing it home from France, for that matter?"

"And why didn't your parents sell the boat?" Briggie asked again. "Like you said, twenty years ago it would have been worth something. Why just lock the doors and let it go to pieces?"

"None of it makes any sense," Alex sighed, sitting on a nearby stool. "If Edward Borden was Grandfather's first cousin, he would be my first cousin twice removed. Why haven't I ever heard of him?"

Sergeant Lindsey was busy copying the contents of the will into his notebook.

"Save yourself some work, Sergeant," Alex advised. "A seventy-year-old will has no bearing on the case, believe me."

The sergeant straightened up, looking relieved. "Yeah, I guess you're right. Sure is hard to read."

"It's not going anyplace," she reassured him.

The sergeant returned to the bay window, where he resumed his seat, stretching his long legs out in front of him.

Briggie was looking speculative. "It's another line of inquiry, Alex."

"Where could it possibly lead?" she asked, defeated. "I'm sure Edward's long dead. If he were alive, he'd be over ninety, for heaven's sake."

"Perhaps they were close at one time and then had a falling out," Briggie guessed. "Perhaps they even joined up together. Maybe he had descendants. It's a lead on your genealogy."

"Yes." This was exactly the sort of thing she had been looking for when she searched the attic. But was there anything here to help solve her father's murder? "If I don't get arrested, maybe I'll try to follow it up."

"We haven't heard from the good lieutenant today," Daniel remarked. "I wonder what he's up to."

"Probably raising Cain in Kansas, trying to get at my psych records."

"He's not going to have any luck on Saturday."

The telephone rang. Startled, Alex glanced at the wall where it hung. "Speak of the devil. Maybe that's him now."

It rang twice more before she managed to answer it.

"Alexandra?"

"Yes?"

"Bob. Your cousin Bob."

"Oh."

"Are you all right?"

"Aside from being suspected of murder. You've heard about the murder, I suppose?" Fifteen years ago Bob had been an aspiring journalist. Perhaps he had made the big time by now.

"In fact, I discovered the body. Didn't they tell you?"

Alex sat down abruptly. "No. Tell me."

"Well, there's not a whole lot to tell. Your mother was pretty upset about something. She called me at work and more or less demanded that I come over right away."

"Did she give you any idea what she wanted?"

"No. She was sort of hysterical. You know . . ."

"So when did you get here?"

"About eleven-thirty. I don't get off til eleven. I'm night manager at McDonald's."

Not the big time, then. Somehow, it didn't surprise her. "How did you get in?"

"The front door was open. Unlocked, I mean. Turned out your mother was passed out upstairs."

"And?"

"Everything was dark except the living room, so that's where I went."

Alex intervened quickly, forestalling his description of what he found. "Did you see a coffee cup?"

"No. The police asked me that. There wasn't anything but that Tranquilor bottle. It was clear he'd died of cyanide. His face was bright red."

Closing her eyes, Alex fought down rising anger and nausea. "Why did you call, Bob?" she asked at last.

"I just wanted to know if they knew anything more."

"Working on a story? 'How I Discovered the Tranquilor Murderer?'"

"Hey! Your dad was my uncle, you know. I probably saw a lot more of him than you did!"

That hurt. Instinctively, she struck back. "I guess that makes you another suspect, doesn't it?"

"Yeah. Don't think you're the Lone Ranger, Alex. By the way, your mother's awake now."

"Did she call you?"

"Yes. She wanted to know what I'd told the police about her phone call to me that night."

"Did you tell them about it?"

"As a matter of fact, I did. I was in a pretty awkward spot, you know. Showing up at eleven-thirty and all that."

Alex was silent for a moment, weighing the tone of his voice. "You think Mother did it, don't you?" she said finally.

"Hey, hold on! Who says I think she did it? I just didn't want the police to think . . . Well." He paused. "In fact, I know she didn't do it."

"You do? How?"

"I saw someone leaving. A car, anyway."

Alex inhaled sharply. "What did it look like?"

"It was dark, remember? Totally overcast."

"Did you tell the police?"

"As a matter of fact, no."

"Why not?"

"It could have been you, Alex."

"It wasn't! You don't even know what kind of car I drive!"

"No. I don't. What kind of car do you drive?"

"I'll be darned if I tell you!" She slammed the phone in its cradle. Taking a deep breath, she tried to calm herself. Bob hadn't changed. He still brought out the brat in her. Sergeant Lindsey was regarding her intently.

"That was my cousin, Bob Borden," she said finally. "He saw a car leaving here the night of the murder. He didn't tell the police." Shrugging at the sergeant, she explained, "He's an aspiring journalist. He cares more about a story than he does about his own neck. Or mine, for that matter."

Getting to his feet, Lindsey asked, "Mind if I use the phone, ma'am?"

While the sergeant reported Bob's telephone call, Alex sat down on a stool in front of the will. "A car. I wonder if he really saw one."

"Does he make a habit of lying?" Daniel asked, pulling up a stool next to hers. Briggie remained standing, squinting at the will through her half-glasses.

"Yes. Almost from day one. His father died when we were still kids, and he used to make up all kinds of stories to get money out of my father. I imagine he comes in for an inheritance under his will, too. His dad was kind of a ne'er-do-well, as they say in Scotland. There's not much money in his family, as you probably gathered."

"How so?" Briggie queried, peering over her glasses.

"Well, Uncle Richard was the baby, and I guess my grandmother spoiled him. She died when he was still in his teens, so my grandfather always made special allowances for my uncle's irresponsibility. He had sort of a storefront title at the plant. Didn't do much but got a good salary for it. He went through every penny, apparently. I remember an enormous house in Lake Forest, and he drove a red Corvette. You can imagine the rest, can't you? One night he got drunk and was going about eighty down Sheridan Road when he hit someone. They were both killed."

Briggie sighed. "And his wife?"

"Oh, she's still alive. They sold the house years ago and moved out to Mt. Prospect. Mother said that after the life insurance ran out, Grandfather made them an allowance. Daddy probably continued it. I imagine they still live in the same house. Bob says he's the night manager at McDonald's."

"Any animosity toward your Dad for not giving him a job at the plant?" Daniel asked.

Alex wondered. "Maybe. I've been away for fifteen years, remember. When I left, Bob was just starting in the Medill School of Journalism at Northwestern. All he ever wanted to do was be a reporter."

"Poor kid," Briggie said, pushing her glasses up onto the top of her head.

"Not that poor. Dad must have paid his tuition. Northwestern isn't cheap. And he graduated."

"Woodward and Bernstein probably endowed him with unrealistic expectations," Daniel remarked.

Alex nodded. "You got it. I'll bet you anything he works days selling ads or doing obits for the Mt. Prospect paper and thinks he can solve this thing and write the big scoop that will make his career."

Sergeant Lindsey hung up the telephone, and there was a silence.

Sighing, she remembered another thing Bob had said. "Mother called him today. She's awake. I guess I'd better go see her."

* * *

The closer they got to Evanston Hospital, the more rigidly Alex held herself. As long as she concentrated on Grandfather, on the puzzle she was trying to solve, she felt connected to Daddy. It was as though he were looking over her shoulder. But now, as she neared a confrontation with her mother, she couldn't push reality away any longer. The reality was that her mother was now a widow. Why had she ever begun this?

Daniel, at the wheel of his rented Taurus, advised her simply: "She's probably in a state of shock, Alex. She's not going to be particularly reasonable."

"It wouldn't be terribly unreasonable for her to blame me for Daddy's death," she said bitterly.

"Look, I won't deny that you were somehow the straw that broke the camel's back, but this situation didn't blow up overnight. Has it ever occurred to you that this thing with your grandfather might be responsible for your mother's alcoholism?"

Startled, Alex could only stare at him. Why had she never made that connection?

"From your father's letter, I'd say it was a fairly high-voltage situation if they tried to keep you out of it," he continued. "This secret, whatever it is, destroyed your family system, probably drove your mother to drink, did a lot of psychological damage to you, and ended up by getting your father murdered. You are a victim just as much as your parents are."

He held up a hand as she started to protest. "I know I sound like a shrink, but bear with me. By approaching them, you were trying in your own way to end the dysfunction, to bring everything out in the open. Your father agreed that was the right thing to do. Okay? The fact that he was murdered does not mitigate that. What it means is that someone involved in this thing is psychotic and just plain evil."

"My mother won't see it that way," she said tightly. The hospital loomed into view.

"We'll be in the lobby waiting for you," Briggie told her resolutely.

Alex took a deep, steadying breath. "No. I want you to go to the Evanston library," she told them, beginning to hunt through her canvas carry-all. Grasping a dog-eared envelope, she passed it back to Briggie. "There's Grandfather's death certificate. Why don't you see if you can get an obituary?"

"That's what you really want us to do?" her friend asked.

"Yes," Alex replied. "Grandfather is the key to everything. I know it."

"Here we are, Evanston Hospital," Daniel announced as they arrived before the brick building. "How long will we be gone, Briggie?"

"Forty-five minutes at the outside."

Getting out of the car, Alex forced herself to walk through the hospital doors. At the information desk, she was directed to room 208. Approaching her mother's room on the second floor, she was momentarily jolted out of her preoccupation by the sight of a policewoman sitting outside the door. Was she a suspect then, or were they merely protecting her?

"I'm here to see my mother," Alex told the large, redheaded woman.

"Identification," she requested flatly.

Fumbling in her bag, Alex finally came up with her wallet and pulled out her driver's license. The redhead took it in her large, freckled hand, checked Alex's face against the picture, handed it back, and made a note of the name on her tablet, then gave a slight nod in the affirmative.

Alex went in, the policewoman following. Her mother appeared to be asleep. Approaching the bed, Alex studied her face. The skin was papery white and crumpled, as though the bones underneath had shrunken. For once, she wore no makeup. She didn't look like Mother.

The tension eased. This was an old woman. A sad old woman. A victim, as Daniel had said.

As she stood staring, the eyes fluttered open. It took Amelia several moments to recognize her daughter. "Alexandra? You're home, then? Where's your father? Have you had dinner?"

Heart contracting, Alex recognized the dialogue. It was in the old pattern, the one that had been set when she was in high school and had come home to find her mother passed out across her bed.

"Mother," she whispered, taking the woman's cold hand in hers, "you're in the hospital."

Looking around frantically, Amelia tried to orient herself. Noticing the policewoman sitting in the corner, she looked back at her daughter. Then she shut her eyes. "Joe," she whimpered.

Alex squeezed her mother's hand and bent down to kiss her forehead. "I'm sorry," she whispered helplessly, feeling ashamed. She had scarcely even considered her mother's grief.

Tears rolled out from under Amelia's eyelids and she withdrew her hand, covering her face. Alex pulled a tissue out of the box on her table and handed it to her. She didn't know what to say.

"I don't know how he could do this," her mother moaned behind the tissue. "It's not like him to leave me. And the police . . . the scandal . . . ."

"He didn't, Mother," Alex said quietly.

Amelia looked up, eyes bright with tears. "What?"

"Daddy didn't commit suicide."

In an instant, her mother's expression changed. The eyes sharpened and narrowed. The mouth tightened. "Of course he did, Alexandra." All the grief had gone from her voice.

Instinctively, Alex withdrew from her, apologizing, "No. I'm sorry to contradict you, Mother, but he couldn't have. You see, he wrote me a letter . . . ."

The eyes flitted away and then back. Was there alarm in them? "A letter?"

"Yes. He had plans. He told me . . . ."

Amelia nodded quickly, cutting her off. "I don't want to discuss this, Alexandra." With her eyes, she indicated the policewoman. "I'm quite certain it was suicide."

Alex sighed. So it was to be business as usual. Denial. "I'm afraid you're going to have to face it, Mother," she said, heavily. "Daddy was murdered. The police have evidence. You see, the coffee cup with the poison was under the couch . . ."

Her mother's eyes flickered. "Where is this letter?" she asked tightly.

"Here." Alex searched through her bag once more, and finding it, handed it over reluctantly.

Scanning it quickly, Amelia sank back on her pillows, murmuring "Thank heavens" as though she had been given some sort of reprieve.

Having braced herself for an outburst, Alex was relieved. "I agree," she said with feeling. "You'll never know what that letter meant to me."

Her mother's nostrils flared, and she pressed her lips together in a firm line. Rising straight up in bed, she attacked. "You misunderstand me, Alexandra. I'm simply relieved that Joe wasn't misguided enough to give in to your totally insane curiosity."

Wide open, Alex felt the blow full force.

"Can't you see what you've done?" Amelia demanded.

Alex felt the onset of panic. Her head began to fizz. Her limbs were seizing up.

"If you hadn't come back, hadn't asked those questions about your Grandfather, this never would have happened. Your father would be alive!" Her mother's rage spewed out, distorting her face into the mask that recalled Alex's worst dreams.

"Have you any idea how much your father and I have suffered? Of course not! All you can see is yourself—yourself and your precious grandfather. We've done every conceivable thing to protect you, and now you've succeeded in getting your father killed!"

"Get out," the frightened girl inside Alex whispered. "Get away from this person who hates you so much."

Forcing her frozen limbs to move, Alex plucked her letter from the bed, stumbled past the policewoman, and left the room.

Clutching the letter to her breast like a bandage, she was lanced with fresh pain. Daddy had been so full of hope for the future. He would have made everything all right. He had loved her, and now he was dead. He was dead because he had loved her. Mother was angry at her because he was dead. Mother was angry because he had loved her.

Alex couldn't stop the tears. Sobbing audibly, she avoided the elevator and ran down the staircase.

Once she was out of the hospital, she walked blindly down the street, unaware of the hot, bright sun. She was torn open, trapped in the dark place where her nightmares happened. Everything was spilling out—love, hate, guilt, grief.

What had happened to that blessed numbness? Where had it gone? Why was she still moving, feeling? Why couldn't she shut off the pain?

SEVEN

It was dark and cool in this place she had found. Someone's yew hedge arched over her like a protective arm, screening her, hiding her from the world. Alex cried bitterly, her grief fresh and acute, as though the loss of her parents had happened today instead of all those years ago.

What had gone wrong? What had robbed her of her parents' love, murdered her father, and made her mother an enemy?

Now she had her mother's enraged, frightened face as a companion to the last picture of her father, head in hands, bowed under her own anger.

Where did all the anger come from?

The question posed itself against her grief. Focusing on it, she allowed reality to pull her back into the present. She was no longer a helpless child but a responsible adult. There were reasons for the things that had happened.

Where did all that anger come from? Alex knew suddenly that she had grasped the fundamental issue.

When Stewart had died, it was winter. After receiving the news, she had calmly put on her coat and walked out into the snow. With no sense of destination, she had wandered through the glen, up the craggy hills, and over the snowbound heather, her mind blank and deadened. Night had fallen early in the gloom. The thickly clouded sky had been dense, the dark absolute. If it hadn't been for her dog, she might have died, calmly curling up against a rock and waiting to freeze to death. But Stewart's Akita had been dispatched by the neighbors to find her and bring her home. Years before, Stewart had laughingly christened the dog Providence because she was everywhere at once.

There had been no reason for Stewart's death. It had made a mockery of the universe. For a long time nothing had made any sense. The remote anger and reasoning of the terrorist had nothing to do with Stewart, nothing to do with her. There was no cause and effect.

But this was different. She must not make the mistake of thinking that the two things were remotely the same. Heavenly Father had sent Providence and Briggie and Dr. Brace after Stewart's death. She was simply a victim of mortality with all its attendant trials. There was no other way for her to come to grips with her loss except through the love and caring of others, but in this case there were *reasons* for the loss. There was a genesis to the whole sad story.

She could and must untangle the mess, discover the cause for the effect, find the murderer for the murder. It was time the anger ended before it scarred any more lives. This is what her father would have wanted. His death would have some meaning if she could find the reasons and end the cycle of fear and anger. They had lost their chance to be a family in this life, but life was eternal, and maybe there was still a chance for them in the next.

Fishing in her bag for a tissue, Alex blew her nose resolutely and left her hiding place.

* * *

"Why would your father's letter upset her so much, Alex?" Briggie wanted to know.

They had adjourned to the white beach between the park and Lake Michigan. Alex had removed her shoes and was trickling the sand through her fingers.

"It wasn't the letter. She was actually quite relieved about that because Daddy didn't disclose the horrible secret. She didn't get really upset until I told her the police knew it was murder."

"But *why* did she want it so desperately to be suicide?" her friend demanded.

"Because of the alternative," Daniel answered.

"She's afraid, Briggie," Alex explained. "That's what finally got through to me after I finished my pity party. She's terrified."

"Of the murderer?"

"I don't know."

There was a long silence. Then, Alex asked at random, "Doesn't anger most often arise from fear?"

Daniel answered. "It can. Or out of a sense of a great injustice."

"But," she insisted, "doesn't it still come back to fear in the end? I mean, when Stewart died, I thought I was so angry because it was so unjust, but maybe it was really because I was afraid. That the universe made no sense, I mean. That there was no one in control."

He nodded. "I think you're right."

Briggie was pawing through her canvas bag. "I'm just a simple farm gal from Idaho," she said. "I've got to get things down in black and white before they make any sense to me. Let's make a list."

Alex grinned suddenly, and Daniel laughed. "Right, Briggie. Myers-Briggs would dub you SJ sent to peg us dreamy NF's down with logic and keep us from floating away."

Alex patted her friend on the knee. "Interpreted, that means that you're the practical one of the bunch."

"Question: Why is Amelia frightened?" Briggie wrote the words on her long legal-sized notepad.

Alex responded, "Possible answer: She's afraid she knows who might have done it. She knows that if he or she thinks she suspects them, then she could be next."

"Or, how about this?" Daniel contributed. "She's afraid Alex will find out the truth and put herself in danger."

"Come on, Daniel! You didn't see her. The woman thinks I'm responsible for the whole thing. She's not the least bit worried about me."

"You can't expect her powers of reasoning to be functioning very well, Alex. From what you said, the idea that the police knew it wasn't suicide was a genuine shock. You were the bearer of bad tidings. Her instinct was to blame you."

"But the point is, why was it bad tidings? I mean, for me it was a relief to find out it was murder rather than suicide. As usual, Briggie has gone to the heart of the matter. Why was she so much angrier when she found out it was murder?"

"She must know something," Briggie concluded. "Something dangerous. No wonder they have a policewoman guarding her."

Daniel said. "This insistence on suicide sounds like denial to me."

"Okay. So what's she denying?"

"The truth. Possibly the fact that there's a blackmailer involved and she knows who it is. She called Bob that night. Maybe it was to try and persuade your father not to tell you the family secret. Her interests were in seeing that he played along with the blackmailer. Possibly Bob's were, too."

"But why would a blackmailer kill Daddy?" Alex asked, tossing up a handful of sand in frustration. "It'd be killing the goose that laid the golden egg!"

"Not if he thought your mother would continue the payments."

Putting her fingertips to her temples, Alex shook her head. "This is getting too complicated. I hope you're taking notes, Briggie."

Her partner read: "Re motive: Was murder committed to prevent J. B. from revealing secret? Re suspects: Blackmailer may have killed to protect his income. Query: Would Amelia continue to play along?"

"It reads exactly like Dorothy L. Sayers," Alex grumbled. "This can't be real."

"What we need is food," Daniel proposed.

Ignoring him, Alex began to dig a hole. "You know, I don't think we're really going to get to the bottom of this until we find out what it was that everyone was so steamed about. Let's forget blackmailers and everything for the time being and go back to Grandfather."

"Right," Briggie agreed, turning to a new page. "Let's write down everything we know about him, starting with his obit."

"That's right," Daniel said resignedly. "Alex hasn't seen the fruits of our investigation."

"Ok Sherlock, just what have the two of you been up to?"

Briggie reached in her bag and handed him a sheet of paper.

Clearing his throat, Daniel began: *"Meat-Packing Magnate Mourned. Joseph Borden, president and owner of Borden Meats, died quietly in his home last Wednesday. He is survived by one son, Joseph, Jr., two grandchildren, Alexandra and Robert Borden. Another son, Richard Borden, was killed in an auto accident in 1965.*

"A resident of Winnetka for fifty years, Mr. Borden was married in 1930 to the former Alice Spinner of Evanston, who predeceased him in 1952. Services will be held Saturday at the Tompkins Funeral Home, Evanston. Interment at Evanston Memorial Park Cemetery."

"Short and sweet," Alex remarked, still digging her hole.

"That was the *Evanston Review,*" Briggie remarked. "The *Trib* had a longer article that we copied, but it was all about Borden Meats. You can read it later. The personal details are the same."

"There aren't many, though, are there? It's like the death certificate. Well, hopefully the military records will tell us something more substantial. I should have ordered them years ago."

Briggie had begun a bio sheet, reading aloud as she wrote: "Birth: 1895? Marriage: 1930 to Alice Spinner. Death: 1970. Residences: Winnetka 50 years. Other Info: Served in France, presumably 1917–1918. Made will in 1917 leaving estate to Edward Borden, cousin from St. Louis. Was not married at that time. Parents dead. Was acquainted with Harold Simpson. Sent his widow money after the war."

"I was forgetting about Sarah," Alex said. "But I still don't see that she's terribly relevant."

Briggie filled Daniel in on the saga of Sarah Simpson, while Alex sat silently, watching two toddlers run through the ripples that passed for waves on Lake Michigan. Then, shifting her gaze, she stared down the shore at the Chicago skyline and thought about her grandfather. A tall, distinguished-looking man. Plenty of white hair. Distant blue eyes. Scar on his temple from the war. Same high-bridged nose as her father. Typical North Shore executive. What in the world could he have done to cause all this havoc?

Briggie had finished her talc. "Why did he keep her picture, though, Alex? Why didn't he give it back to her?"

"Perhaps he was schizophrenic," Daniel offered lightly. "Sarah was the wife of his other personality."

"Good try," Alex told him, dropping a pinch of sand in his ginger curls. "But I'm afraid Harold was a real, documented person. He had two kids and a juicy obituary. I even have his parents' names somewhere."

"And your grandfather? What was his life like before the war?" Daniel persisted.

"I have no idea. Isn't that funny? I know more about Harold Simpson than I do about my own grandfather."

"Let's just do bio sheets on Harold and Sarah," Briggie suggested. "Maybe something will occur to us.

"Harold: Born . . . what did his obit say?" Scrounging in her canvas bag, she came up with the photocopy. "He was twenty-five when he was killed. That means he was born in . . . 1893." She read on further. "Parents: George and Ethel Simpson. Married?"

Alex fished the photocopy of the marriage announcement out of her own bag. "July 1914," she said.

Consulting the obituary, Briggie finished, "Died: November 1918, a week before armistice. Knew Joseph Borden, who must have taken the picture of his wife from his effects."

"We don't know nearly as much about Sarah, because we never looked up the obit," Alex said.

"But her daughter did say she'd been dead for sixty-two years, didn't she? So we have a marriage in 1914 and a death in 1930. Children: Mary and Harold Simpson, Jr. There!"

Tearing the three sheets out, she laid them in a row on the sand and studied them.

"The more I think about it, the stranger that story is," Daniel mused, squinting over the lake. "I mean, if he took her picture from Harold's dead body or whatever and went to all the trouble to find Sarah and send her money, why didn't he return the picture?"

"Probably it just got jammed in the back of his bureau, and he thought it was lost. Or else he just plain forgot about it," Alex mused.

"I think I've got it!" Briggie crowed suddenly. Biting her lower lip, she studied the sheets avidly. "There's nothing to contradict it in the evidence, and it makes sense of everything!"

"What does?" Alex demanded

"I'll bet you a million bucks Harold Simpson never died in France. Maybe your real grandfather, or rather the real Joseph Borden, did. I think Harold Simpson impersonated him. Weren't Joseph's parents dead?"

"Briggie! That's impossible!" Alex objected. "It's the craziest thing I've ever heard!"

"I don't think she's an SJ, after all, Alex," Daniel remarked sadly.

"Listen!" Briggie's eyes had grown large, and she was talking with her hands. "It would explain so much. The picture, the old will, everything your parents did. Don't you understand? The estate didn't belong to them! It belonged to this Edward."

"Yes, and what about Edward?" Alex asked. "For that matter, what about all the friends Joseph had left behind? They would know Harold Simpson wasn't Grandfather . . . I mean Joseph Borden."

Daniel stood up, stretched, and pulled both women to their feet. "I'm hungry."

Briggie pursued her point as they walked back to the car. "Maybe there was a resemblance. Maybe that's what put it into Harold's head in the first place. Edward lived in St. Louis. Maybe he and Joseph didn't know each other very well."

"But why would Harold Simpson keep the will?" Grasping at this one question to steady her, Alex felt as though she had just been thrown on a high speed merry-go-round.

"It was a holograph!" Briggie exclaimed. "He needed it to learn the real Joseph Borden's signature."

"But why keep it?"

"No reason not to. It was supposed to be his. As a matter of fact, it would strengthen his claim to being Joseph Borden."

Alex was silent. They had reached the car, and Daniel was unlocking the doors. "Briggie, do you realize what you're saying?" she burst out. "If you're right, my grandfather committed bigamy—my father was illegitimate."

"No, no!" Briggie was really excited now. Oblivious of Daniel holding the door open for her, she thrust the bio sheets at Alex. "Look! When did Sarah die?"

"1930."

"And when did your grandfather marry your grandmother?"

"1930." Alex looked at her friend, and the light dawned. "Is that what put this whole thing into your head?"

"Why would he wait so long to get married? He'd been home from the war twelve years. He was a prosperous businessman. If his death certificate has the right date of birth, he was thirty-five years old when he got married."

"And you think he had scruples about being a bigamist after everything else he'd done?"

"He might not have thought the impersonation was such a terrible thing. Maybe Joseph Borden even suggested it when he knew he was dying."

Alex got into the car. "Never in our entire acquaintance have I known you to come up with such a cockeyed idea," she said to Briggie evenly. "You can't actually expect me to take this seriously!"

Daniel slid in beside her and started the car. "It's enough to give anyone an identity crisis. I wonder what Dad would make of it?"

"Your dad?"

"Yes. You see, in addition to everything else, it's undoubtedly what they call a nice legal problem. Following Briggie's hypothesis, that would make Simpson guilty of fraud in the matter of the inherited estate. But then he takes the money and makes more money with it. Who inherits that money? The rightful heirs or your father or a combination of the two?"

Alex's head was spinning. "And what does all this make that old woman in the nursing home?"

Biting her lip, Briggie worked it out. "Mary Montgomery would be your half-aunt. Here, look at these descendency charts I've sketched."

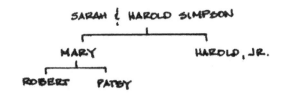

"I don't believe it!" Alex said resolutely. But just then the oven-hot car reminded her of the stifling attic, Sarah's picture, and something else.

"*Grandfather's name was Joseph, wasn't it?*" she had asked her father on the last day of his life. "I mean it wasn't Harold Joseph or anything like that?"

If there wasn't any truth to Briggie's theory, why had her question stopped her father in his tracks? He had stood absolutely still on the staircase for at least fifteen seconds.

"Briggie?"

"Hmmm?" Her friend was squinting through the back window, obviously lost in the intricacies of her theory.

"I hope you're wrong."

EIGHT

They dined at Hackney's; however it was not a cheerful meal in the least.

"Remember the $200,000 mortgage?" Briggie asked. "It fits, too."

"You mean blackmail." Alex said flatly, toying with an onion ring. Her Hackney burger was untouched.

"Who?" Daniel asked, looking from one of them to the other. "Have a heart. I'm new at this."

Briggie smiled at him kindly. "It's just that you don't have all the facts. You see, when we went to see Mary Montgomery, she told us that she had seen some letters from Joseph Borden to her mother. That's how she found out he was sending Sarah money. Mary didn't seem to think he did it out of charity, but she wouldn't get more specific."

"Even so, it doesn't fit, Briggie," Alex told her. "Mary didn't act as though she thought Joseph Borden was her father. She knew something, but it wasn't that."

"He could have been intentionally misleading in the letters."

"Something like: 'Here's the dough. Signed, your friend, Joe?'"

Briggie polished off her Hackney-burger. "You need to eat that," she told Alex, indicating her untouched dinner.

"C'mon Briggie, admit it. It doesn't fit."

"Think back, Alex. What happened when you suggested that your grandfather might have been sending her money out of charity?"

"She got angry," Alex recalled, handing her burger over to Briggie. "I can't eat it."

"In fact," Briggie said while she neatly sawed the burger in half, "she said that in her opinion it wasn't charity but more like . . . then she had her seizure. Perhaps she realized she'd gotten a little carried away and almost let the cat out of the bag." Briggie placed half of Alex's dinner on Daniel's plate.

Exasperated, Alex put both elbows on the table and leaned closer to Briggie. "Listen to me! You're talking about my grandfather! Someone I knew! Somebody I loved! He wouldn't have done those things. He just wouldn't!"

Her friend put down the hamburger. "Take it easy, honey. There's no reason to come unglued. You know how I love to horse around with theories. It's what we always do."

"This time you're theorizing way ahead of the data," Alex told her firmly.

Back at the house, they were greeted by Officer Gentry, who had obviously relieved Lindsey. "You planning to sleep here tonight?" he asked.

"Mrs. Poulson and I are," Alex answered. "Does that mean you will be, too?"

He smiled, revealing a mouth full of braces. "I won't sleep, ma'am. I'm on duty. Lieutenant O'Neill's orders are that no one is supposed to be left alone in the house."

"Okay," Alex said resignedly. She went to the kitchen, turned on the light, and sat down in front of the will, forcing her tired mind to read it once more. Daniel was hunting through the cupboards.

"Anyone know where the coffee is?"

"Second cupboard on the left," Alex said absently. "Or at least that's where they used to keep it."

"I'm beat," Briggie declared.

Remembering her friend's long drive the night before, Alex forced a smile and gave her a kiss. "Don't let your little theory keep you awake, Briggie. I'm going to disprove it tomorrow. "

Her partner looked at her affectionately. "That's my girl. Why don't you hit the sack?" Turning to Daniel, she admonished, "You shouldn't be drinking coffee at this time of the night."

"It's only decaf," he said. "Go to bed, Briggie."

"You can have the Bronte suite," Alex told her, "the horrible green room at the end of the hall."

"Why do I get the feeling I'm being banished?" she complained.

"Oh, there's a bathroom next door," Alex assured her. "Indoor plumbing. You'll be fine."

When Briggie had gone upstairs, she turned to Daniel. "What about you? Are you going to stay?"

Plugging in the old percolator, he came and sat opposite her. "It depends. Do you want me to?"

"Your landlady is probably waiting to pounce on you," she temporized.

He grinned. "Show a little sympathy for the poor woman. She can't help herself."

"Doesn't she have a husband or something? Who's Lee?"

"A female roommate. Sue's divorced."

Alex nodded. "That settles it, then. You'll be much safer here. No divorcees. All we have are murderers and batty widows. You can have Daddy's room."

For a moment, they grinned at one another. Then Alex shifted her gaze back to the will.

"You're really ticked at Briggie, aren't you?" he said.

"My grandfather was *not* Harold Simpson."

* * *

Later, in her mother's big double bed, she stretched out beneath the scented sheets and tried to order her mind. Tomorrow was Sunday. What should they do next? Briggie would want to go to church, of course.

Then . . . but she had forgotten. Daniel would have to go back to Kansas City. End of triumvirate.

The thought added to her misery. The fact that it added to her misery made her still more miserable. Closing her eyes, she remembered the tough security of his wrestler's body as he had held her close in the little room at the airport. It seemed like eons ago. He had stroked her hair. No one had held her or stroked her hair for a very long time.

Rolling over, she threw the tangle of sheets away from her body, deliberately set about displacing thoughts of Daniel with memories of Stewart, and then slowly fell asleep.

* * *

A noise awakened her. At first, she didn't realize she was awake. Registering automatically that the back door had just shut, she wondered idly what time it was and who was going out. There was another sound, and suddenly she jerked awake. Someone had just upset the umbrella jug by the back door. She had done it numerous times herself. Was it Officer Gentry?

Perhaps she had better find out. Climbing out of bed, she descended the stairs lightly and crept through the entryway, her bare feet making no sound. In the dining room, she halted at the swinging door that led to the kitchen. A wavering, yellow light was moving through the slit underneath. A flashlight. Not Officer Gentry, then. Who could it be?

Easing the door just a crack, she could see the light reflecting off the mirror on the butcher block. The intruder was examining the will. A heavy odor of French fries filled the air.

Suddenly angry, she pushed the door open the rest of the way. "What do you think you're doing?"

The flashlight moved to her face, blinding her. Heedless, she moved toward it. "What do you want?" She was dimly aware of someone's tread on the staircase.

The owner of the light jerked around and made for the door. Still dazzled, Alex heard him charge the butcher block, sending the glass table top rolling and then crashing to the floor. Like a slow-motion sequence in a film, its shattering seemed to go on forever. Against this sound, the back door slammed, and the intruder disappeared.

A split second later, she heard the front door. Whirling, Alex ran into the entryway and stared out into the night. It was easy to see Briggie in the moonlight, her white Royals nightie giving her the appearance of a plump fairy as she sprinted across the lawn to her Bronco. Another shape, this one rotund and not quite as fast, was lumbering down the driveway from the back of the house.

Briggie emerged, backside first, from the Bronco, her thirty-aught-six rifle in hand. Meanwhile the rotund shape had made it to the street and was making track across the drive towards what looked like an aged Ford Pinto.

Her partner took aim. "Hands up!" she cried.

Ignoring her, the intruder flung open the car door, tossed something inside, and dove in after it. The something appeared to be Alex's canvas bag.

"Hey!" she yelled, running across the lawn. The car started.

Alex heard a shot and her automatic reflex was to duck from flying buckshot. There was a burst of gravel by the back tire. With the vague idea of blocking the car, Alex ran into the street. Briggie yelled at her, "Out of the way!"

Another shot. "Darn!" she exclaimed as the Pinto disappeared around the corner. Running after it, Alex heard someone shout, "Mrs. Campbell!"

It was no use, of course. The idiot had gotten away with her bag.

Wandering back to the house, she was amused to see Briggie, deer rifle in hand, explaining events to an obviously chagrined Officer Gentry.

"What's going on?" Daniel demanded, his ginger hair standing on end. He was dressed in her father's pajama bottoms.

"Dear Cousin Bob just made off with my bag," Alex explained. "Briggie almost got the rear tires, but I spoiled her aim." Looking over at Briggie she said remorsefully, "Sorry, Briggs."

"Cousin Bob?" Briggie asked. "Is that who it was?"

"Without a doubt. He was fat, cowardly, and smelled unmistakably of French fries."

"Lots of burglars probably eat at McDonald's," Briggie countered, inspecting the scope of her rifle. "Darn, I couldn't hit the broad side of a barn with this. I'm going to have to have this bore-sighted." Turning back to Alex, she admonished, "I don't think you should jump to any rash conclusions here." She climbed back into the Bronco to replace her rifle.

Alex, pointedly ignoring the policeman and trying to keep her eyes averted from Daniel's naked chest, went back into the kitchen, where she examined the back door. "Lots of burglars don't have keys to the back door," she said with satisfaction.

"What's that?" the policeman asked.

"The back door," she told him. "It wasn't forced. He had a key."

"I'd better call the station."

"Yes," Alex said. "I think you'd better." Turning to Daniel, she said, "Don't you think you're a little informal?"

* * *

Lieutenant O'Neill's eyes were more bloodshot than the last time she'd seen him. "What would your cousin want with your purse?" he asked firmly.

They were seated in her mother's sitting room, for want of a better place. Daniel, arrayed in her father's red paisley bathrobe, was leaning negligently against the door frame. O'Neill had preempted the position of authority behind the desk. Briggie and Alex shared the couch. Officer Gentry stood awkwardly behind his chief.

"There was a letter," Alex told him. "I was going to give it to Sergeant Lindsey today, but I forgot. It was from my father."

O'Neill smote his forehead and swore lengthily. "A letter, was it? Have you ever heard of evidence? Don't you know this is a murder investigation?"

"Daniel saw it," she told him. "He'll tell you what it said."

Relating the contents of the letter, Daniel finished by saying, "It sounded as though there might have been some financial shenanigans involved. If so, someone had a pretty good motive for murder. He or she wouldn't have been anxious for Mr. Borden to set things straight if they were going to lose by it."

"*If* such a letter even exists!" O'Neill expostulated. "I wouldn't put it past you three jokers to have staged this whole thing tonight."

"With a policeman in the house?" Alex asked innocently.

The lieutenant grunted. "Says he fell asleep. The shots woke him. Shots! I'm amazed he didn't roll over, thinking it was a car backfiring. Obviously, he underestimated the kind of characters we are dealing with." Turning, he addressed his officer, "For future reference, Gentry, the police do the shooting. The suspects aren't allowed to have guns."

"Briggie's not a suspect!" Alex protested.

"Partner to one, apparently." He looked the older woman over suspiciously. "Thirty-aught-six. I wouldn't have picked you for a deer hunter."

"Only in season," Briggie assured him primly. "But I'm a widow woman, you know. Sometimes I need a little extra protection."

The lieutenant responded to this by instructing the red-faced Gentry to impound the rifle. Then, shaking his head, O'Neill turned once more to Alex. "Now, *IF* this letter exists, how would your cousin know about it, and why would he want it?"

Alex dropped her eyes. This part was going to be dicey. "I visited my mother in the hospital. She was pretty upset by the letter. I think maybe she told Bob about it. She saw me put it in my bag."

"Now we're getting somewhere. Will you kindly explain why she was upset?"

"You had someone in the room!" Alex remembered suddenly. "She can verify the letter. She was taking notes."

O'Neill nodded. "Yes. I haven't read the details of her report yet, but Officer Hawkins said your mother gave you a pretty bad time. Accused you of your father's death, in fact."

"It wasn't like that," she insisted. "My mother is . . . well, let's just say she'd rather not face things. She still thought that Daddy's death was suicide. She thinks I'm responsible."

"But according to you, the letter contradicts that idea altogether," O'Neill said with doubt in his voice.

"She's not always entirely rational," retorted Alex.

"In fact, she's an alcoholic," the lieutenant stated flatly. "But that doesn't explain why she would send your cousin over here for the letter."

"I'm not sure she did. He could have taken her key pretty easily. Or he might even have had one of his own already. My cousin is . . . well, impulsive. He thinks he was born to be an investigative journalist. He probably wanted the letter for some crazy reason of his own."

O'Neill leaned across the desk, fixing her with his eyes. Suddenly the room was heavy with a palpable silence. For no reason she could name, Alex felt a new sense of dread. Finally, the lieutenant spoke. "Has it ever occurred to you, Mrs. Campbell, that your mother might have killed your father?"

Alex's hand flew to her throat. "No!"

Resettling himself in the chair, O'Neill put it to her. "Take a look at the evidence: her insistence on suicide, her upset about the letter, your cousin's theft, the cyanide in the garage, even the coffee cup . . ."

"We don't keep cyanide in the garage!"

"I thought you hadn't been home for fifteen years, Mrs. Campbell? I assure you, the cyanide in the unused Tranquilor capsules is identical to that in the wasp bomb in your garage."

Alex felt Daniel's eyes on her. He moved to seat himself on the arm of the couch next to her. She slipped one of her hands into his.

"She would have messed it up," Alex protested, trembling. "Daddy would have suspected something and caught her. He was always having to get her out of messes. He watched for them."

"Was Mr. Borden found in his pajamas?" Daniel asked.

O'Neill frowned. "No. Fully clothed. Slacks, button-down shirt, smoking jacket."

"Then it probably wasn't Alex's mother who murdered him. You see, he wrote his letters in bed. We found the letter to Alex in the little traveling desk he used. It was clearly written after the time of her visit. So, at one point in the evening, he was already undressed and in bed. Doesn't it make a lot more sense that if Mrs. Borden was staging a suicide, she would do it in the bedroom, where it would have looked more natural?"

Glaring at the three of them, O'Neill growled. "I'm going to have to put a permanent watchdog on all of you. Is there any other evidence you're keeping back?"

Alex thought quickly of the will in the kitchen. Both Lindsey and Gentry knew about that. Let them take the heat. If the lieutenant guessed her mother had a financial motive . . .

"What were you saying about the coffee cup?" she asked.

"Just the sort of thing a drunk would do," he told her. "Set the whole thing up and then botch it by kicking the cup under the couch."

She and Daniel exchanged a look. Unfortunately, this idea had the ring of truth. It was *exactly* the sort of thing her mother would do.

Briggie spoke up, "If Mr. Borden was dressed, it means he was expecting company. Alex says he always received his friends in the study. So whoever it was, it wasn't a friend."

Knowing that Briggie was in danger of destroying their credibility entirely with her cockeyed theory of impersonation and blackmail, Alex intervened hastily. "Perhaps it was my cousin," she suggested. "What were the terms of my father's will? Didn't Daddy leave him something?"

"A sizable chunk," O'Neill agreed.

"Well, I think he's a whole lot more likely suspect than my mother! My mother called him that night. What did he tell you about the phone call?"

"Mainly that she was hysterical. She insisted that he come over right away, that you had been there and upset your father, and that your father was liable to do something Bob would regret if he didn't get there soon."

"What's Mother's version?"

"Your mother," said Lieutenant O'Neill wearily, "claims it's all a blank. According to her, she was blotto from the time she called your cousin until he arrived and roused her."

"But you think she's guilty," Alex said.

"Either that or she's protecting someone."

"Mother wouldn't lie to protect me, Lieutenant."

Daniel slid an arm around her shoulders.

"You'd be surprised at all the things mothers will do," the lieutenant said, standing up. "I'll be straight with you, Mrs. Campbell. I think your mother did it. But I haven't ruled you out entirely. Or your cousin. You'd better keep your nose clean from here on out. No more Three Musketeers. Got it? No more deer hunting in Winnetka, Mrs. Poulson."

The three of them promised devoutly to be on their best behavior, but Alex's mind was already racing ahead to tomorrow. She knew Briggie's was, too. If the only credible suspects were herself and her mother, maybe they ought to pursue her crazy theory after all. They had to do something.

NINE

"Somehow," Alex said at brunch, "none of this seems very real."

She and Briggie had just returned from sacrament meeting at the local LDS Church. Fortunately, no one had known who she was, and the name Campbell had no associations with the man who had just been murdered. It had been comforting to pretend for a little while that everything was normal, that this was just another Sunday.

Since her conversion, Alex had drawn strength and comfort from the ordinance of the sacrament and its promise of the Spirit. While sitting with her head bowed, waiting for the tray to be passed, once again she felt the warm, comforting mantle enfold her. Something unknotted deep inside. The shield she wore for the world dropped away as it had the morning before, and for a brief space of time, she allowed herself to be vulnerable and loved.

Now they were home. Briggie had found some ancient oatmeal in the pantry and managed to prepare a scratch meal. Unfortunately, her many talents did not include the art of cooking. The food was scarcely palatable.

Bleary-eyed from lack of sleep, the trio sat around the dining room table, drinking weak hot chocolate made from a very stale mix that Alex suspected of being slightly rancid. Sergeant Lindsey sat a few feet away, notebook in hand.

Alex realized that the reality of what she had felt in church seemed far greater than the fact of her father's murder.

"You're disassociating," Daniel told her, rubbing the day's growth of ginger beard on his chin. "It's okay. It's normal under the circumstances."

Alex stood up, looking at Daniel. "Stop it! Just stop it," and wandered to the window. "If only I hadn't been so darned determined on getting my own way. My father was clearly in distress. I should have recognized that. I should have *talked* to him instead of yelling at him. Maybe he would have told me something."

Briggie sighed. "We all have regrets, honey."

Alex hugged herself as she felt tears starting. "I was trying to do the right thing, Briggie. How did everything go so wrong?"

"We're not at the end of the story, remember? And your talk with your father wasn't the beginning. It's been years in the making. We're just now starting to unravel it."

Alex felt Daniel's eyes on her back. Turning around, she challenged him. "What are you thinking?"

"I'm thinking how incredibly brave you are."

"Brave?"

"Most people who have lived with a dysfunction will do just about anything to avoid the truth. You're striding into the middle of this, ready to take on all comers. It's impressive."

"Thank you, Dr. Grinnell." Leaving the window, she returned to her seat and laced her fingers in front of her on the table. "Okay, guys, where are we?"

"Are you sure you haven't underestimated your cousin?" Briggie asked.

"Lazy people can be amazingly feral," Daniel contributed.

"What's that supposed to mean?" Briggie asked as she gathered plates.

"Fox-like," Alex interpreted. "Bob is not fox-like. He's marshmallow-like."

"Whatever did he do to earn your everlasting scorn?" Daniel wanted to know.

"He was a crybaby and a tattletale," Alex said sharply.

Lindsey, whose presence they had all forgotten, was fidgeting in his chair. "Mrs. Campbell . . ."

"Yes?" She turned to him in surprise.

"I wouldn't ordinarily tell you this, but for your own safety . . . well. It isn't a good idea for you to discount your cousin altogether."

"Why? Do you know something that I don't?"

"Just that he's disappeared. We've put an APB out on him. He never came home last night. Your mother says she hasn't seen him since yesterday afternoon . . . and she did tell him about the letter."

Alex envisioned Bob going underground and laughed shortly. "Briggie probably scared him to death with her rifle. I can see it all now," she said. "Keep your eyes peeled for a rotund fry cook in a trench-coat and sunglasses."

"I still don't think O'Neill had any right to take my rifle," Briggie said stoutly. They had been hearing variations on this theme all morning. "Couldn't you ask your father about it, Daniel?"

"I'm afraid my father would object to your gun on completely unrelated grounds, Briggie," Daniel chuckled. "He's morally opposed to hunting."

"I might have known . . ." she grumbled, hands full of crockery. Pushing the swinging door with her backside, she went on through to the kitchen.

"Okay, guys. Let's concentrate. Blackmail." Alex put her fingertips to her temples and closed her eyes. A moment later, she opened them, puzzled. "It doesn't make sense to me that a blackmailer would *kill* Daddy on the off chance that Mother would keep up the payments. It just doesn't fit. It's too risky."

"Maybe he did it because your father would have nothing to lose once he came out into the open with whatever it was," Daniel speculated as Briggie came back through the door. "Maybe he was afraid your father would go to the police and press charges."

"Mother wouldn't have liked that," Alex objected after a moment. "It would just add fuel to the fires of whatever the scandal was. I don't think he would have done it."

"But did the blackmailer know that?" Daniel wondered.

"There's another thing," Briggie pointed out as she stacked cups. "Alex's dad was killed shortly after he wrote her that letter. He'd just decided to tell her whatever it was. Do you seriously think he'd call the blackmailer on the phone and warn him about what he was going to do?"

"I see your point," Daniel conceded.

Briggie sat down. "I have a better idea. If my theory about Harold Simpson is right, then the blackmailer was probably one of his descendants who somehow found out the truth. He or she could blackmail your father, even though your grandfather was dead. The estate he inherited really didn't belong to him; it belonged to Edward Borden or his heirs. Are you with me?"

Alex sighed. Daniel nodded.

"Now. If your father decides that he's going to make the stuff public about your grandfather being Simpson and not Borden, that means the money's going to go to Edward Borden or his descendants, right?"

"Some of it, anyway. Remember the nice legal point I mentioned," Daniel reminded her. "Alex's father might have been entitled to the value added to the original estate."

"Let's put that aside for the time being. I don't think any of the Simpsons are likely to be well versed in the law. According to their reasoning, if they were getting money out of Alex's dad, they would have felt they were entitled to it. Assuming Harold Simpson was Alex's grandfather, let's not forget he was their father or grandfather, too. They would have felt they should have had some of his money."

"But once he tells the truth, the money's gone," Daniel concluded. "It goes to Edward's heirs. They can't get part of what's not there."

"Right. So it's not exactly a straightforward blackmail situation. They would have had a big stake in the truth not coming out, too."

"How does that get us around the problem of their finding out what he intended to do in time to kill him?" he objected. "Don't these people live in Des Moines?"

Briggie pondered. "We don't know that. Mary Montgomery's brother, Harold, Jr., might live around here."

"He'd be awfully old," Alex protested. "And Daddy would hardly call him up and tell him what he was going to do, anyway."

"No," Briggie admitted. "But your mother might—the same way she called Bob, thinking maybe they could help persuade him not to do it."

"Instead, they murder him," Alex finished, shuddering.

"It's no wonder your mother's terrified," Briggie said, getting to her feet. "Even if she'd passed out upstairs, she's got to have some idea who did it."

"They probably didn't even know she was here," Alex murmured. "Thank goodness she's in the hospital under guard."

Once again they had forgotten Sergeant Lindsey, who was clearing his throat. "I think they moved your mother this morning, ma'am. She's in a psychiatric hospital now, out near Mt. Prospect. The lieutenant can give you the phone number, but you don't need to worry. She's safe enough."

Alex sighed deeply. "I hope she's trying to dry out."

"Well, Sergeant," Daniel addressed him. "What do you think of our theory?"

"A little hard for me to follow," the young man admitted, grinning. "I'd appreciate a few more details. Who's Harold Simpson?"

Alex chuckled. "Ask Briggie. Believe me, we're not holding out on you. It's just such a crazy idea; we thought O'Neill would explode if we handed it to him on top of the rifle episode. We need more evidence—a lot more evidence."

"Then we promise to tell you all about it," Briggie added soothingly. "Right now I believe I'll call Nonnie, if it's all right with you, Alex. It's Sunday, so the rates will be low."

"Nonnie? Your daughter Nonnie?"

"Yes. She's the one who lives in St. Louis," Briggie explained to Daniel, "I should have thought of it ages ago, Alex. She can get hold of the military records at the National Personnel Records Center. I'll give her what we've got and have her dig up the war records on Simpson and Borden tomorrow. She can give it to me over the phone and then Fed Ex copies to us."

"Good idea," Alex conceded. "Maybe she'll find something to settle this thing one way or the other."

A moment later they heard her on the kitchen telephone.

"You know, we keep talking about blackmail," Alex mused, "but the only evidence we have are Mary Montgomery's claim that Grandfather sent Sarah money and that $200,000 mortgage from twenty-odd years ago. That doesn't make sense. If the Simpson heirs are involved in this, the way Briggie thinks they are, they'd would have something to lose. I mean, the blackmail payments must still have been going on."

"Blackmailers are never satisfied," Lindsey agreed.

"You're wondering if there's any way we can find evidence of payments, right?" Daniel asked.

Suddenly she struck her forehead with the heel of her hand. "Why didn't I think of it before? The bank statements! They're in the attic."

"I somehow doubt your father would have written a check to his blackmailer," Daniel objected.

"There might be something." Alex was already halfway to the stairs. Daniel and the sergeant got up to follow her.

* * *

When they had brought the box of statements back downstairs, Alex doled them out three ways. "I don't exactly know what we're looking for."

"Checks written to cash," Lindsey suggested.

"Of course," she said.

It didn't take them long to find them. In 1980 there had been quarterly checks made out to cash for $20,000. By 1989, the amount had escalated to $50,000.

Sergeant Lindsey was doing calculations on his notepad. "All in all, he paid out a million two hundred and fifty thousand dollars in cash during the '80s. That's a lot of money."

"Did he ever gamble, Alex, or anything like that?"

"I doubt it, but how do I know?" she asked, throwing up her hands in irritation. "He could have had a million secret vices!"

"A gambler wouldn't be quite so regular in his habits," Lindsey remarked woodenly.

"Thank you, Sergeant." Alex replied. "That only leaves drugs. Now I suppose you're going to suggest that he was addicted to cocaine, Daniel."

Daniel registered surprise at the venom in her voice.

Clearing his throat again, Lindsey said, "The autopsy didn't reveal any evidence of drug addiction, ma'am."

She stood and walked over to the window. The checks had shaken her; there was no doubt about it. They were evidence of something real. Blackmail had seemed possible in the abstract. But now? It was difficult to swallow. But then, why should anything be so difficult to swallow after murder?

Closing her eyes, she tried to picture her father's face, but its image and comfort refused to materialize. All she could remember was his letter. What was the phrase about the secret he was going to tell her? "You must be a little patient. It is not my secret alone, and there are legal and other messy ramifications that will be unpleasant."

"I guess it *must* have been blackmail," she sighed, returning to the table. "Everything fits with Daddy's letter. Somehow, it had to do with Grandfather. Briggie's probably got the whole thing figured out, as usual. Doggone it, I wish I'd given that letter to you, Sergeant! Why don't you take these bank statements before someone makes off with them too?"

Watching the policeman fit the statements neatly back into the files labeled in her father's precise printing, Alex suddenly felt that she couldn't take in one more revelation. Her head was spinning and her heart was aching with a sudden rush of grief. "I'm taking a walk," she told them.

Going out of the patio door from her mother's sitting room, she walked into the garden and ventured down to the rose beds. There, strolling blindly through the neglected, overblown flowers, she tried to reconcile what she had just found out with the life she had known.

Was Daniel right? Had this whole mess been responsible for her mother's alcoholism? She tried to remember when it had begun. Forcing herself to look back, her principal memory was one of terrible isolation. There had been the long, frightening afternoons when she had arrived home to find her mother lying across her bed, heavily asleep and fully dressed. At first, she hadn't known what was wrong. She had thought her mother was ill. It wasn't until the behavior had become habitual that she had noticed the smell. And then, one day, she had found a bottle in mother's bathroom. Chivas Regal, Scotch.

She had been horrified. In some sense, it was as though her mother had died. For weeks Alex had huddled, terrified, in her room, wondering what she should do. Gradually, a feeling of helplessness had grown within her, and she realized there was nothing she could do. It didn't matter how patient and loving she tried to be. It didn't matter how good her grades were. Nothing helped. Her mother kept doing it.

Alex now saw that she had finally developed a kind of coping mechanism. On arriving home from school, she had ceased to check on her mother at all. Instead, she changed clothes and escaped the hollow house by taking her little Scottie for a long walk. Sometimes she had walked into the little town center and bought a candy bar, eating it in small nibbles to make it last the long way home. Other days, she had chosen to walk down by the lake, taking an obscure comfort in its vastness. Against something so large, her emptiness seemed tiny.

When it began to grow dark, she would walk home, knowing there were at least two hours before she could expect her father. To the accompaniment of her transistor radio, she had done her homework, taken a bath, and rolled her hair.

Homework! That was it. *It had been her sophomore year—the year following the summer Grandfather had died.* She remembered now, because she had been studying geometry in school. It had been difficult for her, and she had cried over it because there was no one to help her. Her mother had always been very good at math.

So. It looked as though Daniel had been right. Her mother's drinking was most likely linked to this whole mess with her grandfather.

And her father? Was that when he had started spending such long hours at the office?

She remembered only that it was almost always around eight when she heard the door open downstairs. Running to meet him, she would catch sight of his worried face as he peered into the dining room.

"Well, how about a tuna sandwich?" he would say, his voice echoing with eerie heartiness through the lifeless house. "I'm famished."

She would make him a tuna sandwich and heat some soup. They would eat together at the bar in the kitchen, both carefully avoiding the subject of Mother, acting as though this were a perfectly normal evening.

Denial, of course. And what a lot he had to deny! It was a wonder he hadn't taken to drink too. The strain must have been tremendous—mother's drinking, blackmail, a fifteen-year-old daughter who was to be kept in ignorance. And she still didn't know the worst—the hold the blackmailer had held over her parents.

The house had been happy once. The pictures in the attic documented that fact, even if she had forgotten it. Now she could see that it was only after she had lost one person, her grandfather, that she seemed to lose everyone else. How odd that she had never connected the losses! But a child wouldn't. She had thought that somehow she had done something wrong, that it was her fault everyone had withdrawn.

Her poor father. In the midst of everything, he had to have known it was no kind of life for her. When she had fallen into depression, he wouldn't have been surprised. Probably sending her to Paris, the happiest place he could think of, had seemed like the best answer. She was to be the survivor, sent away from the sinking ship in a lifeboat. He could only hope that she, at least, would make it to shore. And hadn't she? For a time life had been very good. She would never had met Stewart had they not sent her to Paris. She would never have had those ten happy years in Scotland, would never have met Briggie, would never have found the gospel, which had healed so much of the hurt . . .

Alex realized she was carrying a handful of fallen rose petals. Stimulated by their fragrance and her gentle, nostalgic mood, a long lost memory stirred: sometime, many years ago, she had walked here in this garden with Mother, picking up the fallen petals. They had taken them inside and put them in a jar—a special jar she kept in her room. Her mother had added other magical things—oil, spices—and all during the winter she had been able to open up the jar and smell the roses.

Above the jar had hung a carefully worked cross-stitch: "Memory is the power to gather roses in winter." Putting the petals up to her face, Alex breathed in their memories and allowed her tears to fall unchecked.

* * *

Sometime later Daniel found her, seated Indian style, in the middle of the garden. Her face held an expression he had never before seen there. Though she had obviously been crying, the sharp tension was gone from her jaw, the lines smoothed between her brows. And her eyes. They had an expression he supposed the Scots would describe as fey—she looked as though she were seeing some sort of private vision.

It was only with tremendous reluctance that he could bring himself to disturb her. "Alex."

She looked up at him, smiling a sweet smile he had never seen before.

"I'm afraid Lieutenant O'Neill is here again."

TEN

When Alex got back to the house, rose petals now clenched in her hands, Lieutenant O'Neill was sitting with Briggie in the dining room, looking as though he hadn't slept at all.

"What about this cousin of yours?" he asked her. "Has he been in touch with you?"

Alex let the rose petals in her hands fall to the floor. "No. I haven't heard from him. Sergeant Lindsey says he's disappeared."

"His mother claims she hasn't heard from him either."

Alex thought briefly of her Aunt Grace. Poor woman.

The policeman was staring at her impassively, and his sergeant's countenance remained as wooden as ever.

What were they thinking? "I don't like my cousin very much," she told them, "but I don't see him as a murderer."

"Then why has he disappeared?"

Sighing, Alex shrugged. "Your guess is as good as mine."

O'Neill glanced at his sergeant again and then surveyed the three of them with interest. "Lindsey has intimated that you have some sort of theory up your sleeves. If you have, the time to tell me is now, boys and girls."

Briggie responded readily. "It's just an idea about Alex's grandfather. We think he might have been an impostor. We've ordered his military records to see if there's any discrepancy with what we know about him."

"An impostor?" O'Neill turned to Lindsey. "You know anything about this?"

"I gather it's a person called Simpson, sir. From Des Moines."

"Any connection with the murder?"

Lindsey looked uncomfortably at Briggie. "I don't know. But," he indicated the box on the table, "we do have evidence that Mr. Borden was being blackmailed."

"Blackmail?" O'Neill looked hard at his sergeant, and then rolled his eyes heavenward. "I suppose it was just a little detail that slipped your mind. Blackmail!" He sat down again, heavily. "Would it be asking too much for you to tell me about it?"

Alex nodded at Briggie, who continued, "Well, our suspicions were aroused by the $200,000 mortgage the Bordens took out shortly after Mr. Borden, Sr.'s death. I believe Sergeant Lindsey gave it to you."

"Right," the lieutenant acknowledged. "Some rigmarole about its being taken out for home improvements but no evidence that it was used for those purposes."

"There was more to it than that, Lieutenant. You see, Mr. Borden, Sr., made a kind of religion about avoiding debt. This house was paid for. There is no reason for that mortgage. The timing was interesting, too. It was taken out immediately after Alex's grandfather's death."

"Go on."

"Well . . ." Briggie glanced at Alex.

"Go ahead," Alex sighed. "You might as well spill all of it . . . everything."

Taking a deep breath, Briggie launched into her theory regarding Harold Simpson's alleged impersonation, the original Borden will leaving everything to Edward Borden, the blackmail checks and Simpson's possibly blackmailing heirs, and finally, Amelia Borden's hypothetical phone call to them that might have ended in murder.

It was a daunting performance. When Briggie had finished expounding her theories, O'Neill was clearly dazed.

"Now let me get this straight," he said after a moment. "You think this Harold Simpson from Des Moines switched identities with Borden, who may or may not have been killed in France, and then proceeded to come back to a city and business where Borden was well known and step into his shoes?"

"Joseph Borden's parents were dead," Briggie stated. "And there may have been some superficial resemblance between the men."

"What about this Edward Borden?"

"He lived in St. Louis. They may have been distantly related."

"So your idea of motive is that this money really belonged to Edward Borden, his heirs, and the Simpsons knew this and didn't want Mr. Borden, Jr., to reveal this information because then they'd lose the source of their blackmail income?"

Briggie nodded.

"And you think Mrs. Borden called them up and told them this might occur, and they hot-footed it over here from Des Moines . . ."

"We think there must be some local connection . . ."

" . . . and put cyanide in his coffee." O'Neill looked at all of them. "Have I managed to grasp the main points?" he inquired.

Alex thought the whole theory more improbable than ever. "Now you see why we didn't bother you with it," she said.

"Tell me about these heirs," the lieutenant replied thoughtfully.

"It'd be easier to draw a descendency chart," Briggie told him.

She borrowed a piece of paper and pen from Sergeant Lindsey and proceeded to do so.

"First the Bordens," she said, sketching in lines and writing names. "We're assuming Alex's grandfather and Edward were first cousins."

Briggie finished her chart and pushed it across the table for the officer to see.

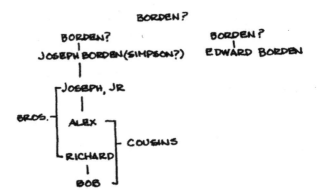

"Okay," the lieutenant said, nodding. "I've got that. What happened to Uncle Richard?"

"Killed in a car wreck," Briggie answered shortly as she drew the second chart. "Here." She displayed the rough diagram of the Simpson ménage.

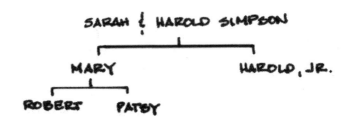

"Now," Briggie continued with satisfaction, "the only one we've met is Mary Montgomery, Simpson's daughter. Alex and I visited her in the nursing home."

Alex envisioned the sparse and sad surroundings of Mary's little room. "It sure didn't look like she was getting extra income from anywhere," she said. "It was the bleakest place you ever saw—one bed, one dresser, one chair, one tiny window."

"And the other heirs?" O'Neill prompted.

"A divorced daughter, Patsy, who works at a truck stop, and a son, Robert, who is a Las Vegas entrepreneur, as she put it," Briggie finished.

The lieutenant's look became speculative. "Las Vegas, eh? That might be worth checking into. Vegas is an ideal place to eat up big amounts of cash. The FBI could be real cooperative with that end of things, always presuming of course that this isn't an idle fantasy. How about this Harold, Jr.?"

"Mary's brother may or may not be alive. He may have heirs too. We haven't checked into that yet."

"I'm surprised." O'Neill gave his head a shake as though he had water in one of his ears. "Well, well," he muttered, sticking his thumbs into his waistband. "That's quite a theory, Mrs. P."

"What do you think?" she asked.

"Craziest thing I ever heard. Think you can find this brother Harold?"

"No problem," Briggie told him.

"Experience says the obvious suspect is guilty nine times out of ten." Beating his fingers on the box Lindsey had set down beside him, the lieutenant stared thoughtfully at Alex. "But there is the blackmail to explain. If it weren't for that, I'd say that old will of Borden's gave your mother a stronger motive than ever. She stands to lose everything she has if Borden, Sr., was a fraud. Where is it, by the way, this will?"

"In the kitchen," Alex said. "Sergeant Lindsey has taken due notice of it. We haven't been keeping back evidence."

O'Neill's expression was rueful. "Any more of that goes on, and one of you spends the night in jail, I promise you."

"We'll let you know the minute we find Harold, Jr.," Briggie pledged.

"You do that. But be careful. Don't go asking if he's a blackmailer. That's our job." He paused, surveying them in turn, a ghost of a smile on his lips. "It's probably all a can of worms, but if by some remote chance these people are involved in the murder, it could be dangerous." He grunted and stood up. "Just to keep things stirred up, I believe I'll put the FBI onto this Montgomery character in Vegas. He could be linked to organized crime, which could add an entirely new and dangerous dimension to the case. You never know." He motioned to Lindsey. "Well, it's been an interesting morning. Sergeant's coming with me. Stay put, Mrs. Campbell, and stay in touch."

The two policemen walked to the door. "Oh, I almost forgot. The coroner wants to know where to send your father's remains. Is there a particular funeral home?"

Alex was struck dumb by the question. "The funeral," she said after a moment. "I forgot all about it. He'll have to have a funeral."

"It's up to you, of course," the lieutenant said, "but these things can attract a lot of press. Unless you have strong feelings to the contrary, you might just want to have a private service."

She nodded. "I guess they should just send him to Tompkins in Evanston. They did Grandfather, I think."

"Fine."

"About my rifle, Lieutenant . . ." Briggie began.

"No," O'Neill interrupted. "Absolutely not." With that remark, he let himself out the door. Following his chief, Lindsey astonished them all by looking back over his shoulder and winking at them.

"Well, Briggs," Alex remarked when the police cruiser had pulled safely away, "you wowed him. I can't believe it."

Her partner sighed. "It's a darn shame about my gun, though. Particularly on account of Daniel leaving."

"Speaking of which," he said, rising to his feet with a stretch, "I have a plane to catch in a couple of hours." He addressed Alex. "Would you care to run interference for me while I get my gear from Susan's?"

"Can you hold the fort, Briggs?"

Her partner nodded absently. "I've still got all that glass in the kitchen to sweep up. Then I've got to see what I can do to take care of that will."

"We won't be long," Alex told her.

The Taurus was like a kiln. Daniel cranked the air conditioning up as high as it would go. For the first while, they drove in silence, Alex still trying to assimilate the morning's events, not the least of which was her new perception of her parents.

"You were right about Mother," she said finally. "Her drinking is related to Grandfather's death. I figured out that she started the fall after he died. She'd be on her bed, passed out, when I came home from school."

Daniel took this in. "You know, I don't think I should leave," he said finally.

"You have your practice and Marigny," she said automatically.

"Dad and Marigny get along fine. And Brenda can handle my emergencies. I'd be no good anyway, worrying about what's going on up here."

Alex felt warmed by his words. "It's Briggie's cooking, isn't it? She's seduced you."

Daniel negotiated one of Sheridan Road's many bends. "Briggie's cooking notwithstanding, I don't think you should be staying alone."

"There's always Grandfather's revolver—"

"Pistol, please."

"Do you think I should get it out of the boat?"

"It would be a whole lot more satisfactory if I stayed on and we left the pistol where it is."

"What horrible thing do you think is going to happen? Even *my* karate could fend off Cousin Bob."

Daniel was silent for a few moments. "It's not just physical danger that I'm worried about, Alex. You've been through a heck of a lot in the past few days. You're holding up incredibly well—amazingly well, as a matter of fact. But I can't help worrying about you."

"Worrying about me how?" she asked suspiciously.

"Don't be coy. You know what I mean."

Something in her hardened. "You've been so human, Daniel. Do me a favor and leave Dr. Grinnell out of this."

She watched Daniel clench his jaw underneath the stubble. "Why do you make it so hard, Alex? Just because I'm a therapist doesn't mean I'm not allowed to worry about you."

Alex didn't answer. She didn't have an answer. All she knew was that when Daniel started referring to her mental condition, she felt violated. She hadn't given him that right.

"You use my profession like a weapon, did you know that?" Daniel accused. "Every time I get too close, you throw it at me."

"Don't you see?" she exploded finally. "That's just it! You walk into my psyche uninvited. I can't keep you out. How do you think that makes me feel?"

"Why can't you just relax? I don't think of you as a patient. I care about you as a person. Is it so horrible that I want to help you get through this in one piece?"

"If I need help, I'll call my psychiatrist," she said stiffly.

"Great!" he expostulated, pulling into Susan's driveway. He slammed out of the car and went into the house.

Alex laid her head back on the headrest. The day only needed this. Just last night she had been longing for Daniel to stay. Now she was pushing him away. Why? Why did she keep doing this?

Would it make any difference if he had another profession? Probably not. This squabbling had an all-too-familiar ring. It brought back memories she had forgotten about: Stewart standing on a rocky outcropping against a gray sky, looming over her, his eyes black and stormy with anger. "Forget your parents! They're twisted, sick! Forget them! Start a *new* story! I *love* you, Alex. You can trust me. Feel it. Look at me! Think! Do you honestly believe I would ever abandon you?"

In the end, of course, she had given in to Stewart. He hadn't meant to get killed, of course, nor had her parents asked for the complications in their lives that had destroyed their family. That didn't make it hurt any less, however.

The thing about Daniel was that he hadn't given her any choice. He saw too much, he knew too much. With no effort at all, he had walked right into her mind, ignoring all her personal boundaries. He knew exactly what she needed. He was more than ready to give it. But life was just too chancy. Whenever she loved, there was the potential of loss. How could she ever feel really safe again?

Then Daniel was back in the car with her. Tossing his overnight bag into the back seat, he consulted his watch. "Four-thirty. I can just make it, I think."

"Aren't you going to shave?" she asked.

"No time," he said.

They were silent the rest of the way to Winnetka, Alex trying with difficulty to shore up her resistance. She wished he would say something, even just reach for her hand across the seat, but though she longed for this, she couldn't take back her words. If she were willing to risk falling in love again, she wanted to be a woman, not a mental case. She was barely holding her own, and she knew it. It was terribly important that she did this alone, that she followed this thing with her parents through emotionally, and that she did it using her own hard-won skills. How else could she ever graduate in her own mind, if not in Daniel's, from the status of "psych patient"?

Unfortunately, all of this reasoning didn't lessen her awareness of him sitting next to her in his blue jeans and the turquoise shirt that showed his biceps. She was keenly aware of the set of his jaw, his hands clenching the wheel, and his eyes glued to the road. She had put that tension there. They were already connected. Didn't her heart speed up whenever he entered the room? And in spite of her fighting the feeling, he *did* make her feel safe. One part of her longed to trust him, to give in, to let him hold her, protect her, love her; the other part of her was busy building walls to keep him out.

"I'm sorry, Daniel," she said when they reached the house.

He turned toward her, and his eyes seemed to see her struggle.

"Thank you for everything you've done. It's just . . ." she broke off, unable to say what she wanted to say.

"Rotten timing," he finished gently. Reaching across the seat, he caressed her face lightly with one finger. "I'm sorry I was so touchy. Keep me posted. And tell Briggie the cocoa's rancid."

Biting her lip, she slowly opened the car door. She didn't want to leave him like this. She ached for him to stay. Getting out of the car was like swimming against the killer current in Loch Fyne. Closing the door gently, she stood on the curb and watched him drive away. As the car disappeared, her tears fell freely, and she went into the house and had a good cry.

"Why did you let him go?" Briggie demanded. "He would have stayed."

"I was afraid." Alex blew her nose miserably.

"Of Daniel?"

"Don't be obtuse, Briggie. You know what I mean."

Her friend embraced her tightly. "You're only thirty-five years old, Alex," she said firmly. "You can't live the rest of your life without caring for another human being."

"I care for you," Alex said, giving her friend another squeeze.

"Poor Daniel."

They spent the afternoon doing domestic chores. Alex telephoned to cancel her credit cards, spoke to the funeral home about holding a private funeral the next day, and telephoned Memorial Park, where her grandparents were buried. Yes, there were already two plots prepaid for in the same lot as the senior Bordens. Alex instructed them to get one ready for a burial the next day.

Then Briggie insisted that they go grocery shopping. "After all, we can't live on stale oatmeal," she said. Afterward, Alex instructed Briggie to house the Bronco in the garage. "Might as well make ourselves at home," she said. "Who knows how long O'Neill will take to decide I didn't kill my father?"

Briggie managed to reposition the will using the sheet of glass that covered her dresser top. It remained sitting on the butcher block table in the center of the kitchen, as much of a mystery as ever.

After a late, overdue meal of tacos and refried beans, Alex confessed to exhaustion and went to bed before it was even dark.

She dreamed she was at the cemetery, standing by her father's open grave. The bishop was just finishing his prayer when she heard a muffled sound from inside the coffin. "He's alive!" she screamed. "Daddy's alive!" Grabbing a convenient crowbar off the ground, she climbed into the grave and began prying open the lid of the smooth oak casket. The wood splintered. "Don't worry, Daddy," she cried frantically. "I'll get you out."

She had spoken aloud, and the words awoke her. Moonlight streamed in through the window, casting eerie moon-shadows on the wall. Her dream retreated slowly, but the sound of splintering wood did not.

Someone was breaking into the house.

ELEVEN

She wondered, climbing out of bed . . . had Bob forgotten his key? What a nuisance he was.

Far groggier than she had been last night, Alex stumbled from the room and made for the stairs. What did he want this time?

The lights should have warned her, but as sleepy as she was, they merely puzzled her. Reaching the bottom of the stairs, she heard a sound coming from the living room. The police had sealed the living room. No one was supposed to be in there. Suddenly, she was completely awake and terrified. What if it was the murderer? What was he looking for? Listening carefully, she could hear another sound, this one coming from the kitchen. Unless she went back upstairs, she was trapped, the living room on one side, the kitchen on the other.

Suddenly the swinging door to the dining room opened, and she was confronted by a man in a purple T-shirt with a black stocking mask pulled over his face. He held a crowbar in his hand. Screaming, she whirled towards the front door and tried frantically to unfasten the bolt. Another man grabbed her from behind. Wrenching herself free, she spun around and kneed her attacker in the groin. Now the purple T-shirt was there. Kicking out wildly at the hand that held the crowbar, she failed to connect as he side-stepped neatly and brought the weapon high above his head. She dodged as he brought the heavy bar down, narrowly missing her head and crashing painfully on her shoulder. She cried out and bolted for the stairs, but that was the last thing she knew.

* * *

She was in some kind of vehicle. Maybe they were going to Minnesota. It always took so long to get there, but the time passed quickly if she slept. She would go back to sleep. It was hard to sleep with the noise, though. What was it? It sounded like a siren. Like in the movies.

Someone was lifting one of her eyelids. "Can you hear me, Mrs. Campbell?"

"Who are you?" she managed to mumble, turning her head to look around. Pain stabbed behind her eyes, and she squeezed them shut, remembering. "Is this an ambulance?"

"That's right. You're coming along fine."

Suddenly the vehicle stopped, and the doors at her feet were flung open. Dozens of hands seemed to grab hold of her stretcher, and soon she was being wheeled through bright corridors. The light hurt her eyes, so she closed them.

A man with a big flat face and a blue shirt sat next to her. He had a badge. Seeing her eyes open, he asked her, "Mrs. Campbell, did you recognize who it was?"

Dimly, she remembered a stockinged face. She tried to shake her head, but it hurt too much. She closed her eyes.

* * *

Daniel had been asleep when the telephone rang.

"Daniel? It's Briggie."

"What's wrong?"

"Alex is in the hospital. She's been hit over the head with a crowbar."

Briggie's hysterical, he registered automatically. Then the meaning of her words hit him. "Crowbar? Someone hit her?"

"Someone broke in. Oh, Daniel, she only comes out of it for a few minutes, and then she goes back under."

"What do the doctors say?"

"They're worried. She was hit pretty hard."

He tried to remember what he had learned about blows to the head, but his thoughts sheered off into panic. "Do they think she'll live, Briggie? Tell me."

"They're worried about coma. Pray for her, Daniel."

Winnie. He could call Winnie. Winnie would know what to do. "I'm calling Dr. Brace. Where are you?"

"At the pay phone in the lobby of the Evanston Hospital."

"Give me the number. I'll call you back when I've talked to him."

Briggie went back to her seat and thrust her knotted hands between her knees. "Please, God. Don't let her die."

Even though it was the middle of the night, she had called the local missionaries, who were on their way to administer to Alex. She prayed they would hurry.

Lieutenant O'Neill was coming toward her, looking like thunder. He mustn't see her crying like this. Fumbling in her canvas bag, she located a handkerchief just as he sat beside her. She blew her nose.

"What in the world is going on?"

"It's her house," Briggie said stubbornly. "How was she supposed to know the murderer was downstairs? She probably thought it was her cousin again."

"What makes you think it was the murderer? The story was in the papers. Borden killed. His wife in the hospital. No mention of a daughter. Good chance for a professional looter." He shook his head angrily. "I shoulda had somebody there."

"It wasn't a looter. Looters don't take wills."

"Wills!" O'Neill exploded. "What wills? For crying out loud, woman, if you know something, spill it!"

"They stole the old will. The one we told you about. The one that left everything to Edward Borden. It was in the kitchen."

Lieutenant O'Neill swore.

* * *

At last the telephone rang. Snatching up the receiver, Daniel barked, "Winnie?"

"I got through," the psychiatrist told him. "She's in and out of consciousness. The blow didn't come down squarely; she must have moved. She has a bad concussion, and they're hoping there's no brain damage. Right now, they're just watching her vitals and keeping her head packed in ice. They'll do a CAT scan in the morning. What's going on anyway?"

He'd forgotten Winnie didn't know. "The latest Tranquilor murder. . . . was her dad."

The doctor swore. "It never even occurred to me it would be the same Borden. How is she handling it? Why didn't she call me? Why didn't *you* call me?"

Picturing a healthy Alex sitting up indignantly in bed, he said, "She'll be mad as fire that I called you now. She's trying to prove to us all that she doesn't need us any more."

Sighing, Winnie said, "What are you going to do now? Is there anything she'll *let* you do?"

* * *

"Briggie? Have the doctors told you anything?"

"She's sleeping now, not unconscious." Daniel could hear the relief in her voice. He heaved a sigh of his own. "She had a blessing."

"What?"

"The missionaries came and administered to her. Since then, she's stabilized. I'm convinced it's a miracle. The doctors were really worried, but now they say she's probably out of danger. We'll know for sure when they do the CAT scan, but I'm confident."

Daniel thought this over. He wasn't sure he believed in miracles, but he didn't like to rule them out altogether. The main thing was that Alex was better. "What should we do?"

"I've been thinking."

"Yes?"

"Could your father possibly take a trip to Des Moines?"

"Dad?"

"Yes. What would make Alex feel better than anything is if we could solve this murder. We need to talk to Mary's daughter, Patsy. I'm not leaving this hospital. I thought maybe your father could see her—you know, in his legal capacity."

Daniel was beginning to see. Chuckling at Briggie's diffidence, he pictured his father's reaction: "The woman's a menace, I keep telling you!"

"It'd be just the thing to start off the week. You want him to pose as a searcher of missing heirs, I suppose?"

"Well, that's what he is," Briggie countered stoutly.

"Whose will is he supposedly probating?"

"Daniel, your father and I have our differences, but I certainly wouldn't want him to get disbarred. Can't he be sort of fuzzy about it? Technically, we are looking for the heirs of Joseph Borden. If my theory's right, and Joseph Borden was Harold Simpson, they would come in for part of Alex's father's estate, wouldn't they?"

"A very nice point. Father will love it."

"Just make sure he gets all the letters and photos . . ."

"Consider it done."

* * *

"The woman's an absolute menace! She's crazy!" Richard Grinnell expostulated a few hours later over breakfast.

"Dad, Alex was almost killed. Briggie can't leave her." Daniel waited a moment to let this detail work on his father's emotions. "This Mary Montgomery sounds right up your street. A salty old gal. You'll love it."

"It has, of course, occurred to you that I could be disbarred for misrepresentation?"

"Nonsense. Alex is your client. You are looking for the heirs of Joseph Borden. He may be Harold Simpson. It's a nice little mess for you."

"Yes." His father had turned speculative, an appreciative gleam in his frosty blue eyes. "I wonder . . ."

"Umm?" Daniel went back to his shredded wheat, confident his father had swallowed the bait.

"I'll have to look up Illinois statutes, of course, but if Alex's grandfather *should* turn out to be Harold Simpson, it'd be interesting to know how the courts would award the value he added to the Borden estate."

"Precisely. You still have your Illinois bar membership, haven't you?"

"Yes, I still get an estate there occasionally."

"Consider yourself hired. I'll mention it to Alex when I see her."

"You're coming with me."

* * *

A thunderstorm pelted Des Moines as their plane landed.

"We'll need a boat," Richard Grinnell growled.

"Have you decided what line you're going to take?" Daniel felt like Archie Goodwin, trying to keep the eccentric Nero Wolfe up to the mark. His father had been sunk in what Daniel hoped was thought during the whole of the twenty-minute flight.

"The name's Simpson?"

"You got it."

"Someone who might be a distant connection of theirs has just passed on. We found this picture of Sarah in his possession." The old lawyer broke off and fixed his son with an accusing look. "You're certain that woman will get it here?"

"Briggie was going straight to the airport this morning to find some willing soul who was flying to Des Moines. It should be waiting for us at the U.S. Air desk."

They had pulled up to the gate. As the plane shut down its engines, Daniel got to his feet and pulled their carry-on luggage out of the overhead rack. Shouldering both bags by their straps, he felt like a Filipino water boy following the rich American.

His father went straight to the U.S. Air desk, demanding the envelope Daniel had said would be there. A petite black woman handed him a small manila envelope.

Grunting, Richard undid the fastening and shook the picture out. Daniel winked at the woman behind the counter. "Thanks."

Wordlessly, his father moved off, staring at the picture as he went.

"Careful, Dad," he warned as an electric maintenance cart swerved to avoid him.

"Where's a phone? Let's call that place and tell the old woman we're on our way."

"Over there," Daniel indicated a bank of telephones dead ahead. "Who am I, by the way?"

"My son, of course. She'll infer you're in practice with me—which you would be if you had any sense."

Refraining from comment, Daniel set down his bags and looked up the number of Lilac Haven nursing home.

* * *

"Mrs. Montgomery?" Richard Grinnell entered the room as though it were a stage. "I'm Richard Grinnell, attorney at law." He extended a hand to the old woman, who clutched it with obvious suspicion. Daniel watched as she took in the thick white mane of his father's hair, always reassuring to any client.

Appearing to relax somewhat, she turned her gaze on him. "This is my son, Daniel." Richard paused, allowing Daniel to shake the dry little claw. "I hope we're going to have good news for you."

At this, the woman's eyes turned shrewd. "How's that?" she asked sharply.

"I believe a young lady visited you recently. She showed you this picture." Richard pulled Sarah out of her envelope. Mary held out her hand for it.

"Said she was a Borden."

"Right. Well, it looks as though there may be some connection between the two families. We have an estate question to settle and were wondering if you might be able to help us. Mrs. Campbell is my client."

"What d'you mean, connection?"

"We're not precisely sure. But it looks as though your mother's heirs might be entitled to a legacy under Joseph Borden's will." Daniel noticed that his father refrained from specifying *which* Joseph Borden. "Do you have any old letters or photos that might prove the connection? All we have to go on is this photo."

The woman laughed wheezily. Daniel darted a glance at the oxygen in the corner and hoped he wouldn't be called on to administer it.

"If there was any connection, as you put it, it sure wasn't legal."

Daniel blinked, but his father took the comment in stride. "Exactly what do you mean?"

"I mean, they weren't married. He sent Ma money. After she died, I found the letters. You think she might have been his mistress?" The old woman grinned serenely, obviously under the impression she had delivered a bombshell.

"Did you save his letters?" Richard asked smoothly.

"Well, I don't know about that. Patsy's got 'em, if I did. She has all of my Ma's things. When I moved in here, I gave 'em to her. Everything was in the cedar chest—Ma's wedding gown and such like. Anything important, Ma put it in the cedar chest. I've never been through it."

"Patsy's your daughter? May we have her address please?"

The woman eyed them sharply, her little black eyes darting from one to the other. "How do I know you're who you say you are, anyway?"

Daniel's father put his hand in the breast pocket of his suit and pulled out his wallet. From this he extracted one of his business cards and handed it to the old woman. She studied it solemnly.

"All right. Now. What about this legacy? How much is it?"

Richard smiled his most soothing smile. "As to that, it's too early to say. It's one of those things the courts will have to decide. It could be quite a substantial amount. But the important thing at the moment is to prove the relationship. There are other Sarah Simpsons in the world, you see."

"But that picture! That's my ma. I said so."

"Yes." Richard smiled again. "You said so. But judges and courts might want something other than your word."

Thinking it was time for him to get into the act, Daniel pulled out his pen and pocket address book. "Could we just have your daughter's address and telephone number, please?"

* * *

Five minutes later, in a mood of restrained jubilation, they were back in the rental car. Mary's daughter Patsy worked at a truck stop on I-80. She didn't go to work until three o'clock. It was now just ten-thirty, and they had her home address.

"Pull over at the first gas station, and we'll ask directions," Daniel's father directed with subdued eagerness in his voice. Daniel reflected that it was taking an extreme act of will for his father to remain detached enough from the case to sustain his antipathy to Briggie. They were far too much alike under the skin.

The problem had begun over baseball. Richard Grinnell, a Cardinals fan since the year one, considered the Royals nothing but an upstart expansion team made up of would-be movie stars. Bo Jackson had been beneath contempt. George Brett was a washed up has-been with a pretty face, "all show and no go." Briggie might have been able to handle any other sort of insult with more equanimity, but the Royals were too dear to her heart.

Undaunted by Richard's imposing physique and social and professional status, she had retaliated by reminding him that the Royals had beaten the Cardinals in the 1985 World Series. This had led to the inevitable argument about the disputed "call" that would forever polarize Missouri's baseball fans. The umpire Don Denkinger had made a video-documented bad call in the ninth inning of game 6 that had cost St. Louis the win that would have clinched the Series. Instead, the Royals had advanced to play another day. Winning game 7 handily, they had become the first team in history to win the World Series after losing the first two games at home. This ignominious fact had now become permanently linked in Richard's mind with Briggie, whom he considered to be representative of, if not responsible for, the entire affair. Over the year they had been acquainted, they had managed to differ on every issue that presented itself, from dogs vs. cats to gourmet vs. country cooking.

While his father inquired for directions to Patsy's trailer park, Daniel used the pay phone to call his florist in Kansas City. He ordered a dozen yellow roses to be wired to Alex with the message "Sleuths, Inc., hot on the trail. Get well soonest. Love, Daniel."

* * *

The trailer park was near I-80 and not too difficult to find. Pulling through the stone gates, Daniel observed that for a trailer park, it wasn't bad. There was a large pond with ducks and a willow tree, and most of the trailers were double-wides with permanent moorings. Patsy's was slate blue with a garden of multicolored dahlias behind a manicured juniper hedge.

"Mrs. Sawyer?" Richard inquired of the petite woman with the gray-streaked ponytail who answered the door. "I'm Richard Grinnell, attorney at law," he paused handing her a card. "Perhaps your mother has telephoned?"

"Yes." The little woman stepped aside, inviting them to enter. "You're here to look at Grandmother's things."

The trailer was unexpectedly opulent. The carpet was a deep, cushiony gray. A scrubbed pine china closet held a collection of Delftware, and a white Bauhaus sofa was graced by a marble slab coffee table that held an antique china bowl full of pomegranates. On the walls were framed reproductions of Monet's *Water Lilies,* which had been on exhibit in Chicago a couple of summers before. Patsy had clearly created her own world, separate from the sparse upbringing she must have received from her mother.

Dressed in pink shorts and white silk shirt, Patsy had to be in her fifties, but her trim figure and unselfconscious hairdo still suggested youth. She led them to the corner of the living room where the cedar chest resided. "Here it is. It would probably work best if you just looked through it yourself. I really have no idea what would be important and what wouldn't."

"That would be fine," Richard replied gracefully. Daniel knelt to open the chest.

The smell of cedar was almost overpowering. It had obviously been years since anyone had looked inside. A shallow tray fitted the top of the chest. In it were various and sundry items—baby shoes, baby pictures, envelopes containing locks of baby Mary's hair. Harold, Jr.'s, first lost tooth occupied another envelope. Of Mary's father, there was no sign. Disappointed, Daniel carefully lifted the tray and placed it on the floor beside him.

What appeared to be a carefully preserved wedding dress occupied most of the bottom layer. It was wrapped in layers of tissue. Daniel was loath to touch it, but his father began systematically unfolding the tissue. There, tucked inside, was a supply of 3" by 4" envelopes inscribed in fading pencil. The return address was A.E.F., Company D, 105th Division, Somewhere in France.

Richard's hands trembled slightly as he gathered the letters, stood up, and went to stand near the lamp that overhung the dining room table. Daniel finished the job. There were no more letters. The main thing he had expected to find was not there.

Richard had disposed of one letter and was now carefully removing the second one. "Ah. Here we go. *My C.O. is from Chicago. He runs some kind of meat packing company. If we both make it through, he's going to give me a job after the war. Would you like to live in Chicago?*"

Daniel rose and came to peer over his father's shoulder. "What else does he say?"

"Just that they're billeted with a French family. He suspects Lt. Borden of being sweet on the daughter. *'Can't see it myself; she's just a skinny little thing.'* Talks about the food. *'Mainly bread and we're lucky if we get that. For days on end sometimes, the only thing we see is hardtack—kind of a flour and water cracker. Hard as the dickens. We reckon we oughta make mortar shells out of it. Win the war quicker, and then we could get some decent food anyway.'*"

Together they read the rest of the letters, finding only an occasional reference to the "C.O." Daniel felt himself irresistibly drawn into a vision of water-filled, rat-ridden trenches. For the most part, Simpson was cheerful. *"Received your letter today. Am glad you are feeling some better. When I land my job at Borden Meats, we'll get some help for you. Hope Mary is through teething. I have her picture inside my helmet. She brings me luck whenever we go over the top. Haven't had so much as a nick. C.O. wasn't so lucky. Got hit with some shrapnel right near his eye. Bled like a pig, but no permanent damage."*

Daniel filed the information about the wound for future reference. Alex would probably know if her grandfather had a scar near his eye.

The last letter was dated October 24, 1918. "Near the end of the war," Daniel's father commented.

Daniel remarked, "Nineteen days."

Their hostess entered at this point with glasses of lemonade on a white enamel tray.

"That looks great," Richard told her absently as he arranged the letters by date. "This is all there is?"

"That's all she kept, anyway. I've never read them. Did you find what you were looking for?"

"I'm afraid not. There are no letters from Joseph Borden here, only from your grandfather."

"Were there supposed to be? Who is Joseph Borden?"

"He was your grandfather's commanding officer. From these letters, it looks as though they developed quite a close friendship. Your grandfather was going to get a job at Borden Meats after the war."

Patsy handed him his lemonade. Her hand shook slightly.

"How different things could have been," she said quietly. "Instead he was killed, and Grandmother and Mother had to live with his parents. Mother grew up at the Simpsons. She hated it there, I'm afraid."

"According to your mother, Borden paid your grandmother some money from time to time. Is there any other place she might have kept his letters?"

"No. If they're not in the cedar chest, they're gone. That's all that's left of Grandmother."

"What about notification from the War Office about his death?" Daniel asked. "They used to issue a certificate. Would you have it in a frame somewhere?"

"No. But Gran died before I was born. I have no idea what she did with it." Turning to Daniel, she handed him a glass.

"How about photos? Are there any of those around?" he asked her.

"Of Grandfather, you mean?" Pausing, she tried to think. "You know, it's strange, but I don't think there are. Mother hasn't got any in her room at the home."

"What did she do with her things when she went into Lilac Haven?"

"Oh, she had an auction. I got first pick before that. Her brother Harold's widow lives in Albuquerque now, but I don't think she would have been interested in a photo of Grandfather."

"Perhaps she liked the frame," Daniel mused. "Those old frames from the twenties are worth something these days."

"I don't think so, but I can call her if you like."

"That's all right, Mrs. Sawyer," Richard interjected. "It's long distance. If you've got the number, we can phone ourselves. Also, do you happen to remember which auction house she used?"

Looking at his father in admiration, Daniel observed, "Yes. They'd have kept an inventory, wouldn't they?"

* * *

The rest of the day was taken up following this lead. Walker Bros. Auctioneers finally located an inventory of the sale. Perusing it carefully, Daniel and his father noted three possibles. "Photograph in mahogany frame. Photograph in mirror glass frame. Photograph in burled walnut frame." They made a record of the purchasers, and for a few moments hope reigned. But after three telephone calls, they were disappointed. Each of the purchasers had thrown out the photographs and held no clear memory of their subjects.

"Just one of those family photos. You know, a guy trying to look like a gent—hair all slicked back."

"A little girl on her mother's knee."

"A man in a uniform. He had a long nose, I remember. Wasn't much to look at so I threw it out, I'm afraid."

Richard blasted his way back to the nursing home.

"Don't you have a single photograph of your father?" he demanded brusquely of the old woman.

Mary Montgomery replied with some spirit, "I don't know what you want a photograph of *him* for."

"Wasn't there a picture of him in uniform? Do you remember it?"

"No. There wasn't any picture like that. I *should* have remembered. The only picture was one of my Grandmother Simpson, holding me on her knee. I sold it at auction."

"You sold two other pictures, too. One of a man in a uniform."

Mary shrugged. "It must have been in the bureau, then. The auctioneers just came and pulled everything out on the lawn. I was too done up to pay much notice. They went through everything and made some sort of list. I have a copy somewhere, but I guess you've already seen it."

"And you have absolutely no recollection of your father?"

The suspicion that seemed to come so easily to Mary Montgomery returned. "He left home when I was two, Mister. What does it matter what my dad looked like? He's dead, isn't he?"

"Buried in France?"

"I suppose. Mother never said."

Richard took an abrupt leave of the old woman, who was becoming increasingly indignant. Feeling the role of Archie Goodwin forced upon him once more, Daniel gave a thumbs-up as he went out the door.

* * *

They managed to find a Steak and Ale, where they had an overdue meal. It was four o'clock. "There's still Harold's wife in Albuquerque."

"I don't hold out much hope for Harold's wife," Richard grunted. "I smell a cover-up."

"Oh, for crying out loud. Now you even sound like her."

"Who?" Richard bristled.

"You know who . . . Briggie."

His father merely quelled him with a glare, and for some moments they ate in silence. "You really think there's something to it, huh?" Daniel ventured finally.

"You're the psychologist. What does it look like to you?"

"Denial. Sarah saved all of her husband's letters, but anything to do with his death was destroyed. She probably waited for him to come home all her life."

"But the pictures. You're forgetting the pictures. Wouldn't she keep them out in that case?"

Slicing his excellent prime rib, Daniel considered. "It depends. She might not have liked the uniform. It might have reminded her too much of the truth."

"But what about the other one? The one with the slicked-back hair?"

"That might have been anyone. Her son, her husband."

* * *

At six o'clock, Daniel telephoned Briggie at the hospital pay phone, as arranged.

"How's the patient?"

"Chomping at the bit to get out of here. The CAT scan was good. She's really better, I think. Still has a headache to beat the band, though."

"Is she taking calls, yet?"

"Yes, they have her in a regular room now. Now tell me, did you find out anything?"

"Nothing positive. Borden was Simpson's C.O. He was going to give him a job after the war. We didn't see any of the letters he sent Simpson's widow. I don't know whether she threw them out or whether someone else, like the blackmailer, got hold of them in the meantime. No surviving photographs. No notice of his death. No certificate from the War Office. Nothing."

"There's a good reason for *that*," Briggie told him. There was a barely discernable trace of smugness in her voice.

"Spill it, woman."

"My daughter looked up the military records today. She just phoned."

"And?"

"Harold Simpson went missing at the end of the war. Missing, presumed dead. No body was ever found."

"You're kidding!"

"Interesting?"

"No wonder Alex is chomping at the bit."

TWELVE

But Briggie," Alex protested from her hospital bed, "we *saw* the obituary. You have a copy of it!"

"I brought it," Briggie told her. "Listen: *Date November 3, 1918. Mrs. Harold Simpson was informed today by the War Office that her husband has been killed in France. Private Simpson had served with honor in Company D, the 150th U.S. Infantry Division. No details are available at this time. The soldier leaves the widow and two children, Mary and Harold, Jr.*

"The son of longtime Des Moines residents, James and Irene Simpson, the deceased was well-known for his athletic ability during his years at Cleveland High School, where he broke all-conference track records in the high hurdles. School fellows remember him as cheerful and fun-loving. 'Harry was always game for whatever was going,' Charlie Glover remembers. 'None of us were surprised when he enlisted.'

"Private Simpson will be buried in France alongside his wartime compatriots. There will be a memorial service at the Creekside Methodist Church on Saturday morning at ten o'clock."

Leaning back on the pillows, Alex pinched the bridge of her nose. "It doesn't make sense."

Briggie scraped her chair closer to the bed. "Daniel says there wasn't any telegram from the War Office or any certificate. I've seen those certificates. Joy Lewis has her father's framed. The Army sent them out. They say that so-and-so died with honor in the service of his country. Sarah would have saved something like that if she had had it."

"So you think she just called the newspapers and gave them the story? Why would she do that if it wasn't true?"

"What if her husband wrote to her, telling her he was going to switch identities with Borden? He might have told her to give it out that he was dead. Meet me in Chicago, etc."

Alex's head throbbed. Something was wrong with Briggie's argument, but she couldn't think it through.

"Another thing. Mary Montgomery says she never saw a picture of her father. Well, it seems that before she went into the home she had an auction. She was in bad shape, so she left everything pretty much up to the auctioneers." Here Briggie stopped and grinned. "Daniel and Richard are really catching on, you know that? They got the inventory list and found three photographs sold for their fancy frames. They got hold of the people who bought them, and of course they'd thrown away the photos in them, but one person remembered an old picture of a soldier, and another one said there was someone in a suit with slicked-back hair. They asked Mary, and she'd never seen either one. Said they must have been stuck away in her mother's bureau."

"So?" Alex queried irritably. She could see where this was leading, of course.

"Well, can you tell me why her mother would put the pictures away if her husband had died honorably?"

"I give up."

"The letters were gone, too."

"What letters?"

"The ones Mary says her mother got from Borden. The ones that came with the money."

Alex sighed. "The blackmailer must have them, then. Those letters probably tell the whole story."

"Exactly." Briggie looked triumphant.

"What are you planning next?" Alex grumbled.

"We've eliminated Harold, Jr. He's dead. His widow lives in Albuquerque. So I guess all we can do now is wait for the military records. Nonnie's FedEx'ing them. They should be here tomorrow. Maybe they'll give us some more ideas."

"What did they say about Grandfather or, I guess I should say, Joseph Borden?"

"He was invalided out right before armistice. Head wound."

"Head wound!"

"Right. Some shrapnel caught him right near the eye."

"Briggie!" Alex sat straight up in her excitement, ignoring the sudden blinding throb behind her eyes.

"You've thought of something?"

"Yes! Grandfather had a scar. On his temple. From the war. Was Harold Simpson wounded?"

Her friend's forehead wrinkled in puzzlement. "Nonnie read me the records. I don't remember anything, but then, I wasn't looking for that."

"I'll bet he wasn't." When Briggie didn't challenge this, Alex lay back against her pillows, her mind racing. "What if Simpson deserted, and Sarah knew it? Wouldn't she give out that he had been killed? What if he had a French girlfriend? What if he wrote her that he wasn't coming back?"

"In that case, why would she save her wedding dress and all his letters from the war?"

"She put his picture away, remember."

"Just answer me this: Why was Joseph Borden paying her money, and who was blackmailing your father?"

They were actually glowering at one another when Doctor Norris entered on his evening rounds. "You're doing much better, Mrs. Campbell," he remarked, studying her chart. "How's the pain?"

"There. But I don't want any more painkillers. They make me too sleepy."

"You *need* bed rest right now."

"How long before I can get up?"

The doctor stroked his beard. "Mrs. Poulson has told me quite a bit about your situation. I understand why this is difficult for you. But you've got to realize that head injuries are tricky things. You were hit hard. We really need to observe you for a couple of days."

Alex sighed and her eyes filled with the tears that had lived so close to the surface ever since the blow on her head. "Darn!" she said. Reaching for a tissue, she blew her nose.

"Briggie! I just remembered. Daddy's funeral was supposed to be today."

"All taken care of. Don't worry, honey."

"You need to be worrying about yourself right now," the doctor cautioned. "You were very nearly killed, young lady. If you promise to stay put, I'll take you off the Demerol. I don't like to use it longer than necessary. Can you take codeine?"

"It gives me migraines."

"Hmm. Well we'll see how you do on regular Tylenol, then. But stay down. Can you promise me that?"

Alex nodded half-heartedly towards Briggie. "I've got my jailer here. Don't worry."

When he had left, she pulled the blankets up to her chin and said abruptly, "Briggie, I don't *want* Harold Simpson to be my grandfather. If he was, he's a liar, a cheat, and a whole lot of stuff I don't want to know about. Daddy was right. I should have left it alone."

The tears began again. Swamped with guilt and depression, she felt again the weight of what she had done. "My father's been murdered all because of my own self-righteousness. I thought I had some kind of divine right to the truth! I thought my *parents* were the bad guys."

"Honey, you're getting a little carried away. That bang on the head is making you weepy. And the Demerol's got you looking at the black side of everything. You're not responsible for this mess. It started years before you were thought of. And if Harold Simpson turns out to be your grandfather, well, he's just one link in a chain. We all have rotten links."

For once, Briggie didn't even begin to understand Alex's feelings. The thought came to her that Daniel would, but she pushed it away relentlessly. "I loved Grandfather. And besides that, it just doesn't fit, Briggie. It makes nonsense of my entire universe. My grandfather just couldn't have been the father of that poor pathetic woman in the nursing home. He couldn't have deserted his wife and family, lied, cheated and then lived as serenely and quietly as he did. Harold Simpson would have to be cunning to carry it off. His own background was entirely different. Grandfather wasn't cunning. He was just plain smart—in a very understated, un-showy way. And his face was *bony*. That woman in the nursing home looks like a pudding."

Her friend walked around the bed and sat on the edge, looking into Alex's face. She was the same no-nonsense Briggie who believed in facing up to the truth. "You're really angry at me, aren't you?" she asked.

"Oh . . . a little, it just, well . . . I just wish I'd never heard of Harold Simpson."

* * *

On their way to the airport, Richard Grinnell suddenly inquired, "Where does that Patsy woman work?"

"Truck stop on I-80. Apache Flats or something," Daniel answered.

"That far from here?"

"North and east." Daniel wanted to get home. They'd failed in their mission, as far as he was concerned. He was feeling tired and defeated.

"Turn around. We need to talk to her again."

"For crying out loud," Daniel expostulated. "We'll miss our flight. It's the last one to Kansas City tonight."

"What's happened to all your knight-errantry? I thought we were trying to help Alex."

"Don't pretend this has anything to do with Alex. You're just pandering to your warped curiosity."

"I want to find out who had an opportunity to take Borden's letters out of that chest. You got me started on this. I'll be jiggered if I'm going to quit in the middle. Now turn around."

The truck stop was a fairly prosperous one with a clean, brightly lit coffee shop. Patsy worked the cash register.

"How long before your break, Mrs. Sawyer?" Richard asked her.

Daniel had the feeling that she wasn't altogether thrilled with their reappearance. "Twenty minutes," she said, her reluctance obvious.

"We'll buy you a cup of coffee."

"The chest was just sitting there in Mother's house. She kept it at the foot of her bed."

"Did she ever tell you what was in it?"

"Oh, yes. Old letters, Gran's wedding dress. Not very interesting to kids."

"What about after you grew up?"

"It was still there."

"Now then." Richard cleared his throat ominously. "Suppose you tell me, do you remember anyone ever looking in that chest?"

"Why? Is it important?"

"Some letters are missing. They're what we call evidence. Without them, I'm afraid we'll never be able to prove any relationship between your grandmother and the deceased."

Patsy eyed him warily. "Just who is this deceased? If he's Grandmother's vintage, he'd be over ninety."

Amused, Daniel watched his father stir his coffee with measured deliberation. "Joseph Borden had a son to whom the property went. The son just died. It's his will we're probating," he admitted.

"I didn't know lawyers did this sort of thing. I thought they hired detectives or something."

"My detective is in the hospital, unfortunately. This looked like such a mess that I've put the whole thing off longer than I should have. Now I'm paying the price. I've got to do everything myself. Now. Who took those letters?"

"It could have been anyone in the family, I suppose. But why would they?"

"Maybe they wanted the stamps," Daniel interjected. "Might have been valuable."

"I would think the French stamps would have been more valuable," she challenged. "Those letters are still there."

"Mrs. Sawyer," Richard peered at Patsy earnestly. "Don't you want to help us? Don't you want this legacy?"

"Not particularly. I'm not even sure I believe in it."

"The Borden estate is considerable."

"But why should any of it come to us?"

The old lawyer cleared his throat, delicately this time. Daniel decided it was time for him to take a hand. "There's a possibility that Joseph Borden, Sr., may have had an affair with your grandmother."

"So? Even if that was true, why should he leave her anything in his will?"

"We have no idea," Daniel breezed. "Ours is not to reason why, you know."

"I don't believe you," she said flatly. "If he left her anything, it would have come to Gran under his will, not his son's. I don't know what you're up to, but my break is over. If you gentlemen will excuse me?"

"So much for the Perry Mason act," Daniel murmured after she was gone. "We didn't get a thing."

"Oh, yes we did," Richard said, his voice rich with satisfaction. "That woman knows something. Why else would she be so evasive? And another thing. About the stamps . . . that was inspired, by the way," his father paused to acknowledge handsomely. "Did you notice what she said? *The letters from France were still there.* She's looked in that chest, and she's pretty familiar with its contents."

"She'd have had to be less than human not to go through it after we left. She'd want to know what was so interesting." Daniel paused as another thought hit him. "Or how about this? She looked through it before we came, after her mother called. She read the incriminating Borden letters, saw what her grandfather had done, and removed them."

"Impossible," his father pronounced firmly, opening his wallet and placing a five on the table. "No cedar odor in the air when we got there. That chest hadn't been opened in years. Those letters didn't disappear this afternoon."

"So what do you propose now?" Daniel asked wearily as he stood up. "I've got a kid and a practice in Kansas City."

"There's a six A.M. flight in the morning. We've got a little job to do yet tonight."

"Little job? That sounds ominous. You're not Phillip Marlowe, you know."

"You're behind the times, Son," his father replied with spirit as they exited to the parking lot. "This is the nineties. V. I. Warshawski . . . maybe."

"You haven't got the legs."

THIRTEEN

Daniel was cursing himself in three languages by the time eleven-thirty rolled around. He and the distinguished Richard Grinnell, Esq., still wearing their charcoal-gray suits, were concealed among the thick lilac bushes behind Patsy Sawyer's trailer. Using the screwdriver on Daniel's Swiss Army knife, his father had shown amazing adeptness at unfastening the sliding window above them. It was now fractionally open. He claimed that the window was over Patsy's kitchen sink, and that her telephone was next to it.

"Who's she going to call at eleven-thirty, for crying out loud?"

"Whoever took those letters, we shook her up. She'll want to pass on a warning."

At that moment, they heard Patsy's car. Daniel crouched lower and prayed the seams of his suit would withstand the punishment.

Hearing the door open, they saw the light switch on simultaneously. Then there were sounds: "Oh, Momma's good pussy. You ate your dinner," the opening of the refrigerator door, the sound of a pop-top being released, and finally the lifting of the telephone. Dad had been right, then. Looking at his father, who was straining to hear, Daniel remembered his slight deafness. Miming the act of telephoning, he pointed to the window. His father smiled in satisfaction.

"Johnny? Pat. Listen, I've had a couple of detectives here today. I'm worried."

Silence while the other party spoke.

"They looked through the chest. Ma told them about the letters, bless her greedy little heart. They handed her some story about a legacy."

Silence.

"You're pulling my leg! You're sure it's the same Borden?"

Squawking loud enough for even Daniel to hear.

"If he was murdered, then these guys could've been plain-clothes men. Or FBI!"

More squawking.

"They told Ma they were lawyers. Showed their business card and everything. What have you done with the letters?"

Silence.

"Okay. Just so you realize you're in for a nice, long stretch if they're found. You didn't murder Borden, by any chance?"

Louder squawking.

"All right, cool off. You do live in the neighborhood. When did it happen, by the way?"

Silence.

Patsy swore. "That was my night off. I hope they don't come looking in this direction."

Silence.

"Okay. Sit tight. 'Bye."

* * *

Who was Johnny? Daniel started to stand up, but his father clamped a heavy hand on his shoulder and signaled for silence. After an eternity, during which his feet went numb, Patsy finally moved off toward her bedroom at the other end of the trailer.

"Got 'em!" his father crowed when they had finally reached the safety of the car.

"Not unless you can tell me who Johnny is."

"Isn't he the brother?"

"No. He's named Robert, and he lives in Las Vegas. Whoever that was must live in Chicago. She said he lived in the neighborhood of the murder."

But his father wouldn't be robbed of his victory. "That woman'll know who Johnny is," he said, still smug.

"What woman?"

"Brighamina. If there's anything she's good for, that's it! Daniel, do you realize what we've done? We've found the blackmailers!"

But Daniel, far from feeling elated, had slid into a funk. "Alex won't thank us for proving Briggie right. And there's still the murderer to catch."

"Give us time, Son. Give us time."

There was silence as Daniel drove through the deserted streets to the old Fort Madison Hotel. He thought about all Alex had been through in the past five days, physically and emotionally. Even a person in peak mental health would have difficulty handling it, particularly after that blow on the head.

"I'm going to Chicago tomorrow," he announced finally.

"What about your child and your practice?"

"Brenda's taking my emergencies. She'll just have to do it a little longer. And Marigny would probably rather be with Kelly anyway." Prior to their hasty departure for Des Moines, Daniel had arranged for his daughter to stay with her best friend.

"Well," his father said complacently, "That's fine. I was going there anyway. Seems to me we need a little consultation."

* * *

Lying in her hospital bed, Alex kept her eyes closed. The morning sun was unmercifully bright. If only the nurse would come in, she would tell her to close the curtains. It had been six days since Daddy was killed. She wished Briggie would get back. Her head throbbed with every beat of her heart.

The door whooshed, and Alex opened her eyes.

"Good morning, my dear!" It was Daniel's father, carrying an enormous begonia. Behind him was Daniel, looking harassed, as he so often did in his father's presence. Her heart bumped into her throat, and she felt the tears starting again.

Daniel approached her. "Two black eyes. How becoming."
He brushed her hair back from her forehead. His father
tactfully turned his back and put his offering on the bedside
table next to his son's roses. Daniel kissed her gently between
the eyes.

"What are you doing here? Briggie said you were in Des
Moines!"

"Mission accomplished, my dear!" Richard Grinnell
beamed. And then, warily, "Where's Brighamina?"

Alex grinned. The man was looking around as though he
suspected Briggie of concealing herself somewhere. "Cook
County Probate Court, poor soul. She'll probably be there all
day. She's looking for my grandfather's will."

"We need her," Daniel's father said petulantly. "She's got
to find this Johnny joker. He's the blackmailer."

Alex's head throbbed sickeningly. "What are you talking
about?"

Richard Grinnell told her his story, while Daniel sat on the
bed, holding her clammy hand.

So, Briggie had been right. The Simpsons were
blackmailing her father. It must be true, then. Harold Simpson
must have been her grandfather. Alex withdrew her hand from
Daniel's.

"Well?" Richard Grinnell clearly felt he ought to be
congratulated.

"You'd better phone Lieutenant O'Neill," she said
resignedly, sitting up. "This Johnny'll be the murderer, most
likely." Tentatively, she swung her legs over the side of the bed.
"I'm going to get dressed."

But before she could move any further, the door swung
open and a salmon-uniformed volunteer entered with a fat
envelope. "You need to sign for this, dear. It's Federal
Express."

Taking the envelope, Alex signed with a suddenly shaky
hand. She had forgotten about the military records. There was
the matter of the scar still to be explained.

Ripping the envelope hastily, she fished inside for the
records. The top one belonged to Joseph Borden. Laying that
aside, she began to scan the other one. Harold Simpson.

Here it was. She skimmed the description and vital statistics.

Height: 5' 10." Grandfather had not been a tall man. She didn't know his height precisely. *Weight: 165.* Well, that could change. *Hair: Brown.* That would change too. *Eyes: Brown.* Her pulse exploded in wild clamoring, and her head began to spin. That was something that didn't change!

"Hallelujah! Here's the proof. . . . Grandfather was *not* Harold Simpson," she announced, tossing the document onto the bed. "I don't need to read another word."

Richard Grinnell snatched the papers. "What?"

Throwing her arms around Daniel in sudden exuberance, she buried her face in the soft blue knit of his polo shirt. "Grandfather's eyes were blue!"

Clasping her to him, Daniel chuckled. "Round 2 to Alex. This *will* be a shock to Briggie."

Richard regarded them in puzzlement. "But the letters, the telephone conversation. It couldn't have any other explanation!"

"I don't know about that," Alex said happily. She shrugged. "I don't know how Sarah's picture got in Grandfather's bureau either. All I know is that Grandfather was not that sickening Harold."

But Daniel's father refused to join the rejoicing. "Then what was the secret? Why was your father murdered?"

Her head pounded. "I don't care, Richard. I don't want to know."

"Someone killed your father," Daniel reminded her gently. "And someone almost killed you."

FOURTEEN

"What we need is a conference." Richard Grinnell announced. "Things are definitely getting out of hand. This case is like an octopus."

"It's up to Alex, Dad."

Alex, suddenly immensely tired, lay back down. Facts swam through her brain like iridescent fish, flashing and then darting out of sight. She heard the rattle of the lunch cart.

Opening her eyes, she waved her tray away. "No thanks."

"What insensitive idiots we are!" Richard declared as the nurse with the lunch cart departed. "Taxing you with all of this. I'm sorry, my dear." To her surprise, the older man approached her bed and kissed her cheek. "I'll take Daniel away for lunch, and we'll wait downstairs for Brighamina. You take a nap."

Alex closed her eyes, sliding immediately into the black tunnel of sleep.

* * *

The room seemed shrouded and quiet when she woke up. Someone had pulled the curtains and closed the door. A carton of apple juice stood on her bed tray. Suddenly thirsty, she opened it and poured it into a paper cup. What time was it? Fumbling for her watch among the debris on her tray, she finally ascertained that it was four o'clock. She had slept for four hours at least. And was the better for it. Where was everyone?

Moments later, the door cracked marginally as someone peeked in. "I'm awake," Alex sang out.

Her friends trooped in, one by one, Richard carrying a yellow legal pad, Briggie a box from the bakery, and Daniel a cardboard holder fitted with four cups.

"How are you feeling?" Briggie asked. "You've had a long sleep."

"I'm definitely better," Alex replied. "Is that something to drink?"

"It's orange juice," Briggie declared stoutly. "Lots of vitamin C."

"What's in the box? I'm starved."

"Éclair's. We're going to have a tea party."

Briggie opened the box while Daniel seated himself precariously on the low windowsill and his father sat on the big chair in the corner. She handed around the pastries.

Waving the legal pad, Richard told her, "We've been having a pow-wow. We've got it all down on paper. Do you want to hear it, or should we save it for later?"

"You might give her time to eat," Briggie observed tartly.

"No," Alex intervened. "I want to hear what you've come up with. Just so long as you realize that Harold Simpson could in no way, shape, or form have been my grandfather."

"We do realize that," Daniel's father agreed. "But it leaves us in a heck of a bind."

"Tell me."

"Okay. . . . Fact: The man known as Joseph Borden had in his possession a picture of Mrs. Harold Simpson, Sarah, presumably taken on the occasion of her engagement."

"Fact: Joseph Borden was Harold's commanding officer in the war. They were good friends, and he planned to give him a job after the war.

"Fact: Joseph Borden was wounded in the head near the end of the war.

"Fact: Harold Simpson wrote home about this in the last letter, which is still in the cedar chest. He maintained that he himself hadn't gotten a scratch.

"Fact: Alex's grandfather had a scar on his temple.

"Fact: Alex's grandfather had blue eyes.

"Fact: Harold Simpson had brown eyes.

"Fact: Harold Simpson is reported by the military to be missing, presumed dead at the end of the war, some weeks after Borden received his head wound.

"Fact: Sarah Simpson reported her husband dead on November 3, 1918.

"Fact: There is no evidence of Simpson's death among his wife's things.

"Fact: Harold Simpson's daughter, Mary Montgomery, claims Joseph Borden sent money to her mother.

"Fact: The letters that would have accompanied this money are gone from the chest where they were once kept.

"Fact: All pictures of Simpson were kept out of sight.

"Fact: Sarah's granddaughter, Patsy Sawyer, is overheard calling someone named Johnny to report that some 'detectives' visited her about the Borden letters. She inquires whether the letters are safe and tells him that if they are found, he is 'in for a long stretch,' implying blackmail.

"Fact: When Patsy learns of Joseph, Jr.'s, death, she asks Johnny if he murdered him, as he 'lives in that neighborhood.' Implication—Johnny lives in Chicagoland, probably an active member of the blackmailing team.

"Fact: Johnny denies murdering Borden."

Richard came to a full stop. Wiping her fingers with a napkin, Alex took a final sip of orange juice. "You've forgotten a few things."

"Fine. What are they?"

"Fact: Joseph Borden, Jr., and Amelia Borden destroyed any trace of Joseph, Sr., upon his death, except for his boat.

"Fact: Concealed on the boat is a will made in 1917 leaving everything to Joseph's cousin Edward.

"Fact: Joseph, Jr., takes out a $200,000 mortgage on his house immediately following his father's death.

"Fact: Joseph, Jr., and Amelia refuse to discuss Joseph, Sr., with their daughter.

"Fact: When Joseph, Jr., decides to disclose the family secret regarding Joseph, Sr., he is murdered.

At this point, Richard Grinnell looked up from his frantic scribbling to eye Briggie accusingly. "How could we leave that out?"

"Fact:" Alex continued calmly, "A letter written to Joseph, Jr.'s, daughter, Alex, disclosing his intention is stolen by his nephew, Bob Borden, who promptly disappears."

"Who's Bob Borden?" Richard demanded.

Alex proceeded relentlessly.

"Fact: At least two men break into Borden home with a tire iron and clobber me."

"Fact." added Briggie. "Borden's will of 1917 is stolen."

"You didn't tell me that," Alex protested.

"You were in no shape, honey."

Alex put her hands to her head. It had begun throbbing terribly. "That's really strange," she murmured. "Why would they want the will? And for that matter, how would they even have known we had it?" She pinched the bridge of her nose. The Tylenol just wasn't doing the trick. "They were pros, believe me. Who would hire pros to go steal a seventy-year-old will?"

"It's weird, all right," Daniel agreed.

"So! What conclusions can we draw?" Richard asked peremptorily, turning to a fresh page.

Alex fell back against the pillows and closed her eyes. "First of all, what did you find out today, Briggie? About the will?"

"Nothing that would explain your parents' actions." She passed a photocopy to Alex. "It's a pretty standard will. He leaves everything to your dad, except a provision for Bob and his mother. Oh, and the boat. It explains about the boat. Your grandfather left it to you. That must be why it was never sold."

Alex looked over the pages, but her eyes were suddenly dim with tears.

Grinnell looked at Briggie, reproach in his eyes. "You didn't mention the will downstairs."

"I'm sorry. Your news about this Johnny person and the blue eyes knocked me right off my feet. This is the queerest puzzle I've ever seen."

"Who is Johnny, Briggie? Do you have any ideas?" Alex queried, laying the will on top of the military records on her bed tray. She was getting quite an assortment of documents. "There's got to be some explanation for this Simpson angle. If Grandfather wasn't Harold, what was the connection between them?"

"Well, Johnny could be a son of Patsy's, or a nephew. We don't know anything about her brother, Robert Montgomery, or her uncle, Harold Simpson, Jr., except their names."

"What about her ex-husband?" Daniel broached tentatively. "There was a certain hostile quality to the conversation."

"All of these things are easily checked," Briggie said briskly. "Richard, you're so nice and authoritative. Why don't you call the Iowa state offices tomorrow and find out who Patsy's husband was? I'd say she was probably married about thirty years ago—say 1958–1962. They ought to have birth records, too, if she had any children."

Alex lowered her head to conceal a smile. Richard was obediently recording his orders.

"What're we going to do if we find this character?" Daniel asked warily. "Storm his castle and retrieve the letters?"

"That'll be a job for Lieutenant O'Neill, I think," Alex mused. "He'll be thrilled to get his hands on someone."

"Hold it," Richard protested. "I don't know this O'Neill, but is he really likely to understand the letters' importance? I doubt he has half the facts we do."

"That's a point," Briggie admitted.

"Dad just wants an excuse to launch upon a life of crime. O'Neill's okay," Daniel told his father. "I didn't think so at first, but he's got brains. He can figure it out. Besides, if we give him the name and address of the blackmailer, maybe he'll give us a peek at the letters."

"That only works in books, Son. O'Neill's not going to show anything to any interested relations of a principal suspect."

"Why did they want the will?" Alex asked again. "And how did they know about it?"

"Which will?" Briggie and Richard chorused.

"The one they stole when they conked Alex over the head," Daniel elaborated. "For detectives, you two certainly seem to have a rather loose grasp upon the salient facts."

"It's just that there are so many!" Briggie sighed. "And they point in so many different directions."

"The thing to do is divide them up," Richard proposed. "I'll call Iowa tomorrow to try and get Johnny's identity. What're you going to do, Brighamina?"

"I'm staying with Alex. Her karate seems to have let her down."

"The police still have your gun, Briggie," Daniel reminded her. "Protecting Alex is clearly a job for a brown belt." He indicated himself.

But Alex wasn't listening. She had remembered something. "Guys, be quiet a minute. *Who knew about the old will?*"

"Sergeant Lindsey," Briggie remarked.

"Officer Gentry," Daniel added.

"And Bob Borden," Alex finished. "He was studying it when I caught him in the kitchen."

"I thought Bob had the constitution of a marshmallow," Daniel objected. "Are you fancying him with a crowbar now?"

"Just listen! That other Tranquilor murder. The widow. Remember where it was committed?" Alex challenged. "Mt. Prospect!"

"You think Bob is the Tranquilor murderer?" Briggie was incredulous.

"For the love of Mike!" Richard expostulated. "Someone explain who Bob Borden is."

"My cousin, my father's nephew, an heir under his will. Also, the one my mother called to try to get my father to change his mind about whatever it was he was going to tell me, and the one who showed up and 'discovered the body.' When Mother told him about the note my father wrote me planning to set the record straight about Grandfather, he let himself into the house with a key and stole it. At the same time, he saw the will, but I surprised him before he could take it. He disappeared. Later that night, the will was stolen."

"You've revised your opinion of your cousin rather drastically," Daniel observed.

"I never liked him. Maybe I underestimated his greed. He could have hired some rough boys. He's too much of a coward to run the risk of Briggie's deer rifle two nights in a row."

"But, Alex," Briggie remonstrated, "if your grandfather wasn't Harold Simpson, then Bob's inheritance wouldn't be jeopardized. What would his motive be?"

"I don't know what the Simpsons have to do with it," Alex remarked, suddenly exhausted. "But they're obviously involved, because they were blackmailing Daddy about something to do with Grandfather and their precious Harold. Bob must know about it."

"It doesn't gel, Alex," Daniel told her. "We still need a motive. And no matter how scared he was of Briggie, I still can't see Bob hiring a couple of thugs to get the will—"

Throwing up her hands, Alex exclaimed, "Maybe Lieutenant O'Neill was right! Maybe they were just looters!"

"Specializing in seventy-year-old wills?" Richard queried. "No, I'm sorry, my dear. Granted, the behavior of your cousin is strange, but I still think our best line of inquiry is the Simpson letters. I'll call Iowa first thing in the morning."

"Then why did they take the will?" Alex demanded again. No one answered her.

* * *

Later, when Daniel and Richard had gone out for dinner and Briggie was dozing in the corner recliner, the telephone rang, its insistence startling Alex out of her ruminations.

"Hello?"

"This Joe Borden's daughter?" The voice grated, obviously disguised.

"Who wants to know?"

"Answer the question."

Alex almost laughed. "You watch too many gangster movies."

To her surprise, the voice chuckled. "I write the scripts, honey."

"Is this Bob Borden, by any chance?"

"Never heard of him."

She wasn't convinced. "Where are you, Bob? What've you done with the will?"

"Bob Borden's not my department. What I'm calling to tell you is this: Butt out. Leave things alone. You're a pretty girl. We want you to stay that way."

"Who are you?"

"Someone who doesn't want you to get hurt."

It sounded too much like something out of *The Godfather.* "You're Robert Montgomery, aren't you? Patsy's brother."

"I'm nobody you ever heard of."

Alex was suddenly chilled. "How did you know where I was?"

Silence.

This couldn't be real, she thought. "Are you the one who attacked me?" she demanded.

There was no answer. Her heart pounded in her ears. "Did you murder my father?"

The caller cut the connection.

FIFTEEN

Alex sat with her hand on the telephone, trembling.

"Who was it?" Briggie demanded.

"You'll never believe this, Briggs," she said quietly, "but unless someone was playing some kind of joke, I think it was someone connected to the Mafia."

"Robert Montgomery! The Las Vegas connection."

"Whoever it was knew I was in the hospital."

"I'm calling Lieutenant O'Neill." Briggie moved to the telephone by the vacant bed on the other side of the room and dialed the lieutenant. A minute later he asked to speak to Alex.

After giving him the details of the conversation, she asked, "Does that sound like the Mafia? I mean do they really talk like that?"

"What did he say when you gave the name Montgomery?"

"He ignored it."

"I'm sending a guard over for your protection."

"That'll make four," she told him wearily. "Nothing against the Winnetka Police Department, but even unarmed, my friends are a lot more use to me than Officer Gentry. Somehow I can't see him making a very good showing against a couple of gangsters."

"There'll be a guard on your door tonight. I'm sending Lindsey over in the morning," O'Neill growled. "You stay put, young lady. And tell your friends to do the same."

Police guard or no, Briggie insisted on sleeping in the recliner, but nothing further happened that night. The following morning brought Daniel and Richard with more flowers—daisies, this time. Richard, who had clearly been shopping, sported a new mint-green golf shirt and a pair of khaki Dockers. Daniel wore a pink fluorescent T-shirt declaring "BOOMERS RULE" in chrome yellow and black stripes. Alex had never seen it before. It fit beautifully.

"Peacocks," she remarked to Briggie, who still wore the blue polyester slacks and white Royals T-shirt of the day before.

"I've already phoned Des Moines," Richard announced. "They're getting the information for me. I'm to call back at ten."

"In the meantime," Daniel announced, "we're here to relieve Briggie."

"We've had a threat." Briggie told them about the telephone call of the night before.

"You called O'Neill?" Daniel asked.

"Of course. There was a guard on the door all night, and he's sending Sergeant Lindsey over this morning," Alex told him with a sigh. "Do you suppose it really was someone connected to the Mafia? It seems so bizarre."

"Actually, they make much more convincing villains than Cousin Bob," he mused. "Your father could have set Robert Montgomery up in some sort of racket with that $200,000. He's under 'protection' of the Mafia, and now the Feds are nosing around. They don't like it."

Pulling the covers up to her chin, Alex groaned. "So now we're up against a possibly homicidal fry cook, a blackmailer named Johnny, and some Las Vegas gangsters."

Briggie was bitter. "Most likely they're all armed to the teeth, and the lieutenant can't do anything but take away my deer rifle."

"Deer rifle! I understand it's been nothing but trouble . . . why did you bring it in the first place, Briggie?" Richard exclaimed.

"I'm a farm girl, Richard," she said coolly, "not a blood-sport enthusiast. I grew up in the Depression. I've had venison in my deep freeze every winter since I was a girl."

"It's not that I don't love you all," Alex said firmly, "but do you think you could go away and let me take a shower before my fourth bodyguard shows up?"

Briggie left with Alex's key to the Borden house, where she would freshen up. She made plans to meet Daniel and Richard in the hospital lobby at ten o'clock. In the meantime, Richard was going to plan the day's agenda and Daniel would check in with his office.

Relieved at her privacy and the relative lack of pain in her head, Alex moved cautiously out of her bed and into the bathroom. Briggie had laid out her soap, razor, shampoo, and bathrobe. While she was showering, she tried to bring the chaos in her mind into some kind of order but failed. The attempt only brought the pain back, clamping her head like a vise.

While she was gingerly toweling her hair, she heard the telephone. At first she was tempted to let it ring, but the bell was so loud it hurt. Grabbing her bathrobe, she shrugged into it and went to answer the telephone.

"Hello?"

"Alexandra?"

"Bob?" Alex's knees went rubbery, and she sat down hard on the bed. "Where in the world are you?"

"Look, I need to talk to you."

"So talk!" she demanded, suddenly angry. "It's about time you did!"

"I mean in person. I know who killed your dad."

Alex's heart slammed into high gear. All she could do was clutch the telephone.

"I do, Alex, honesty. I've got evidence."

"Bob," she said finally, closing her eyes against the sudden pain hammering her head, "you *are* an idiot. I suppose you're playing what they call a lone hand?"

He loosed an exaggerated sigh. "If you mean, have I told the police, no. You see, what I've got isn't exactly hard evidence," he admitted. "I need some help."

"My help, I presume?"

"Yes. You're the only one I can trust. If I handle this right, it could make my career."

"What a good thing for you that Daddy was murdered." Bob's narcissism clearly knew no bounds. "And I'm so glad you feel you can trust me. Are you going to tell me who did it?"

"No. No offense, but I'm going to file the story first."

"Then what do you need me for?"

"A witness."

She might have guessed. "Witness to what?"

"Well." He hesitated. "I've got evidence, like I said. And I've figured out an awful lot, but I still haven't got enough. The suspect is going to meet me this afternoon in a public place. He thinks I'm a blackmailer. I want you close by, Alex. No one will believe me if I don't have a witness."

"Bob, this is the lousiest idea I've ever heard!" she cried. "Who do you think you are? Indiana Jones? If this person knows you've got evidence against him, do you think he's going to stand for blackmail? He's already killed once. He doesn't have a thing to lose by killing you!"

"I tell you, it's safe. The guy thinks I'm Mafia. He wouldn't dare do anything."

Despite her lack of affection for her cousin, Alex was becoming frantic. At this moment, Daniel entered with Sergeant Lindsey, saw her attire, and started to back out when she signaled them urgently to stay. She motioned for Lindsey to pick up the extension phone by the untenanted bed. "You idiot!" she told Bob. "You total, complete idiot. He's probably with the Mafia himself! They're in this for real, Bob. They've already threatened me, and they know about you."

That seemed to give him pause.

"Where are you, anyway?" she asked.

"At the cabin."

"What cabin?"

"Oh. I forgot. You don't know. Your folks have a cabin up here at Lake Geneva."

"And when is this person supposed to meet you?"

"Two o'clock. I want you to get here by one-thirty, at least. Then we'll go meet him. It's a public place, but I've got a good spot picked out for you to hide."

"Wonderful." Alex grabbed a pencil and paper off her bedside tray. "Directions, Bob."

"You'll come then?"

"Under certain conditions."

"Like what."

"Tell me who the murderer is."

"Absolutely not."

Alex decided to appeal to his vanity. "We haven't had any luck. How did you find him, Bob?"

"Well," he said, obviously torn between his need for secrecy and his desire to demonstrate his superiority, "remember the car I saw?"

"The night of the murder?"

"Yeah."

"In the driveway?"

"Yeah."

"Well, I did see the license number."

"And?"

"That's all I'm telling you now. Come and meet me, and you can see the murderer for yourself."

"I'm not coming alone. I'm bringing someone with me. By the way, how did you know where to call me?"

"The attack on you was in the papers, how else? Geeze— what'd you think? That I did it or something?"

"Well, there *was* the little matter of the night before, you know, when you stole my bag."

"Oh, that. You knew it was me?"

"Why did you do it?"

"I promise I'll tell you when you get here, okay? But I don't know about your bringing someone with you. Who did you have in mind?"

"A karate brown belt. He could come in handy. Now, are you going to give me those directions?"

Lindsey and Alex wrote frantically for the next minute, and then the conversation ended.

Yanking a comb through her wet hair, Alex winced as she briefed the two men on what they'd missed.

"Could be a trap," Daniel warned. "He could be the murderer himself. Remember the scenario you painted last night?"

"As I recall, you didn't buy it," Alex retorted. "Anyway, I really think he's dumb enough to be doing exactly what he says."

Lindsey said, "I don't like it, ma'am. What's he doing in Lake Geneva?"

"Apparently, my parents own a cabin up there."

Lindsey picked up the phone, consulted a pocket notebook, and dialed.

"Clothes, Alex," Daniel suggested. "We don't do raids in bathrobes. Might keep some people's mind off their work."

Grabbing her suitcase out of the closet, she went back into the bathroom and shut the door.

* * *

"The lieutenant wants you to stay put." Lindsey told her when she emerged.

"Look," she reasoned. "Bob might talk to me. He sure as heck won't talk to you. He wants this story like he's never wanted anything in his life."

"Ma'am, if he's the murderer . . ."

"This morning, I'm prepared to bet just about anything he isn't." She sighed heavily. "But, you're right; I won't bet my life on it." Sitting on the edge of the bed, she tried to think. If only her head didn't hurt so much.

"Dr. Norris hasn't even released you, Alex," Daniel reminded her.

"He will," she told him, absently. Then, addressing the sergeant, she said, "How about this? We get up there a little early. We call Bob and ask him to meet us in a coffee shop or something. You can sit somewhere near us with one of those remote listening devices. We'll get him to tell us the plan, and then you can phone for a SWAT team or whatever to get to Bob's meeting place ahead of time. I won't go anywhere near it, I promise you."

Lindsey appeared to consider. Then he picked up the telephone again.

* * *

Half an hour later, Alex had been released from the hospital, and she and Daniel were on their way to Lake Geneva. Following in an unmarked car were Lieutenant O'Neill and Sergeant Lindsey.

"How's your head?" Daniel asked.

"It still hurts a little," she allowed. "But it feels good to be out of the hospital. I just hope Bob doesn't bungle it."

"Maybe your two black eyes will make him see reason."

"Who do you suppose it is?"

"The murderer, you mean?"

"Of course."

"Johnny, I guess. Which reminds me," Daniel gave a low chuckle, "my esteemed father got the goods. Johnny is John Sawyer, Patsy's ex-husband. He's even in the telephone book, which is a little careless of him, I'd say. Guess where he lives?"

"Not Winnetka!"

"Mt. Prospect."

"Oh, my . . . *he* could be the Tranquilor murderer!"

"Not so fast. Mt. Prospect's a big place. Just because he's a blackmailer doesn't make him a homicidal maniac."

Alex's excitement subsided. "I think that hit on the head did some permanent damage," she sighed. "There's no reason on earth why he should suddenly take to murder days before he would even know my father was going to spill the beans."

"Still, it is strange."

"Maybe he's Bob's neighbor," she mused. "Maybe that's how he recognized the car."

They were driving through Lake Forest now. Alex surveyed the huge trees and hedges, which were all that could be seen of the enormous houses nestled away from Sheridan Road. She vaguely remembered driving this way before Uncle Richard had died. Their house had been right on the lake. The entire eastern wall of the house had been made of windows that looked out over the lake and their private dock.

"Poor Bob," she said. "Mt. Prospect must have seemed like quite a comedown."

"If he took after his father, it was probably enough to warp him for life," Daniel agreed.

Alex settled her head on the bunched-up pillow she had borrowed from the hospital. "His judgment is definitely warped. By the way, what are Briggie and your Dad up to? They haven't gone to Mt. Prospect, have they?"

"I hope not. I'm relying on Briggie's good sense. After the telephone call came, they left for breakfast."

Alex looked at her watch. It was eleven-fifteen. "What do you want to bet they're on their way to stake the place out? It would be just like Briggie to have a friendly little chat with Johnny."

* * *

"Look, Brighamina," Richard said in a low voice. "I think he's coming out."

Parked two houses away from Johnny's brick bungalow, they watched as a tall, lanky man dressed in Levi cutoffs emerged from his garage with an enormous motorcycle.

"It's a Harley," she whispered. "Top of the line. The boys in Raytown would kill for one of those."

"Raytown?" Richard raised an eyebrow. "What do you know about Raytown?"

"Battered women."

"What?"

"I'm a volunteer at the shelter," she said tersely. "Look! He's leaving!"

When the last sounds of the cycle had died away, Richard opened the door and gallantly helped Briggie out of the Bronco.

They had decided in advance that they would pose as door-to-door canvassers.

Starting with the house in front of them, Briggie knocked briskly. The door was opened by a young housewife with a baby on her hip.

"Yes?"

Richard cleared his throat. "We're canvassing the neighborhood regarding Proposition C," he said, holding his Mont Blanc pen poised over a little leather-bound notepad. "Are you in favor of it, ma'am?"

"Proposition C? I'm afraid I haven't ever heard of it. The kids keep me pretty busy . . ."

"We understand," Briggie intervened kindly. "It's the one about the parks. Whether you think they are adequately protected at night, you know. We're on the Neighborhood Watch committee."

"Oh. Well, to tell you the truth, I've never really thought about it. I mean, I wouldn't dream of going into one of the parks at night."

"That's just the point," Richard told her. "Shouldn't our citizens, who pay heavy taxes to maintain our parks, be allowed to enjoy them?"

"Well, yes. I suppose so."

"We also think the ponds should be stocked," Briggie elaborated. Richard looked at her sharply, but she only smiled wider.

"Stocked?" The young mother was puzzled.

"Bass would be nice."

* * *

By the time they reached Johnny's door, Richard was simmering. They had canvassed four houses, and Briggie had elaborated upon her performance at each one. "Would you mind telling me why you found it necessary to waste all that time? Bass!"

"I don't lie too often," Briggie explained. "It was so much fun, I guess I couldn't stop."

No one answered their knock. Unobtrusively, Richard tried the door, just in case. Locked.

Holding his ear to the door, he appeared to be listening to a voice inside. "Fine," he yelled, "We'll come around to the back. No problem."

Circling the house, they noted the neglected, weed-infested yard. The gate hung crookedly on its hinges but opened easily. The back porch was covered by an aluminum canopy supported by rusty wrought iron. An ancient barbecue grill looked as though it hadn't been used in years. The back door was locked.

Busy investigating, Briggie was startled by a bright marmalade-colored cat leaping out from behind a hedge. He seemed to recognize her at once for a cat lover and began weaving himself between her ankles.

"Well, Brighamina!" Richard declared, mopping his brow with a handkerchief. "What now?"

"I wonder . . ." She peered behind the overgrown hedge through which the cat had materialized. To her great satisfaction, she found that it screened a row of basement windows, one of which was open just far enough to allow Marmalade in and out.

"If a house is open, it's not technically burglary, is it?" she asked.

"Open! Where?"

Holding back the hedge, Briggie displayed her find. Richard's face lit up, and without answering he stooped to investigate.

He grunted. "It's a hand-crank latch. I think I can just reach it."

To Briggie the process seemed agonizingly slow. While her accomplice sweated and swore, she darted back around to the gate and peered into the street. So far no one was taking any notice. The back walls were high, shielding Johnny's yard from the eyes of his neighbors.

When she returned, only the lower half of Richard's body was visible.

"Don't you think it might work better if you went in feet first?" she inquired.

With difficulty, he backed out of the opening and brushed himself off. "It's quite a drop. A person might break a leg," he told her ruefully.

Briggie took a look. "We need a stool or something," she said. Scanning the neglected backyard, she sighted an aluminum lawn chair folded against the rear wall. "Just the ticket," she said.

Lowering the folded chair through the opening, she then managed to pry it open with the help of the rusty barbecue fork. Dropping it gently to the floor, she exhaled gustily.

"That seat's only made of plastic, Brighamina," Richard warned. "It's rotten, too."

"No use complaining," she said briskly. "It's the only thing we've got. If the Lord thought we needed something else, undoubtedly he would have provided it."

Turning around, she gave him her hands. "Now. I'm going to back down through the window. You kneel down and brace yourself against the window frame. I know I'm no sylph, but try to hold on to me till I'm sure of my feet."

It was an awkward, undignified process, but finally Briggie felt the chair underneath her and, shutting her eyes tight in fleeting prayer, let go of Richard's hands. The chair held.

"Okay!" she called triumphantly. "Your turn, Richard!"

SIXTEEN

"This is an awfully leisurely route we're taking," Daniel said.

"Isn't there a faster way?"

"Probably." Alex consulted her watch. "But it's only noon. We've still got an hour and a half, and we're almost to Wisconsin. Is the lieutenant behind us?"

Consulting his rearview mirror, Daniel reassured her.

He looked different in the boomer T-shirt. It was sort of like seeing your minister in civilian dress. Daniel's casual wear normally consisted of Izod polo shirts and slacks.

"I like your shirt," she told him.

"Couldn't resist it," he said grinning. One of the nicest things about Daniel was his grin. Alex gave a mental sigh and burrowed back into her pillow.

* * *

It was one-fifteen when they pulled into the resort town. Daniel stopped the car.

O'Neill and Lindsey pulled up behind them, and Alex opened her door and got out.

"There's a phone booth at the gas station," she pointed out. "I'll call from there."

When she dialed information, however, Alex was disappointed to find out that the phone number to her parents' cabin was unlisted.

The lieutenant assured her that the police had ways around that sort of thing. In a few moments he had the number, and she was dialing it without any clear idea of what she was going to say.

"Hello?"

"Bob?"

"Alexandra?"

"Yes. I'm downtown and starving. Daniel and I are going to have something to eat at the . . ." she looked around frantically for signs of a restaurant, "Swiss Inn. Why don't you come and join us here?"

She sensed his hesitation. "You want to meet in public? You still don't trust me?"

"Not much," she agreed.

"Okay," he sighed heavily. "I'll meet you in a couple of minutes."

Lieutenant O'Neill fitted Alex with a discreet microphone underneath the collar of her shirt. "Now, as soon as he lets out the arrangements, Lindsey and I are gone. We've got a team waiting. You stay put. Under no conditions are you to go with your cousin."

Alex bit her lip. Poor Bob. She really was setting him up. "I'll just tell him we'll follow in our own car," she said. "We'll get lost."

Entering the Swiss Inn, Alex felt her stomach churn. She couldn't even pretend to have an appetite, though the place was charming in a phony Olde World sort of way. The air smelled of gingersnaps.

Informing the maitre d' that they would be joined by another party, Alex and Daniel were shown to a cozy booth in the back of the restaurant. She watched as O'Neill and Lindsey displayed their badges and then followed their host back into the nether regions of the restaurant.

A waitress arrived and poured water. "Would you care for something from the bar?" she asked.

"No thanks," Daniel told her. "We're waiting for someone. We'll just have a look at the menu."

Had she been hungry, Alex would have been tempted by the sauerbraten and red cabbage. As it was, the idea of eating made her ill.

"We have to order something," she murmured. "We can't just sit here."

"Soup," he suggested.

They settled on French onion. Alex sipped her water and checked her watch. "I feel like I'm in a James Bond movie or something."

With a glint in his eye, Daniel lounged back in his chair. "Lieutenant?" he queried lazily. "Have you ever noticed what absolutely spectacular legs Mrs. Campbell has?"

Alex blushed and kicked him under the table. "Where's Bob? He couldn't be that far away."

"He's probably getting into his double-breasted pinstripe. He's got to look the part, you know."

"I believe you're actually enjoying this," she said accusingly.

* * *

Briggie found the light switch while Richard dusted off his new Dockers. Unfortunately, he discovered a triangular tear where he'd gotten hung up on the window.

"I'll mend it," she promised. "Don't worry about it now, for heaven's sake." She looked around her. The basement was fairly bare, furnished only with a metal shelf that appeared to hold hardware and paints.

They mounted the stairs. The ground level of the house proved to be something completely outside Briggie's experience.

"Richard!" she exclaimed.

The basement stairs had brought them into a hallway from which they had an unimpeded view of Johnny's bedroom. The walls and ceiling were mirrored; the bedspread made of synthetic leopard skin and covered with what looked like rabbit pelts. A crystal chandelier hung from the ceiling.

Her cohort cleared his throat. "I'll take the bedroom, Brighamina. It has a view of the front street, so I can keep a look out at the same time."

"I can't wait to see the living room," she remarked. Leaving her partner in crime, she ventured down the hall.

There was a dingy, old-fashioned kitchen, surprisingly neat. Its white enameled cupboards looked far too blameless to be the hiding place for blackmail letters.

She moved on to the living room. Decorated with pictures of Elvis and Willie Nelson painted on black velvet, it was quite bare except for a big screen TV, a stack of videocassettes, and a red plush couch.

Reluctant to insult her psyche with the probable content of the videocassettes, she turned her attention to the red plush couch. It was a hide-a-bed, of course. Making short work of it, she found that it contained no secret stash of letters. There was no desk. The mantle was bare of ornaments, except for a bucking bronco made into a cigarette lighter.

There was nowhere to look except the videocassettes. Sighing, she walked over to the rack and began examining them one by one. As she had suspected, they were pretty bad.

"For the love of Mike!" Richard's voice over her shoulder made her jump. "This is a little raw, Brighamina. I apologize."

"For the male sex, you mean?" Briggie asked wryly. "Don't worry, Richard. I don't hold you responsible. If you go wandering about the barnyard, you're bound to get muck on your shoes."

"Nothing pertinent in the bedroom. There's only one other room. It looks like an extra bedroom. I'll be in there if you need me. How's your hearing?"

"What?"

"I mean, are you getting deaf or anything?"

"Not to my knowledge. Are you?"

"A little. I might not hear if anyone comes. Maybe we'd better stay together."

"Fine. Help me look through these things."

Eyebrows raised, Richard gazed at the cassette she held out to him. "Surely, Brighamina, we don't need to bother with these! The bedroom is far more likely—"

"If I were Johnny, I believe I'd hide them right here . . .

"Hey!" She dropped the cassette she was holding to the ground and inspected the cardboard sleeve. There was an envelope all right. Pulling it out, she read the address aloud,

"Mrs. Sarah Simpson, 121 D. Street, Apt. 12, Des Moines, Iowa. Return address is Evanston, Illinois."

"Well! Open it!" Richard exclaimed.

"You do it," she handed it to him. "I'll keep looking."

Richard opened the envelope carefully and removed the fragile pages. Looking hastily through them, he found the signature. "Very truly yours, Joseph Borden!" he exclaimed triumphantly.

"Johnny?" a woman's voice called out impatiently from the rear of the house.

Briggie froze, staring at Richard. Then her eyes darted around the room, frantically seeking a hiding place. Instead, she saw the front door. In a moment, she had reached it, slid back the bolt, and thrown it open. Richard was at her heels.

"Hey!" the woman yelled, catching sight of them. "Hey! What are you doing?"

They were in the front yard now, sprinting for the Bronco. Briggie's breath was coming in gasps. She only hoped Richard was in better condition than she was and that neither of them would have a heart attack.

The woman was right behind them now, catching up. "Who are you? What do you think you're doing?"

Thank heavens they hadn't locked the Bronco. Flinging open the door, Briggie felt herself being unceremoniously assisted from the rear as Richard shoved her across the seat.

"Keys!" he yelled hoarsely, slamming the door and locking it in one motion. The woman hammered on the door, screaming, "Help! Somebody HELP! Thieves!"

Keeping his face averted from the window, Richard commanded, "Duck. Don't let her see you. It's that Patsy woman."

Briggie found the keys in her pocket and handed them over with shaking fingers. The door to the house next to them flew open, and the young mother came running out. "It's the one with Ford on it," she hissed impatiently.

At last he had it in the ignition. The engine came to life, and they pulled away from the curb with a jerk. Patsy stepped out in front, but Richard showed surprising dexterity, driving up over the curb to avoid her, mowing down a hedge and then taking the corner on two wheels. "Pedal to the metal," he said, "it's a good thing you don't drive one of those sissy little Tempos." They tore down the suburban street at an unholy speed.

"Pray that the license plate is covered with mud," Briggie said fervently. "It usually is."

"I think we'll go to ground in the mall parking garage," he told her grimly. "Just in case."

"You still have the letter?" she asked anxiously.

"Down the front of my shirt. I hope it's okay."

Briggie glanced down to see that she was holding an Astrid Borden music video in her hands. The pop star was standing with her hands on her hips—metal breastplate shining and her purple hair in tiny ringlets.

Without much hope, she slid the cassette out of the sleeve. "I do believe our Johnny has a sense of humor," she said, holding up another letter for Richard to see. "I wonder what Alex's grandfather would have thought about sharing a video sleeve with Astrid Borden!"

* * *

Alex looked at her watch again. One forty-five. Where was Bob?

"Do you think he could have gotten lost?" Daniel wondered.

"Lake Geneva isn't exactly a metropolis," Alex said dryly. "Lieutenant," she said into her collar, "Bob was going to meet his suspect at two. Do you think he gave up on me and went on his own?"

After a few more minutes of futile waiting, the lieutenant appeared in the foyer and motioned to Daniel. Alex was to remain where she was.

Following a short conversation, Daniel waved, and he and Lieutenant Lindsey exited by the front door, leaving Alex with the check and two untouched bowls of French onion soup. Speaking into his walkie-talkie, O'Neill retreated back to the kitchen.

Alex put her aching head in her hands and continued to wait. This was not easy.

* * *

"Okay," Richard said, having berthed the Bronco safely in the parking high-rise. Sticking his hand inside his now dusty mint-green shirt, he cautiously extracted the letter. "Postmark is January 1919. How about yours?"

"February. Same year."

"I'll go first, then." With shaking fingers, Richard unfolded the letter, cleared his throat, and read,

Dear Mrs. Simpson:

I just received your letter today. Now that I understand the situation, I realize that I owe you an apology. Please forgive me for last week.

I have not been well since returning from France and have had some trouble with my memory. The doctor thinks it is only a temporary lapse, but it is unfortunate that I should have had difficulty remembering such a good, loyal friend as your husband must have been to me.

I have since found a picture of you in my belongings. I will be honest and tell you that I do not know how I came by it.

You seemed terribly worried about your husband's fate. My heart goes out to you, but I am afraid that at present I am unable to give you any information at all. Surely the War Office would have contacted you if he had been killed. It seems to me that he must have been taken prisoner in the final days of the war. I pray he will be restored to you soon. I believe the exchange of prisoners is still going on.

I surmise that you are having some financial difficulties arising out of this unfortunate situation. I am certain I owe it to Harold to send you the enclosed check.

When he is safely home, please have him come to me in Chicago, and I will see about getting him a job in my company.

Very truly yours,
Joseph Borden

Briggie sat motionless. Loss of memory. Was it genuine? What *really* happened to Harold Simpson? Had Borden known? Obviously, Sarah had expected him to have information for her.

"Well, Brighamina?" Richard called her out of her reverie. "What does yours say?"

Rousing herself, she slid the paper out of the limp envelope. "It's much shorter," she said.

Dear Mrs. Simpson:

I am afraid I do not know quite how to respond to your letter. What is it exactly that you think I'm guilty of?

It is true that I was wounded in the head. It is certainly not surprising that you didn't notice the wound when you were here, for the very good reason that it is hidden underneath my hair. I lost quite a bit of blood and more than a little of my memory, which I have explained must account for my inability to help you more concerning the matter of your husband.

I gather that for some reason you doubt my identity. I am not really certain what business it is of yours, but I assure you that I am Joseph Borden. I regret once again that I cannot tell you any more about the disappearance of your husband and recommend once more that you contact the War Office.

To help you in your present circumstances, I have enclosed another check, this one in the amount of fifty dollars. I have no doubt that it will tide you over until Harold can be with you again.

Sincerely,
Joseph Borden

"Well?" Richard asked her.

"Something was fishy all right. Alex's grandfather was wounded on the temple, not the scalp."

"Yes," her companion mused. "I remember the letter Simpson wrote to his wife. He said the shrapnel narrowly missed his eye."

They looked at one another. "Well!" Briggie said, folding the letter with an air of finality. "That takes care of that! Alex's grandfather wasn't Harold Simpson, but he wasn't Joseph Borden either."

Richard tapped the steering wheel meditatively. "And Sarah guessed."

SEVENTEEN

Bob did not come. Alex's cold soup was revolting. Pushing it away from her, she wondered what had gone wrong.

A moment later, O'Neill was flying out of the kitchen, motioning her to follow him.

"The check . . ." she protested.

"Leave it," he told her. "We'll take care of it later."

Then she was in the buff-colored Chevy that passed for a plainclothes cruiser. Switching on the ignition, the lieutenant pulled out into the quiet street and laid a patch of rubber as he floored the gas pedal.

"Bad news," he told her. "The murderer beat us to the punch."

"What do you mean?" Alex demanded.

"Your cousin's dead. At least, we think it's your cousin. We'll need your identification."

Alex's head swam, and she put a hand to her temple. "Dead?"

"Murdered. Gunshot wound."

"Where?" she managed. "Where did it happen?"

"Your parents' cabin. Lindsey and your boyfriend just found him."

Dazed, Alex could only remark, "I've never been there before." Her head was pounding so hard she couldn't think.

O'Neill was speaking into his car radio, calling up local reinforcements. "This is Lieutenant Rod O'Neill of the Winnetka Police . . . We have a homicide . . ."

Homicide. She couldn't take it in. Bob, the rotund fry cook, the odious cousin she hadn't seen since she'd left home. Stony-faced, she looked out the window at passing cars. Everyone was staring. Of course. They must be doing sixty. As they screeched to a halt at a red light, she met the eyes of the man in the car next to them who looked at her curiously. She had forgotten her black eyes. He had a beautiful head of white hair. Like Grandfather's. Wincing, she put her hand to her head again and sank back limply against the head rest. She felt clammy and ill. She hadn't liked him, but why did Bob have to go and get murdered?

The cabin was unpretentious—blue-washed cedar with a riot of multicolored dahlias lining the postage-stamp lawn. The front door stood open.

"You stay here for the moment, Mrs. Campbell. I'll send your doctor out."

In a moment, Daniel was with her. Opening the car door, he stooped on the gravel drive next to her. "You look like you've been sick again," he remarked, tenderly twining a rebellious lock of hair behind her ear.

The simple gesture released her tears. Without answering him, she wept into the handkerchief he offered.

"I'm sorry, Alex," Daniel whispered. "I guess Bob was a shade too cocky for his own good."

"Poor idiot," she muttered, blowing her nose. Then, looking at Daniel, she asked, "Is it very bad?"

"Not messy, no. Just one bullet hole in the middle of his forehead. What they call an execution-type killing, I imagine."

"Mafia?"

"Could be."

Alex sighed heavily as two police cruisers, CB's blaring, pulled into the drive behind them.

"Inside!" Daniel told them.

* * *

In the end, identifying the body wasn't as bad as she thought it would be. Bob looked much the same as he always had, except that his hair was thinner and he weighed about fifty pounds more. The red circle in his forehead scarcely impressed her at all. Daniel led her away, and they walked down by the lake.

"Did you and Lindsey turn up any clues?"

"Nothing. Bob had obviously been staying in the cabin. The sink was piled with dirty dishes. His typewriter was set up on the dining-room table, but whatever he was typing was gone."

"What about the ribbon?"

"Gone. The killer thought of that one, too."

"It looked like Bob just opened the front door and got shot. Poor boob. Why didn't he look out the window or something?"

Alex sank down on a bench. "Criminy, Daniel, I can't take much more of this."

* * *

It was late afternoon before they were able to leave. No fingerprints had been found; the murderer had worn gloves. Alex had repeated her account of the telephone call and was corroborated by Lindsey. She had also provided what details she could about Bob's character.

"He wasn't dumb," she had said. "Just obsessed. Obviously he had stumbled on the identity of Daddy's murderer. I think it was because of the car he saw."

But she could give no further insights and in the end was freed to go back to Winnetka with Daniel.

"I suppose Briggie and Richard will be at the house," she guessed. "I'm beginning to hate that place."

"I don't think it's too safe anymore. I'd much rather you were in the hospital."

"Hospital. That reminds me. Mother *couldn't* have done this one. She's in the hospital!"

"Even O'Neill will have to accept that alibi," Daniel said, patting her knee. "So at least one good thing's come out of this."

"Thanks, Daniel."

"For what?"

She reached a hand across and patted his leg. "For being there."

"As long as you want me," he answered solemnly.

* * *

The Bronco was not parked in front of the house. Surprised, Alex went to the door and tried it. "Locked. And Briggie has the key. What do we do now? Where do you think they are?"

"I only hope it's not Mt. Prospect. It's occurred to me that in their present moods, Briggie and my father make rather a reckless combination."

"You don't think anything's happened to *them*, do you?"

"I sure hope not. Let's go eat something and come back later."

Over hamburgers, Daniel speculated about the murderer. "Who knew what Bob was up to?"

"He was so closed mouthed; he wouldn't have said anything to his own mother. I'm sure the only person he told was the murderer."

"Not his editor?"

Alex pondered. "I think he would have worried that his editor would put a real reporter on it. No. This was Bob's big scoop. I think the murderer must have known that too."

"If the murderer had any idea that Bob had talked to you, you're in more danger than ever."

Looking at her hamburger, Alex gave up every pretense of eating.

"It's time Briggie slept in a bed. Tonight I'm staying with you," he said stoutly.

Keeping her eyes lowered so he couldn't read the relief there, Alex toyed with a French fry.

When they returned at seven, the Bronco still wasn't in the driveway. "Where did you spend the night?" Alex asked. "Maybe they've gone to the motel."

"Why would they do that?"

"Search me," Alex shrugged.

The Bronco was at the motel. Daniel raised his eyebrows at Alex and then got out of the car and tapped discreetly on the door.

"There you are!" Briggie exclaimed. "We were beginning to worry!"

"*You* were beginning to worry! What are you doing here? Why didn't you go back to the house?"

"We've gone to ground, as Margery Allingham puts it," Briggie told her. "We're in hiding."

"From whom?" Alex demanded.

"Johnny and Patsy," Richard told her, obviously impatient. Alex noticed a triangular tear in his new Dockers. "Did you catch the murderer?"

"No, I'm afraid not," Alex sighed heavily and entered the motel room.

"You'd better lie down," Briggie advised. "You look done up."

"More Margery Allingham," Alex commented with a tired smile. "I think I will. Daniel can tell you."

When Daniel had finished a curt recital of the facts, Briggie inquired, "When did the murder take place?"

"Sometime between when we called him from the pay phone and when Daniel and Sergeant Lindsey went out to the cabin and discovered the body," Alex contributed.

"So when was that?" Briggie pressed. "Richard, could you get the map from the Bronco? I think he could have just done it."

"Who?" Daniel asked as his father pushed past him for the door.

"Johnny. So what time did you call Bob?"

"Around one-fifteen, wasn't it, Alex?" Daniel queried.

She nodded her pounding head. "Briggie, have you got some aspirin? Why do you think Johnny did it?"

Rooting through her carryall, Briggie came up with a bottle of Tylenol. Daniel went for water.

"We had him under observation. He left Mt. Prospect about noon on his Harley."

Richard had reentered the room with the map. "Nothing easier," he said with a flourish. "Look. All he had to do was get on highway twelve, and it's a straight shot."

"Whereas, we took the leisurely route." Daniel traced their travels up Lakeshore Drive.

Richard went to the telephone and dialed the police. Alex closed her eyes and, in spite of all the hubbub around her, went to sleep.

* * *

What seemed like hours later, Alex woke to find she was alone. Briggie had placed her much-traveled suitcase on the next bed and left a note on top of it. "We've gone down to the police station. Hope you had a good rest. Will be back as soon as possible. Here's the key to the room next door. You and I are sleeping there tonight. Richard and Daniel will stay here again."

Grabbing her suitcase and her canvas bag, Alex went next door to be greeted by the smell of lemon air freshener and an immaculately anonymous room. A hot bath. She would have a scalding hot bath, change into her pajamas, and then see how she felt.

Lying in the steaming tub, she tried to apply her mind to the puzzle. Her mother had not killed her father. Bob had not killed her father. That meant there must be someone else, and that someone else might be Johnny. But if Harold Simpson was not her grandfather, what possible motive could he have for killing her father? If he *was* blackmailing him, which Richard and Daniel's evidence of Patsy's phone call suggested, *where* was he, and why would he kill the goose that laid the golden egg? Their previous reasoning went out the window if Harold Simpson was not her grandfather. And there was another thing: How would Johnny know about the cabin? Bob had arranged to meet the murderer in a public place, not the cabin.

Suddenly impatient, Alex got out of the tub and dried herself off. She hoped Briggie had stuck the military records in her bag. Hastily pulling on her pajamas, she yanked out her clothing and found the documents in the bottom of her suitcase. Harold Simpson's she had already read. He had brown eyes. He was missing at the end of the war. Two salient points. But what about Grandfather's records? Would they tell her anything?

Seating herself at the desk, she turned on the feeble lamp and began to scan the document. Name: Joseph Borden. Age: 22. Hair color: Brown. Eyes: Hazel. *Hazel!* Alex stood up with a jerk, and the chair fell on the floor behind her. Grandfather's eyes had been blue! Sky blue. She was certain of it! Hastily reading through the remainder of the record, she read about the wound to his right temple. Wait a minute. Squeezing her eyes shut, she dredged up a memory.

She and Grandfather were out on the boat. The wind was blowing his hair straight back off his brow. She was standing on his left, cheering him on as he reeled in a fish. No good. She couldn't remember whether the scar was there or not. Another memory. Sitting on his lap when she was young, tracing the scar with her finger. "How did you get that, Grandfather?"

"Shrapnel. A piece of metal. I fought in a war one time. We call it World War I these days."

Arranging herself on the bed in the way she remembered sitting on Grandfather's lap, she realized she had been looking at his *left* temple. The scar had been on the left, not the right.

Alex drew back the covers and went to bed, curling herself into a tight ball. If her grandfather wasn't Harold Simpson, and if he wasn't Joseph Borden, then who was he?

EIGHTEEN

"I'm surprised you're not in jail," Alex remonstrated with Briggie and Richard the following morning over breakfast. They had just completed an account of their adventures of the day before.

"Oh, we didn't tell O'Neill about getting into the house," Briggie said in soothing tones. "Besides that, the house was open, so I don't really think we could be charged with burglary."

Richard harrumphed. "I don't know what law school you went to, Brighamina, but at Yale we learned that burglary is any unauthorized entrance into someone's private home, whether it is open or not."

"Then you ought to be thoroughly ashamed of yourself, instead of which you're carrying on like an aged James Bond," Daniel remarked tartly. "Just what *did* you tell the police?"

"About the phone call you and I overheard. They're searching for the rest of the letters now, I imagine. We also told them about staking the place out and seeing Johnny leave on his motorcycle."

"Heaven help you if Patsy gets into the act!" Daniel groaned. "Do you think she recognized you?"

"He looks like a normal human being in Dockers and a golf shirt," Briggie assured them. "It was as good as a disguise."

"But your license plate, Briggie!" Alex objected.

"Covered with mud," her friend asserted smugly. "Besides, with Johnny under suspicion of murder, do you think Patsy's going to tell the cops that someone stole his blackmail letters?"

Alex chewed her apple pancake thoughtfully. "I wonder if they've arrested him."

"What's bothering me," Daniel remarked, "is motive."

"Yeah. If Grandfather wasn't Harold, they weren't entitled to the inheritance. Would they really murder Daddy on the slim chance that Mother would keep up the blackmail payments? Wouldn't it occur to them that she would go to the police?"

"Maybe they've threatened her," Briggie suggested. "Maybe that's why she's hiding out in the psych hospital."

"Do you think Sarah knew who Grandfather was?" Alex wondered.

"I don't think so," Richard answered. "At least it's not evident from the letters. She just put together that he wasn't Joseph Borden. Because of the head wound."

Putting down her fork, Alex leaned against the back of the booth. "You realize he must have inflicted that wound himself? After her visit?"

"And he didn't know which side it was on, apparently," Briggie added.

"*Who was he?*" Alex demanded. "Here we've had two murders and uncovered a nest of blackmailers, not to mention incurring the wrath of the Mafia, and we're still no closer to Grandfather's secret than we were in the beginning. Do you realize I'm not a Borden? I don't know who I am! Why did I ever start this?"

"It would have to be someone who knew Borden very well, someone who could impersonate him successfully at the plant and among the various acquaintances they had. Did your Grandfather have a brother?" Richard asked.

"I have no idea," Alex said. "I was never able to find the family on the soundex."

"What's the soundex?" Richard and Daniel chorused.

"It's a statewide index by the sound of the last name for 1880 and 1900. In 1900, there were no Bordens with a son named Joseph in Illinois."

"Did you try the neighboring states? Wisconsin, Minnesota?"

Suddenly Alex sat up straight. "Missouri! Edward Borden lived in St. Louis, didn't he, when the will was made? Maybe the Bordens were originally from St. Louis."

"It's worth a try," Briggie said, tossing her napkin on the table. "There's a National Archives branch here in Chicago. Let's go."

While Richard paid their bill, Briggie looked up the National Archives address in the telephone book. "South Pulaski Road. Where in the world is that?"

Placing a telephone call, she determined that the archives were at 7400 South 4800 West. "That'll be quite a drive. We're north and they're way the heck southwest."

"What else is there to do?" Richard asked.

So they all piled into the Bronco and drove for nearly an hour until they reached the address.

Entering the modest building, Alex felt the excitement of the chase course through her blood as she saw the rows of microfilm machines and the large steel cabinets containing the census microfilms.

The soundex code for Borden was derived by dropping the vowels and assigning numbers to the remaining consonants. The code for Borden was B-635. Using the catalog, they found the film number for B-635 in Missouri for the year 1900. Richard fetched it from the cabinets, while Alex staked out a microfilm reader.

With shaking hands, she threaded the soundex film through the apparatus on top of the machine. Then, cranking the reel as fast as she could, she moved to the B-635's. "We might as well check all the Bordens while we're at it," she commented. "That way we might get a line on the mysterious cousin Edward."

They struck pay dirt in the E's. There was an Earl Borden, age 22, married to Molly, who had a son Edward born in April 1898. No other children were listed. Briggie took down the details in her notebook, including the numbers that would lead them to the actual census. "We might find other relatives living near them," she told Richard and Daniel. "And the actual census has more information, like birthplaces for the mother and father of all the family members."

It wasn't until the J's that they found Joseph as a child in the family of James and Susan Borden. "Look!" Alex exclaimed. "His grandfather was living with them! Jacob Borden!"

"Joseph was age five," Briggie mused. "No brothers, just one sister, Margaret."

"They could have had another boy later," Alex said impatiently. "Briggie, do you realize we have a real lead at last? I'm back two more generations!"

"Hold your horses, honey," Briggie said gently. "Remember Joseph wasn't your grandfather."

"Grandfather must have been related. I feel it in my blood. It's singing! I'm going to make a descendency chart."

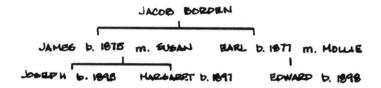

"Now what?" Richard asked impatiently.

"We look in the miracode for 1910. It works just like the soundex."

But neither Borden family showed up in Missouri in 1910.

"Bummer," Alex declared, exasperated.

"Cheer up," Briggie told her. "They'd probably moved to Illinois by then."

Richard, who was demonstrating all the right instincts, insisted on fetching the Illinois miracode and inserting it into the machine. Four heads leaned over the white screen as he cranked through to the B-635's.

"Yes!" Alex exulted in a voice not at all suitable for libraries. "There they are! Earl and Mollie had two more girls born 1901 and 1903. Are you getting all of this, Briggie?"

Her friend nodded. "They lived in La Salle County. Did you notice?"

"Yes, so Daddy didn't pull the county out of a hat after all. He probably thought since Grandfather . . . wait! This is important! If he said La Salle County, he must have known Grandfather grew up there. Even if Grandfather wasn't Joseph, we've got to be on the right track. He must have had a brother."

However, reeling to the J's, they found James and Susan Borden again, with no more children. "No brother!" Alex exclaimed in disappointment.

"Wait, wait," Briggie was excited. "Look! Where did they live?"

"Cook County, Evanston," Richard answered.

"Think, Alex!" Briggie ordered.

Alex's brain did a radical somersault. Grabbing Briggie's notebook, she reread the details. "Edward. Edward grew up in La Salle County. Grandfather's death certificate said he was born in La Salle County. Daddy gave that information. He must have known Grandfather grew up there and thought that's where he was born. I think *Grandfather must have been Edward! The Edward in the will!*"

For a few minutes there was silence as they all took it in. Then Daniel remarked, "Too bad they don't give eye color on the census. That would clinch it."

"They do on military records!" Alex crowed. "We've got to call Nonnie. Briggie, where's a phone?"

"Wait," Daniel insisted. "Don't they have military records here?"

"No, idiot," Alex told him fondly. "If they did, do you think I would have wasted all that time getting Nonnie to find them for me? All they have here are the Revolutionary War Pensions."

From the telephone in the lobby, Briggie placed a call to the indispensable Nonnie, who said she would proceed directly to the Personnel Records Center and call them that night at the hotel.

"Let's just hope he joined up," Alex said fretfully as Daniel held the door open for her.

They drove into downtown Chicago for lunch. Richard insisted that they celebrate the probable finding of Alex's grandfather by eating on the ninety-ninth floor of the John

Hancock Building. The view of the lake was dazzling, but Alex's head reeled as she stood by the glass wall and looked out. She felt as though she would fall straight forward and down one hundred stories to the street where the people were walking like tiny ants. Quickly backing away, she allowed Daniel to lead her to their table.

Alex found it rather amusing to compare their little group with the pinstriped diners. Briggie, having run out of Royals T-shirts, was wearing a madras smock with her track shoes. Richard was wearing another pair of spanking new Dockers with a raspberry-colored polo shirt. Daniel wore stonewashed jeans and another outrageous T-shirt. This one read: "Age and treachery will always overcome youth and skill." Alex's own outfit did nothing to distinguish the company, being a pair of white slacks and the new emerald silk shirt Daniel had bought to replace the red one he had ruined with his squirt gun.

Over Peking duck, Briggie organized them. "Alex, you need to buy a black dress for the funeral tomorrow."

"What about you?" Alex countered.

"I have the navy blue blazer and skirt I wore to church."

"Do you suppose the police would be interested in this stuff about Edward?" Daniel wondered.

"The will!" Alex exclaimed suddenly. "Remember, I couldn't figure out why anyone would want the will!"

"Right," Richard agreed. "We should have paid more attention. Me particularly. It seems this may turn out to be a probate matter after all."

"But if he was the heir, why did Edward have to pretend he was Joseph?" Daniel wanted to know.

"Because Joseph wasn't dead!" Briggie and Alex said together. Then they looked at one another in surprise.

"So what happened to him?" Daniel asked.

Alex put her fingers to her temples. Her head was pounding with the excitement. "Just when it looks like we're finally getting someplace, it gets more complicated again. The records just say he was discharged with a head wound. Did he die en route to Chicago or something?"

"If he did, the question still stands," Daniel insisted. "Edward was the heir. Why would he impersonate Joseph?"

"And where does Harold Simpson fit into all of this?" Briggie demanded.

"And why was my father killed?" Alex wondered wearily.

Since there was no ready answer to that, they ate in silence for a few moments.

"What orders do you have for us, Brighamina?" Richard asked finally. "I don't think Alex would appreciate us all tagging along on her shopping expedition."

"Maybe while Alex is shopping we could do something touristy, like visit the new Comiskey Park," she suggested.

Richard rolled his eyes. "If we must visit a ballpark, it ought to be Wrigley Field. It's everything a ballpark should be . . ."

"You two fight it out," Daniel said, laughing. "I'm going with Alex."

"So what happens afterward?" Alex wanted to know. "Should we visit O'Neill and let him in on the latest?"

"You and Daniel can do that," Briggie told her. "I'd like Richard to drive me out to Mount Prospect, if he doesn't mind."

"I don't," he declared, "but why Mt. Prospect?"

"I think it might be important. I'm going to see if I can get in to visit Alex's mother. Maybe if I confront her with this Edward business, she'll loosen up a bit."

"But she doesn't even know you!" Alex objected. "You'd better wait until I can come with you."

Briggie hesitated, looking at her with an expression Alex couldn't read. Finally, her friend said gently, "That won't be necessary, honey. She knows who I am. We've talked on the phone about you quite a lot over the past couple of years."

Alex was stunned and momentarily speechless. "And you never told me?" she demanded finally.

"She made me promise not to, Alex. Believe me, there were hundreds of times I wanted to."

"You should have!" Alex responded angrily, tears starting to her eyes. "How could you keep a thing like that to yourself? You know how much I wanted a family . . ."

"Hold your horses, honey." Briggie reached across the table, touching Alex's arm. "She told me it was for your own good. Of course, I didn't know what in the world that was supposed to mean, so I discussed the whole thing with Dr. Brace. He said he thought you'd been abused by your mother but that you had blocked it out. He thought that was why your father sent you away."

The idea of Dr. Brace and Briggie discussing her behind her back fueled Alex's anger. "And neither of you thought to ask me? I'm not a child any longer, Briggie."

Never had she felt such anger toward her friend! How much difference it would have made over the past two lonely years if she had known her mother cared about her in the slightest degree.

"Put yourself in my shoes, honey," Briggie pleaded. "The only times she called, it was obvious she'd been drinking. She used to cry a lot. Then she'd ask me how you felt about her. What would you have done if you were me?"

"I'd have let the people involved work it out! Why does everyone think they have to protect me?" Glaring at Daniel as well as Briggie, she demanded, "Do you think I'm an imbecile or something?"

"Hold on, Alex," Daniel said firmly. "I'm innocent. I didn't know a thing about this."

"I'm surprised." Suddenly it was all too much. Mother, Daddy, the murders, Bob, Grandfather's being Edward. As though she could distance herself from everything, she pushed herself firmly away from the table and stood up.

"Where are you going?" Briggie wanted to know. She looked suddenly old, and there were tears in her eyes.

"To buy something to mourn my father in." Alex's own tears brimmed over as she turned away from the table, seeking the elevator.

Once outside, she strode in blind anger down Michigan Avenue, her head bent against the stiff wind that dried her tears as they fell. How could Briggie have kept such a thing from her? She might have reconciled with her parents long ago, long before this horrible thing had happened that made reconciliation impossible!

She might have been a little less aggressive in her desire to find her grandfather. Her father might never have been murdered. They might have had a chance at salvaging some kind of family life. She might even have been able at some point to share with them the healing she had experienced because of the gospel. Now there was no chance of anything. It was too late. Daddy was dead, and Mother hated her because of it.

Raging within, Alex didn't count the blocks she walked. Instinctively she was heading for Marshall Field's in the Loop—Marshall Field's where mother had taken her twice a year to buy her clothes, once in the fall and once in the spring. And they had luncheon upstairs.

Alex had reached the bridge that spanned the Chicago River. Noticing her surroundings for the first time, she was suddenly exhausted. She must have walked a mile at least!

Facing the street, she hailed a cruising taxi, climbed in, and slumped against the upholstery. "Marshall Field's," she told the driver.

It was at the next stoplight that she first became aware of someone staring at her. Looking to her right, she saw a man with white hair in a limousine quickly avert his gaze. For just a moment it seemed as though she knew him.

NINETEEN

Marshall Field's, the block-sized department store, was the same as ever. It seemed eons since Alex had last shopped there. The last time was when she had bought her college clothes. She remembered her Audrey Hepburn coat—black wool, cut in an A-line with big pearl buttons.

But that was another Alex, a child, standing in the distance behind a scrim—the scrim of ignorance. This Alex was a woman with two black eyes and anxiety working in the pit of her stomach.

Wandering idly through the men's furnishings that contrived somehow to smell of pipe tobacco and leather, she fought to still her incipient panic by identifying the thoughts behind it, as Dr. Brace had taught her to do.

There was fear there, lurking behind the more immediate anger with Briggie—the old fear that she would be abandoned, that she had lost her last chance to have a normal family.

Moving blindly into the cosmetics department, Alex willed fresh tears to stay unshed. She continued her analysis, thrusting down the panic that was rising inside her. She had been abandoned years ago. It was over. Done with. The fact that it needn't have been that way didn't change the facts. It had happened.

There was also this growing physical fear, understandable under the circumstances. Two people close to her had been murdered, and she had been brutally attacked. But on another level, wasn't she growing steadily more afraid of what she was going to find out?

Grandfather had been Edward Borden, she was certain. That part of it wasn't too hard to swallow. It was the secret behind the seemingly unnecessary deception that worried her. What had happened to Joseph Borden?

A woman stopped Alex to hand her a sample of Calvin Klein's "Eternity." Smiling absently, Alex slipped it into her bag and continued her aimless drift through the cosmetics department.

What if he had been murdered? She stopped dead in front of the Estee Lauder counter. What if her grandfather were the murderer? No. Not Grandfather. Not the man who had loved her.

"May I help you, dear?" a late-middle-aged woman with dyed black hair asked.

"Not with this," Alex murmured absently, and turning abruptly she sought the escalator.

It would explain so much, wouldn't it? The blackmail, her parents' behavior. They were probably informed by the Simpson descendants, who had somehow arrived at the truth and begun to blackmail Grandfather. When he died, they simply latched on to her parents, knowing they would never want such a scandal to come out.

Climbing on the escalator, she ascended to the women's department, and like a person in a dream began to sort through the racks. Black was in for fall, apparently. There were dozens of dresses to choose from, but few of them were suitable. Embellished with sequins, rhinestones, and black seed pearls they would not have done at all for a father's funeral.

Daddy's funeral. She had become so caught up in the consequences of his death, she hadn't even begun to mourn him. A lump filled her throat, but she swallowed it down with determination. Like Scarlett O'Hara, she would think about her grief tomorrow. Finally selecting a linen sheath with a short jacket, Alex headed for the dressing room.

It would do. Alex grimaced at her complexion. The dress certainly went nicely with her black eyes. Actually they looked less black than green today.

It was when she left the dressing room and went to the counter to make her purchase that she first noticed the white-haired man from the limousine. Looking up from fumbling in her bag, she surprised him staring at her again. She was certain that before he glanced away and began flipping purposefully through the racks of clothes, he had been studying her intently. Was it merely her black eyes? Was it just weird coincidence that brought him to the same floor in Marshall Field's?

The thing was, she felt she ought to be able to place him. Thinking hard, she wrote a check for the wrong amount and had to begin again. She put the man out of her mind.

Suddenly she was hungry. Having left most of her lunch on her plate, she thought how pleasant it would be to go to the tea room again and have a slice of Field's Frango Mint Pie. She and her mother used to finish their shopping expeditions with Frango Mint Pie. Comfort food. Then she would walk the few blocks to the train station and travel back to Winnetka. Perhaps everyone would have forgiven her for her outburst by then.

The tearoom was crowded, but she was finally seated at a table in a far corner. Studying the menu brought back more memories. Coming here with Daddy after a hectic Saturday's Christmas shopping. Daddy. Darn! The numbness was wearing off. Soon she wouldn't be able to run mentally and emotionally from her memories. Dr. Brace would say that was progress, that feeling anything was better than shutting it off. Only if you allowed yourself to feel could you move through the emotion. Otherwise it was there forever, like a bear in a cave, waiting to come out and grab you at the most unexpected moment. But it took lots of faith to face the hard emotions and know that they wouldn't destroy you. Before all this had happened, she was just beginning to nurture that kind of faith. The hard part was trusting God. Trust didn't come easily to someone who had been abandoned.

Alex's anger with Briggie resurfaced. How much it would have meant to her to know that she hadn't been totally abandoned! That somewhere in her mother there had been love and caring, even if it only surfaced when she was drunk.

Suddenly, as she sat there, it was as though a kaleidoscope shifted and Alex had an entirely different picture of her mother. What if her mother had been afraid to feel, too? What if her emotions were so frightening to her that she had to dull them with alcohol so she could bear them?

So intent was Alex on this new picture that she wasn't aware she was staring. When the actual picture before her crystallized, she found she was looking at the white-haired man who was now being seated across the room. She was jerked out of her preoccupation. This was too much. Was he following her?

When he was seated, his profile was to her, and she remembered in a flash where she had seen him before. He had been in Lake Geneva yesterday when Bob was killed. Staring at her from a car window. She had thought how much like Grandfather he looked.

By the time her pie arrived, she was seriously troubled. Why would a perfect stranger, an elderly man, be following her?

No. It was too absurd. It was only that he looked so much like Grandfather. He had the same high-bridged, hawk nose, the same frosty blue eyes. Even his unruly white eyebrows reminded her of Grandfather. Grandfather. Suddenly, Alex's thoughts slammed into racing gear.

After two bites, she grabbed the check and headed for the cashier. She was no longer hungry. There was something else disturbingly familiar about the man with white hair. What she wanted was the public library.

After the air-conditioned store, it felt unmercifully hot outside. Too hot to walk across the Loop. Hailing a taxi, she saw her white-haired shadow exit hurriedly through the rotating doors. He was too late. He could never follow her now. Her heart began to pound, half in exhilaration, half in fear.

"Public library, please," she told her driver.

She would be perfectly safe in the public library. Her hands closed more tightly around the package containing her dress. Was it possible she had solved the mystery at last? If she had, would O'Neill ever believe her? Would anyone believe her?

After paying her driver, she mounted the steps of the regal gray building that was the Chicago Public Library. Traffic whizzed by on Michigan Avenue. Surely with all of Chicago behind her in one way or another, she would be safe. What she wanted was the reference section. Inquiring at the information desk, she was directed to a cozy corner on the second floor.

* * *

"Do you think I ought to have told Alex about her mother?" Briggie asked Daniel. They had just arrived in Mt. Prospect.

"Don't beat yourself up, Briggie," Daniel advised. "You did what you thought was best. I can see why you thought it wouldn't be good for her to talk to her mother when she was drinking so heavily."

"I thought it would just hurt her more. They didn't want her home. Her mother kept saying she was safer with me than she would be with them. That's why Dr. Brace and I assumed it was abuse."

"Under the circumstances, that was a reasonable assumption."

"I felt guilty about keeping it from her. But I kept rationalizing, saying she was better off with me and Dr. Brace."

"And you were right, Brighamina," Richard replied forcibly. "As soon as she stepped foot in that house, her father was murdered."

"But you still think I should have told her, don't you, Daniel?"

"What does it matter now, Brighamina?" Richard soothed. "You've been a good friend to her. The best she's ever had. She's just upset. We're all a little on edge. What's the address of this hospital?"

Daniel gave it to him. "They said on the telephone that it was kitty-corner from the southwest corner of the mall."

Moments later they had drawn up in front of the North Side Institute.

"What are you going to say to Amelia Borden?" Daniel wanted to know.

"I'm going to tell her about Alex's black eyes. If I'm right, I think that will finally loosen her tongue."

"What do you want us to do?"

"Stand by in the lobby, I guess. I don't imagine they'll let me stay with her too long."

The North Side Institute was more like a plush hotel than a hospital. With its pale pink walls, maroon carpet, and enormous posters of water-colored flowers, it was obviously designed to soothe.

"I'm Brighamina Poulson," she announced at the information window. "Would it be possible for me to speak with Amelia Borden for a few minutes? It's an important matter concerning her daughter."

"Just a moment." The strawberry blond receptionist punched a button on her switchboard and spoke to someone on the unit.

"She's in a group therapy session right now, Ms. Poulson. She'll be finished in about ten minutes. If you care to wait, I can have her brought into one of the small conference rooms around the corner. But it will have to be a short visit. She has an appointment with the dietitian at 2:30."

"I'll wait," Briggie informed her.

Sitting down in the lobby, she picked up the day's newspaper and began to read the rather boring account of the campaign funding scandal. Apparently, there were no more Tranquilor murders to report. Richard and Daniel occupied themselves with hospital literature.

"Pretty toney place," Daniel observed. "Their brochures look like advertisements for some glitzy condominium development."

"She can afford it," Briggie said. "I just hope they can help her."

Finally, the receptionist indicated that Briggie should go to the locked door. As it was buzzed open, she pushed her way through and found herself in a long, carpeted corridor. A woman she took to be Amelia Borden was approaching, a dark mustached man at her side. Indicating an open door, he stood back as the two women entered.

Amelia looked hollow. Her eyes seemed to have sunk in her head, and her cheekbones stuck out cruelly beneath them.

"So you're the famous Briggie," she said. Her voice sounded merely tired.

"Well, I don't know about the famous part." Briggie forced a friendly chuckle.

"What did you want to see me about?"

Briggie sat down opposite the tiny woman. The mustached gentleman left, closing the door behind him.

"Has anyone told you that Alex was attacked a couple of days ago?" she asked finally.

"Attacked? Sexually?"

"No, no, nothing like that. I'm afraid it's something to do with your husband's murder. They were professionals and they broke into the house while we were asleep. Alex heard them and went downstairs. She was hit pretty hard with a crowbar. The doctors told us that anyone with a thinner skull would have been killed."

Amelia went white. "They told me about Bob, of course, but not Alexandra," she said in a small voice. Looking at her lap, she began pleating the cloth of her cream colored skirt between her fingers. "What am I supposed to do?"

"Do you know who killed your husband?"

"I was passed out upstairs, like I told the police."

"But you must have some idea," Briggie protested. "You're quite safe here, but what about Alex? She's determined to solve this thing. No one can stop her. She's already out of the hospital. What if whoever it is tries again?"

"It could have been one of several people," Amelia said slowly. "I found Joe, you know. I let the police think Bob did, but I was downstairs before he got there. That's why I was so sure it was suicide. Isn't it ironic? I'm probably the one who kicked the coffee cup under the couch. I was drunk, of course. If it hadn't been for me, the police would have bought the suicide story. But then, there was Alex's letter, wasn't there?"

"She's figured out that her grandfather was Edward Borden," Briggie intervened flatly.

The woman's eyes flew to Briggie's face. "She has? What else does she know?"

"We know that the Simpson family found out about it and have been blackmailing you for years."

The woman bowed her head again. "Yes."

"Do you think one of them killed your husband?"

"No. I think they ordered it done. I think someone from the Mafia came . . ."

"The Mafia? Oh, you mean because of Robert Montgomery. So he was in on the blackmail too?"

Amelia nodded.

"They said Joe's dad murdered their grandfather, Harold Simpson. They said they had proof. Whatever it was, Joe seemed to think it was pretty convincing."

"But why would they kill your husband?"

At this, Amelia's face crumpled and she began to cry. "I called them," she choked. "I actually called that Johnny person and told him what Joe was going to do! It's as though I murdered my husband with my own hands."

"Nonsense," Briggie told her. "Try to think a little more clearly about this. Why would they want to kill him?"

"They knew I'd keep paying, even if Joe was dead. That's why they set it up to look like suicide, of course. He'd been wanting to tell the truth for years. Ever since Alex went to Paris. He missed her terribly. But I talked him out of it. I said Alex would never get over it. She adored her grandfather. And she would be in danger, too, if she came back. The Mafia might have kidnapped her, or threatened to kidnap her if Joe didn't do what Robert Montgomery wanted. They knew all of this. We actually argued it out once in front of that Patsy."

For once, Briggie didn't know what to say. She wouldn't change places with Amelia Borden for a million dollars. The guilt and fear must be tearing her to pieces.

"Would you be willing to give a statement to Lieutenant O'Neill now, Amelia?"

She shuddered. "I've been so frightened."

"Once they've been arrested there would be no reason for you to be frightened," Briggie told her.

"Those people in the Mafia don't forget though, do they? One day I'll be walking down the street and some car will come up over the sidewalk and run me down . . ."

"You're letting your imagination run away with you," Briggie assured her. "The Mafia will make very sure to stay out of this when Robert gets picked up."

"How can you be sure?" Amelia pleaded, her eyes round and frightened.

Briggie made a decision. "There is an attorney out in the lobby. You can write out an affidavit, and Daniel and I can witness it. Spill it all out about the Mafia. It's your best protection. Once they know the police are on to them, they'll lie low, I think."

The mustached man came back into the room. "Time for Mrs. Borden's appointment with the dietitian!" he said breezily.

Drawing herself up, Amelia told him, "You'll have to reschedule it, Dave. I'm sorry, but I need to take care of something important with my lawyer."

Briggie's heart leaped. "I'll be right back, Amelia. Don't go anywhere."

* * *

"Where can I find *Who's Who?*" Alex inquired of the reference librarian, looking at the clock over her shoulder. It was only three-thirty. The day seemed interminable. She was directed to a shelf in the corner. With trembling hands, she pulled out the volume and opened it to Borden. There was the entry she wanted. Her heart was thudding in her head as well as her chest.

Borden, Ronald, U.S. Senator. Son of the late Edward Borden and Cecilia Gray Borden, the senator was born in 1918. Due to the death of his father in the First World War and the death of his mother following childbirth, Senator Borden was raised by his maternal grandparents, Robert Gray and the former Eustacia Young.

Elected to his first term as Senator for the State of Illinois in 1980. Re-elected in 1986. Formerly, served as Congressman, first elected in 1970 . . .

Alex shut the book, her hands clammy and shaking. She'd done it! She'd made the connection. *Cecilia* was the name of Grandfather's boat—the name of his first wife. Cecilia was the mother of Senator Borden. Edward Borden, her grandfather, was the senator's father.

Suddenly her knees felt rubbery, and she sank abruptly onto a hard wooden chair. She repeated her discovery to herself to make it more real. *Senator Ronald Borden, the man with the white hair, was her father's half-brother—Edward's son by his first marriage, born during the war.* Never mentioned. No relationship ever claimed.

Had her father even known? And had Senator Borden known that his father Edward wasn't dead, that he had changed his name to Joseph and claimed his brother's inheritance?

Yes. He must have. Alex put her aching head in her hands. First elected to congress in 1970—the year Daddy had mortgaged the house. Had the $200,000 gone for Ronald Borden's campaign? Ronald Borden must have known about the impersonation. He hadn't been mentioned in his father's (Joseph's/Edward's) will. He would have been angry. He would have felt the money was his right.

Trying to place all the new information was making her dizzy. Pulling out the descendency chart, she added Ronald's data.

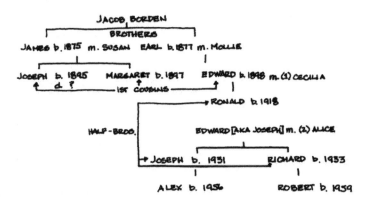

Then she went back to *Who's Who* and studied it carefully. Re-elected in 1986. That meant he was up for re-election this year, 1992. And wasn't he one of the senators involved in the investigation of illegal campaign contributions? It had been all over the papers. She had been seeing it for weeks, never knowing that the scandal would touch her life. The savings and loan magnate, Cornelius Presley, had allegedly bought Borden's influence with his campaign contributions.

Whatever her father was going to tell her about Grandfather being Edward must have been political dynamite. Of course Daddy would have warned Senator Borden, since he was his half-brother. And the senator was conveniently in town, campaigning.

Alex got up. She had to get home, had to tell the others. Then they would decide how to approach O'Neill. After all, it wasn't as though she had what could be called real proof.

* * *

By the time Amelia completed her affidavit and had it signed and notarized by a member of the hospital staff, it was four o'clock.

"Let's get this right over to O'Neill," Briggie suggested as they finally left the hospital.

"Then we need to get back to the house. Don't you think that's where Alex would go? It's closer to the train station."

Briggie looked at him sharply. "You're worried about her, aren't you?"

"Yes. If the Mafia is behind this, they're probably watching the house and the hospital. They already tried to kill her. Don't you see? She's getting too close, and they know it. Bob must have let on about the will. They must have been behind the housebreaking. If she's there alone . . ."

Stiffening in sudden alarm, Briggie instructed Richard as he slid in behind the wheel of the Bronco. "Step on it. How far are we from Winnetka?"

"As the crow flies," Richard replied, "it's not far. But it's all surface streets, and this is Chicago's rush hour."

Viewing the congested street, it seemed to Briggie that she could see red stoplights for miles ahead of them.

Alex hadn't been able to get a taxi, and the walk across the Loop to the train station had taken her a good half hour. Fortunately, the trains were running frequently now. She barely caught the four-fifteen. The ride to Winnetka would only take about half an hour.

Boarding the train, she felt incredibly weary. When she had settled herself in a window seat and the train began to move, she nodded and dozed. It was only when the train made its first stop in Evanston that she jerked awake.

She had to think, she told herself, trying to banish her mental fuzziness. Darn, her head hurt. Where did Harold Simpson fit into the picture? He must fit somewhere. Somehow the Simpson clan had gotten their claws into Daddy. It had to go back to the war. Simpson had never come home. Joseph had never come home. But Edward did. But Edward was Grandfather, and Grandfather would never have murdered anyone.

Why am I so certain of that? She wondered. Probably because he had always been so kind to her. Her memories of him were dim, of course, but she retained a sense of warmth and caring that surfaced whenever she thought of him. There had been so many wonderful days on the lake, cruising into the wind. He had taught her to fish and to steer by the stars. One weekend they had gone away together from Friday night to Sunday night. She had kept house for him on the boat, feeling very grown-up. They had slept in the bunks and eaten her terrible scrambled eggs for breakfast.

Finally, the train pulled into Winnetka. And there was a cab. She had just enough money left for the fare.

Automatically, she gave the driver her home address. It wasn't until she had gotten out and it had pulled away that she remembered. The others wouldn't be here. They would be at the motel.

Well, she could call them, couldn't she? Fortunately, she had recovered her key from Briggie. Letting herself in by the front door, Alex headed for the telephone in her father's study.

There she stopped short. Sitting behind her father's desk, going through the drawers, was the honorable Ronald Borden of the United States Senate.

TWENTY

"How did you get in?" Alex demanded idiotically.

"Your cousin Bob very obligingly lent me his key."

"You killed him," she said flatly. The blood had gone from her head, and her knees were rubbery again. "What are you doing here, Senator?" she asked, hoping her voice sounded brave. "Or should I say, Uncle?"

"Put it all together, have you? I thought you recognized me. How unfortunate." The man smiled the benevolent smile that had won him so many votes over the years. How could she ever have missed his resemblance to Grandfather? There was no hint of ruthlessness in his face. There were even laugh lines around the familiar blue eyes. But this man was a murderer. She was alone in the house with a murderer. It seemed entirely unreal.

"You murdered my father," she accused evenly. Suddenly, she was calm. Her headache had flown, and the rubbery feeling was gone from her limbs. "Why?"

* * *

"There has to be an accident up ahead," Briggie moaned. Ahead of them the traffic went on forever. Lights changed, and still they didn't move.

"Gridlock," Richard sighed. "There's not a thing we can do. We're hemmed in on all sides."

* * *

The senator's hands appeared from underneath the desk.

In the right one he held Grandfather's automatic, pointed squarely at her chest.

"My dear, you know perfectly well why I did it. We're in an election year. I'm under scrutiny already because some twit in Cornelius Presley's office thought she'd act out a scene from *All the President's Men.*"

"But what are you afraid of?"

"Still haven't figured it out? I'll help you." His face turned grim. With his free hand, he fished inside his breast pocket and brought out his wallet. Extracting a dog-eared letter, he tossed it across the desk and said bitterly, "I don't usually carry this around, but I brought it to refresh your father's memory the other day. It is with great pleasure that I am able to reveal to you the truth about your precious grandfather."

Alex took the letter from the desk with surprisingly steady hands and began to read.

Dear Ronald:

I don't suppose anything I write will make you understand or forgive me. All I can do is tell you how things came to be as they are.

When I was on my way home from France in that miserable December of 1918, my prospects were pretty grim. I had a six-month-old son I'd never seen and had no means of supporting. My dear wife, your mother, had died, and her parents, with whom you were living, could not forgive me for joining up. I was having a difficult time forgiving myself. Maybe if I had been there to look out for her, Cecilia's peritonitis would have been diagnosed sooner. Perhaps she might have lived.

The war changed a lot of us. I saw men blown in two, others lose half their heads, still others who took a long time to die there in the shell holes of the abominable wasteland. It was supposed to be honorable to fight a war, but I felt no badge of courage. I was terribly tired, and I suppose more than a little shell-shocked. All I wanted was a peaceful hearth and your mother. I had no hope of either.

This was passing rather grimly through my mind as I traveled west from New York by train. I was bound for Chicago, in hopes that my cousin Joe would give me a job in the meat-packing business. We had seen each other once in France, but that was the first time we'd laid eyes on one another since my family moved to St. Louis when I was fifteen.

It had been a good reunion, in spite of the hell all around us. We'd grown quite alike in appearance and temperament over the years. He knew, of course, that my father's company had gone bust and that he had committed suicide. Then he showed me something that moved me very much. It was his will. He had made me his heir! I was so surprised I don't think I was even able to speak. We both got a bit teary, and he told me to look him up if we both made it through. Then it was time to march. We were bound for different destinations, and that was the last time I ever saw him.

When I look back on what occurred on that train journey, I still feel that there was some sort of divine inevitability about it. Thinking of one thing and another I couldn't sleep, and I went to the dining car in hopes of getting something hot to drink. It was full, and so I shared a table with another soldier. Most of his head was covered in bandages, so I really couldn't tell what he looked like, but his eyes were like burnt-out coal— deep and lifeless. I'm sure you can imagine how shocked I was to hear him introduce himself as Joe Borden! I asked what he did for a living, and he told me he owned a meat-packing business in Chicago. Then I knew he was an impostor. I didn't exactly want to make a scene in front of all those people, so after we finished our cocoa; I had suggested we take a little stroll through the train. We walked down to the end car and stood outside by the gate. I offered him a cigarette. Our conversation, as best I can remember, went something like this:

"You know, I have a cousin named Joe Borden."

"Yeah? Small world."

"He owns a meat-packing plant in Chicago."

With that, I finally saw some life in those burnt-out eyes. Not panic or fear, a sort of sharp cunning. It reminded me of the scavenger rats in the trenches.

"Well, well," he said.

"You are not my cousin. What happened to him?"

The man laughed as though I'd said something extremely funny. "I'm Joe Borden, like it or not."

"I don't like it. Not one bit. Is he dead?" In answer to my question, the soldier merely took out his papers, holding them up so I could see the name Joseph Borden, and then he quickly put them away. As he was putting

them back in the inside pocket of his suit, we took a swerve, and he fell against me. A folded paper dropped, and I stooped to pick it up, unfolding it as I did so. It was the will—the will in which my cousin had named me his heir. He took it from me and replaced it in his pocket.

The fellow laughed again, "Edward Borden, I presume?"

He held out a hand as though to shake mine, and before I knew it, he had a hold on me and was trying to throw me off the end of the train!

I make no apologies for what happened next. It was him or me, and fortunately I was in better condition. I threw him off that train into a forest of trees.

I got off at Erie, Pennsylvania, and hitched rides until I got back into that general area. I didn't know if he was even dead, but if he was, I wanted those papers. It took me days of walking in the snow along those railroad tracks and down into the forests until I found him. I believe his neck had broken. He was lying at a queer angle. Anyway, he was dead.

The papers were on him. I read them and saw that he was being discharged, supposedly with a head wound. Of course there wasn't any wound under those bandages. I don't know how he got away with it—it was a detail that almost tripped me up later on. But I guess in the general mess and confusion of de-mobbing, he got by. There were scores of wounded being transported. I took off the bandages, put my papers on his body, and took my cousin's papers.

I had fully intended to go back to France to look for Joe or his grave, but my intentions never came to anything. That is my only real crime, I feel, and though you condemn me for many things, not searching hard for my cousin is the only thing I really reproach myself with. By the time I was in the saddle at Borden's and had enough money to do it, I didn't have the time. Maybe someday I will. But he must be dead, probably under a marker with that evil stranger's name on it. I wouldn't even know who to look for.

Since you have such bitter feelings, I'm sorry you found out the truth. When your mother's parents went to identify the body in Pennsylvania, they knew it wasn't me, but they were satisfied to think me dead anyway. That's how they wanted things. When I wrote to them from the grave, sending money for you, they made me promise solemnly that I would never approach you. Jealousy, I suppose. Maybe they were afraid that if you knew I was alive, they would lose you. How wrong they were! When you traced the money and found me, it was only to accuse and vent your implacable hatred against the father who deserted you.

I hope this letter will vindicate me somewhat in your eyes, but if it doesn't I'm sure my proposal to settle a large amount of money on you will take away the sting. If there's one thing you're fond of in this life, it seems to be money. I can't say I'm terribly impressed with what you have done with your life. But then, I suppose you hold me accountable for that, too.

I have only one final parting word. The money I am paying you is not blackmail; it is what I acknowledge to be your right. After all, I have sent you money anonymously for years.

You will not be mentioned in my will, for I shouldn't want my sons to have any nasty surprises after I'm gone. But if I should ever find out that you have approached them with this story, your funds will cease.

Sincerely,
Your father

She had nearly forgotten the senator. When she looked up from the last page of the letter, he was studying her intently.

Looking him in the eye, she said, "I don't see what's so terrible about all of this. What in the world are you afraid of?"

"You buy it, then?" he asked with a jaded laugh. "You believe in the stranger on the train and all of that malarkey?"

"Of course I do!" she told him. "I even know who he was—a man called Harold Simpson."

Her uncle's face hardened. "No! There was no stranger on the train. Your grandfather killed his cousin, Joseph, for that will, my dear innocent. My father was a murderer."

"He wasn't," she replied coldly, "but you are."

The man stood jerkily, keeping the pistol aimed. "Turn around and walk out that door."

* * *

In the distance Daniel heard the wail of an ambulance. "At last," he murmured. "Say your prayers, Briggie, and hope this mess will be cleared up soon."

Running a hand over his head, Daniel resisted the impulse to open the car door and begin running. So much adrenaline was coursing through him that he thought he could probably run all the way to Winnetka. Alex was in trouble. He could feel it.

Briggie felt it, too. "They're starting to move up there! Thank you, God!"

* * *

"This'll be a little trip down memory lane," the senator told Alex as followed her across the driveway, gun at her back.

They were headed for the shed where Grandfather kept his boat. Her heart plummeted. Did he mean to murder her in there? No one would find her for months. Forcing her brain into action, she pleaded with the heavens to stall him. "How did Bob know it was you?" she asked desperately.

"He was a cunning brat, wasn't he?" Her uncle laughed a short burst of humorless laughter. "The car belonged to my staff, but once he found that out, he made the Borden connection. The boy showed promise. I can't tell you what pleasure it gave me to shoot a member of the press, no matter how lowly."

They had come to a halt in front of the shed. Its door had been pulled open, probably by the senator when he had retrieved the pistol. The *Cecilia*'s bow showed in the dimness.

"What are you going to do?" she demanded, her palms clammy and her knees weak.

"I have a hankering to see you aboard the *Cecilia*," he told her. "Father willed it to you, didn't he? He used to take me aboard from time to time. It's where we conducted all our business."

Scrambling across the bow at gunpoint, Alex racked her pounding brain. There were more questions. He seemed to like answering them. "It must have been you who sent those thugs to get the will, or was that the Mafia?"

"Mafia? What circles do you think I move in?"

"How did you know about the will?"

"Your egregious cousin Robert. He apparently caught a glimpse of it. For him, it was the last puzzle piece. The very last."

They were on the deck now. Alex turned to face her captor. "Daddy really believed Grandfather was a murderer? Did you show him the letter, too?"

"I showed your father the letter for the first time the night after our father died. It was a shock, needless to say."

"He had no intention of making anything public. He was only going to tell me. What was the real reason you killed him?"

"Haven't you been reading your newspapers? I'm already under investigation. They're tracing my campaign contributions back to the beginning. Eventually, they would have come asking your father about the $200,000 he gave me. In his passion for truth-telling, he might have let it slip that the contribution wasn't voluntary. When I originally blackmailed him, he didn't think he could afford to have it come out that, at best, his father was a fraud and that the estate didn't really belong to him. But the other night, that didn't seem to matter to him anymore. Nothing seemed to matter to him but the truth. He would have told the investigators about the real reason for his campaign contribution without a qualm. And that, of course, would have been the end of my career." He jerked the pistol menacingly. "Now. Down into the cabin, my girl."

"So the main reason you killed him was so the blackmail wouldn't come out? Grandfather was just a side issue?" she exclaimed, bumping her head as she descended blindly into the blackness.

"Let's just call the whole thing a happy coincidence. I was going to have to do something about your father sooner or later. Then suddenly he phones me out of the blue and wants to see me. With the Tranquilor murders all over the front page, it was too good a chance to pass up."

"But he wouldn't have given you away! Daddy wasn't like that!"

"Let's just say your father didn't have a soft spot where I was concerned, and leave it at that."

Alex spoke through clenched teeth. "They'll find you out, you know. You may murder me, but my friends will find you. They know everything that I know."

"Now, now. I'm not going to murder you, you know. You're going to commit suicide. I understand you've been under considerable strain lately, my dear Xandra . . ."

"Don't you dare call me that! Daddy . . ."

"Yes. I know. It was his pet name, wasn't it?"

Alex's fear left her suddenly, and she felt murderous.

"It's so convenient, your being a mental patient. Why don't you just lie down on the bunk, take a little rest."

"I won't!" she challenged, her eyes growing accustomed to the dimness. She could make out his shape now, and the hand that held the gun. "Why should I? If you're going to shoot me, it's going to look like murder, not suicide."

He leveled the gun at her chest. "You really mean that?"

Suddenly, Alex was back at the Baltimore. *Pretend it's just Daniel,* she told herself. *Pretend it's only a squirt gun.*

With a swift front kick, she disarmed her uncle, and the gun went sailing. It landed with a thud against the hull and then slid down onto the bunk. Before he could recover from his surprise, she moved in with her chop to the collarbone, driving him to the ground.

But she wasn't going to have it all her own way. Using his head as a battering ram, the senator charged from his position on the floor. She felt the blow to her stomach. He tossed her up over his back and then stood up, dumping her onto the floor. He was groping for the gun when she scrambled back into position and, ignoring the thunder in her head, delivered a roundhouse kick to his left ear.

Hand on the gun, he pulled the trigger just as the kick landed, and she felt the bullet whiz by her head before embedding itself in the hull behind her.

Borden lay sprawled on the bunk, shaking his head, hand still clutching the gun. Another chop to the collarbone only enraged him further. There just wasn't enough power behind her moves.

Her mind raced as he got to his feet, gun still in hand. What would Daniel do? An upper cut punch.

She got him square in the jaw and then used a chop to the forearm. The gun fell between them, and she kicked it behind him, out of his reach. He was breathing hard now. The space in the cabin was too small for any but the most limited maneuvers. She had to get out, gun or no gun. Her back was to the door. Spinning, she bolted quickly through the galley and up onto the deck. She could hear him behind her. Crawling across the bow of the boat, she felt ancient spider webs brush her cheeks. She leaped to the ground and began to run. Before the senator appeared over the bow, she had concealed herself in the large oleanders that lined the driveway.

He came hunting her, gun in hand. Listening to his rough, raspy breathing, she tried to track his progress. Now!

Leaping out of the bushes, she aimed a kick straight for his stomach. Borden crashed back onto the pavement, his head striking the ground with a dull thud. Alex dove for the gun, aimed it at his chest, and stood over him, breathing hard and praying he was unconscious.

At that moment, the Bronco roared into the driveway, and three people scrambled out, running toward her.

"Alex!" It was Briggie.

"Not bad for a yellow belt," she said shakily.

TWENTY-ONE

Richard, Daniel, and Briggie stood over the recumbent body of the senator.

"Who in the heck is that?" Briggie demanded. "The murderer," Alex announced with weary pride. "Senator Ronald Borden, my uncle, my father's half-brother." Three pairs of eyes beheld her in astonishment. "But you said . . ." Daniel began.

"Give me the gun, Alex," Briggie interrupted. "You're all in."

"Senator Borden!" Richard exclaimed in patent disbelief. Peering closer, he muttered, "I do believe you're right. I didn't know you were related."

"She said she wasn't," Daniel replied. "Isn't anyone going to call the police?" Alex asked. Suddenly, she didn't feel very well. "No . . . wait! You'd better get the letter out of his breast pocket first before he comes to. It's from Grandfather."

Daniel moved to her side and, with an arm around her waist, coaxed her across the driveway toward the patio furniture. "You call, Dad. Briggie can stand guard."

It looked as though Richard might protest, but noting Briggie's set lips and challenging glare, he was silent.

Hours later, when O'Neill had come and gone and an ambulance had sped the senator to the hospital, they were still sitting on the patio. The sun was long gone, and Alex was so tired she felt as though she were floating in a deep ocean of calm.

Everyone had heard the statement she had given O'Neill. Now, it seemed they had a story to tell her.

"Your mother thought it was the Mafia, Alex," Briggie told her. "That's why she was so frightened. That's why they never wanted you involved and that's why they sent you away. Johnny and Patsy were working with Patsy's brother, Robert, who used his Mafia connections as a constant threat. Once your mother realized that your father's death wasn't suicide, she thought it was a Mafia execution. She had even called Johnny herself to try to get him to talk your father out of bringing you into it. She's had a terrible time."

Closing her eyes, Alex sank back into her chaise lounge and tried to take it in. "Her alcoholism . . ."

" . . . was the only way she could deal with it," Daniel finished. "She's been living in constant fear ever since the Simpson heirs first contacted them. They claimed that your grandfather had murdered their grandfather. The 'proof was in Sarah's letters from Harold and your grandfather, I suppose."

"How sad," Alex reflected heavily. "And the letter from Grandfather to Ronald clinched it, I suppose, with the tale of meeting Simpson on the train. Twenty years! Can you imagine? For twenty years they thought Grandfather was a murderer. Daddy died thinking that."

"I don't think your mother really knew anything about your uncle at all," Briggie continued. "She may not even know of the connection. With everything else, your father probably thought she had enough to bear."

Putting her fingertips to her temples, Alex tried to order her spinning mind. "And the senator thought Grandfather had murdered his cousin, Joseph. He didn't believe all the stuff in the letter. But Grandfather didn't really murder anyone. It was self-defense! I wonder whatever really happened to Joseph."

Briggie looked at her with glowing pride. "You'll find out. That'll be kid's play compared to this puzzle. You're the one who put all the pieces together, Alex. The Edward Borden piece, the Harold Simpson piece, and finally the Senator

Borden piece. I can imagine that your father's very proud of you right now, wherever he is."

"Thank heavens he didn't die just because I came home," Alex sighed. "The hardest thing about all of this was that I thought he died because I wanted to do my genealogy. But Senator Borden was already planning his death. My curiosity just happened to coincide with the Tranquilor murders, which gave him the perfect opportunity."

Suddenly, Alex began to cry, silently releasing all the pent-up emotions of the past week.

EPILOGUE

The service for her father was at two, and Alex and Briggie would pick her mother up at noon so they could have a chance to eat lunch. It had been Briggie's idea that maybe she and her mother would need a little time to get used to one another again. There was so much to say. So many memories to straighten out and remake. There was the future, too. It was going to be a rough road for Mother.

Awake long into the night, Alex had considered this, wondering how she might make it easier. Finally, inspiration had come.

"Come and help me, Briggie," she invited after their leisurely breakfast.

"Where are we going?"

"Out to the roses."

Stepping out into the humid August morning, Alex took the air into her lungs in long, deep breaths. Fear was gone. Panic was gone. Anger was gone. There was only a blessed peace, changed by uncomplicated grief. And she had her memories back.

"It's nice that Daniel and Richard could stay for the service," Briggie remarked.

"Yes," Alex agreed. "It is nice."

"What are we going to do?"

"Gather rose petals, all you can find, and put them into this basket. We're making potpourri to take to Mother. She used to make it for me when I was a little girl. I want her to have some good memories in that hospital room."

As in most things, Briggie humored Alex with cheerful gusto. Gathering the velvety, fragrant petals that covered the ground like a pastel carpet, they worked in silence for a while.

"Honey?"

"Mmm?"

"Have you forgiven me?"

"Yes." Alex paused in her petal gathering to give her friend a hug. "I know it wasn't an easy decision for you to make. It's too late to go back now anyway. We've got to go forward."

* * *

Alex's mother asked the same question in the car on the way to the memorial service.

"Alex, dear, do you think you can ever forgive me?"

Looking at her mother, so shrunken and pale in her black dress, Alex felt her heart ache.

"If you can forgive me," she answered. Suddenly they were hugging and crying as they hadn't done for far too long.

"I know I was a brat about Grandfather," she began, "but I was so *tired* of secrets . . ."

"We were only thinking of you," her mother said. "Of course, I realize there is no way you could have known that. It's just that we were so afraid . . ."

Alex could feel Briggie's presence on the other side of her and was aware that her friend was beaming.

"I want to stay, Mother, at least until you're out of the hospital. I want to see you through your treatment."

"But what about your work? What about your young man?"

"They can both wait. Your recovery is the most important thing right now." Alex reached for the little package next to her. "Here. I don't know if I got it exactly right, and this is only a jam jar . . ."

Her mother's face lit at the sight of the potpourri. Opening the jar, she inhaled its fragrance, and her whole body seemed to relax. "Oh, darling, you couldn't have given me anything that I needed more. I can't believe you remembered after all these years." Turning to Briggie, she explained, "It was a tradition we had in the summer. We always gathered memories of roses for the winter."

"This is apt to be a particularly difficult winter, Amelia," Briggie said.

"Yes, I know. But I have Alex now."

* * *

After the brief graveside service, which was attended only by Alex, her mother, and her three friends, Alex wandered away from the group and over to her grandfather's grave. She stood looking at it. A modest marker, it was adorned only with the name he had gone by and the dates that bracketed his life. She must have it replaced. They would have the truth now, if they were to go on and become an eternal family. Also, there was the matter of Grandfather's cousin Joseph. She must find him somehow.

"Are you plotting to have that removed?" Daniel asked. He had come up behind her so quietly she hadn't even heard him.

"How did you know?"

"You have that determined look. I've gotten so I can recognize it. You're setting your house in order. How about Cousin Joseph while you're at it?"

"Briggie and I will go to France. I think he must be buried in a civilian churchyard, since there are no military records."

"That makes sense."

They stood together in silence for a few moments. Then Alex turned to him with sudden resolve. "I want you to understand something, Daniel. Will you try?"

The careful distance they had so scrupulously maintained during the day was bridged in a moment. He took her arm. "Why don't we sit down?"

Once they were seated, however, she found it difficult to go on.

"Is it about Stewart?" he guessed. Alex didn't know how he did it, but for once she was grateful for his prescience. She was having a hard time knowing how to tell him what she had to say.

"Yes, partly." She took a deep breath. "You see, when I joined the LDS church, my ideas of family changed."

"How?"

"Well, part of our faith is that we believe we can be sealed forever to our families in the temple. Even if they've died, we can do the sealing ordinances by proxy. That's the whole reason we do genealogy—to create eternal families."

Daniel was studying her face. "I can see why that would be important to you," he said gravely.

"One day I will be able to be sealed to both my parents and through them to Grandfather."

"And Stewart?" he asked. "Can you be sealed to Stewart, too?"

"I always planned to be." Alex looked down at her lap and concentrated on interlacing her fingers. "You have to wait for a year after you've been baptized. My year will be up in December."

"That sounds like a very healing event to look forward to," he told her, his voice gentle.

She looked at him again and wondered if he could see the sudden anguish she was feeling.

"I *have* been looking forward to it. That doctrine is one of the main reasons I knew this was Jesus' church. I have always known there must be some link beyond the grave. When I heard I could be with Stewart forever, I was comforted. At that time, I had no one else I could call family."

"Why are you telling me this?"

Examining her fingers again, she said, "I can only be sealed to one man. I can only be married once for eternity."

Daniel was very still.

"If really loved Stewart, Daniel. You've always known that."

"Yes." The word sounded sadly hollow.

"But now I guess I'm confused." Raising her eyes, she looked at him unflinchingly. She saw his countenance lift. There was hope in it. "I don't *want* to be confused," she continued. "That's partly why I've fought you every step of the way."

"And now?"

She took his hand between her own. "We'll just have to wait and see what happens, I guess."

She smiled tentatively, and he kissed her with extreme gentleness.

ABOUT THE AUTHOR

G.G. Vandagriff studied writing at Stanford University and later received her master's degree from George Washington University. She worked for five years in the financial field before her children were born. After that, she taught part-time in several different colleges. She was very happy when the day came that she could finally concentrate on her first love: creative writing. *Cankered Roots* is the first of a series of Alex and Briggie mystery novels. G.G. received the 2009 Whitney Award for Best Historical Fiction for her novel *The Last Waltz: A Novel of Love and War.*

The author and her husband, David, make their home on the bench of the Wasatch Mountains in Utah. They have two sons, a daughter, and two healthy grandsons. She can often be found playing in a tent with her grandchildren making up stories. (She is doing her best to encourage them to see the world they live in with a writer's vision.)

G.G. is also an avid traveler. She claims that she must visit Florence at least once a year for medicinal purposes. After spending almost two months there researching her novel, *The Only Way to Paradise*, and a new Alex and Briggie mystery, now she has to journey to Caputo's in Salt Lake City to get her fresh ground sausage.

GG's website and blog are at http://www.ggvandagriff.com. You can follow her on Twitter at @ggvandagriff. She also has a Facebook author page.